The history of that area
I've included in the
first seven chapters.

Enjoy!

from
J. S. Pessani

THIS WE WILL DEFEND

A Novel

by

T.S. PESSINI

authorHOUSE®

AuthorHouse™
1663 Liberty Drive
Bloomington, IN 47403
www.authorhouse.com
Phone: 1-800-839-8640

Published by AuthorHouse 2/23/2012

ISBN: 978-1-4685-4621-7 (e)
ISBN: 978-1-4685-4622-4 (hc)
ISBN: 978-1-4685-4623-1 (sc)

Library of Congress Control Number: 2012901634

DEDICATED

In loving memory of my wife, JoAnn Ubertaccio Pessini

Acknowledgement

My deepest appreciation goes to Mary Douds, a Guidance Counselor at Northern High School in Garrett County, Maryland, for editing the first seven chapters; to Patti Butler, head of the Technology Department at Owings Mills High School in Owings Mills, Maryland, for her complete editing service for the entire manuscript. To Betsy Deem, Math Teacher at Northern High School, for her time in proof reading the manuscript and making note of the few corrections to be made. To Lynn Coburn, English teacher for her time proof reading the final manuscript and to the folks assigned to the Pre-Publishing Review Sections at the National Security Agency and the Department of the Army Pentagon for their time in previewing my manuscript for publication. And to all of my readers who have waited patiently for this novel.

I give a special thanks to L. Friend and First Sergeant Edward B. Kelly 1st A/D 2/1 Aviation B Company Ansback, Germany for their time in checking my manuscript for historical and military accuracy.

And to my family who had supported my endeavors and challenges during the course of eight years in writing this novel.

Thank you!

T. S. Pessini

Also by T. S. Pessini

TRAITOR IN THE WHITE HOUSE

Chapter One—Detection

Frantz Farm
Friendsville, Maryland
Friday, October 1

He placed the cross-hairs of his rifle scope on the center of his target's forehead. He inhaled a deep, cool breath of air and exhaled while applying pressure to the trigger with his right index finger as he whispered, "This one's for my daughter."

ONE DAY EARLIER

Oakland, Maryland
Thursday, September 30th
1300 hours

Skip and Kristine Daggard sat waiting for the traffic light to change at the intersection of Route 219 Garrett Highway and Memorial Drive. His attention was focused on the four Oriental occupants of a maroon colored Geo that was just driving onto Route 219 from Memorial Drive. The question raised in his mind was instantaneous, "What's wrong with that picture?"

He studied the occupants in a nonchalant manner as the vehicle turned left, heading toward the center of Oakland while the female passenger glared at him.

"Are you listening to me?" Kristine Daggard raised her voice about three octaves.

Warm temperatures and a bright autumn sun had created an Indian summer.

"*Skip!*"

"*What?*" Skip Daggard shouted back at Kristine.

Kristine turned around looking between the front bucket seats. "Pay attention, Eilis. This is your father's favorite sport—mentally disappearing."

Skip glared at Kristine then redirected his attention back to the maroon Geo Prism.

Skip jumped and swiveled his head as his blue eyes narrowed to slits.

"Yes, I punched you!" Then she leaned toward Skip as she whispered, "What is so damn interesting about that oriental female? Remind you of 'Nam, or maybe Korea?"

Skip's movement was snake-strike fast. He reached over and pulled Kristine's head forward and planted a juicy one on her wet, red lips. "You haven't learned much in five years have you?"

"Oh yes, I've learned a well-full. We're retired...remember? So whatever is going on in your over-loaded subversive imagination, forget it. We're not spies anymore; just John and Jane Public."

Skip was now three vehicles behind the Geo, which was stopped at the light near Sheetz gas station. He continued to analyze the question in his mind by turning it over and studying it from different viewpoints, but he was not able to grasp any solid reason for his inquiry. Then his subconscious supplied him with the needed information. Skip said, "Korean! They're Korean."

"What?"

"Take out a notebook and pen from the glove box. When you get the chance, write down the license plate number."

The clear, blue sky was bright. The sun warmed his face through the windshield of his Chevy TrailBlazer. "But there is something else... something...something else...what is it?"

Kristine did as she had been directed, but leaned over and punched Skip in his right upper arm again. He maintained his surveillance on the Geo but smiled. This was the woman he had fallen in love with. Yet, he had almost killed her when she had revealed her true identity so he could take out a traitor in the White House.

"Stop," Kristine demanded. "Please, Skip stop."

He followed the Geo through Oakland to the intersection of Route 135 East and Route 39 West. The Geo turned right onto Route 39 West heading toward Kingwood, West Virginia. Skip continued to follow. His vehicle was now two cars behind the Geo. He glanced at her then turned back to his quarry. "I can't," he said, a remorseful tremor in his voice.

She saw the bridge was coming up and prepared to copy the plate number. "You mean you won't. I know you. Once the game begins…"

As the Geo crested the bridge over the train tracks, Kristine was able to copy the plate number: Y7U130AN, DC for the state, and the registration month and year: 09-12. And now Skip was offered a clear picture of the four occupants. He sat straight up and his body became rigid. He turned toward her with a slow, swivel movement of his head. His face was pale-white. "I know what it was," he whispered, "I know what caught my eye. I know what's wrong…they're soldiers."

Kristine stared straight ahead. Slowly, she turned her head toward him. "Oh…my…God! Disengage…please disengage. Skip, please… stop. Make the right after the bridge and let's go to Pizza Hut for supper as we planned."

They were still two car-lengths behind the Geo. Skip sat frozen in place. His words were crisp and clear, "The Communist Coalition force your father and the Russian Secret Service had lost several years ago is here, Kristine. Our enemy is in hiding within the belly of America."

Kristine studied his face. Nothing! "How can *he* do that?" she asked herself although she knew the answer. She had learned more about Skip's horrors and secrets while they were in the hidden room in the Lincoln Tunnel than she had during the two previous years of their engagement. At times, in the middle of the night, she would lie awake sweating, reliving that nightmarish moment when Skip was applying pressure to the trigger of his Colt, its cold muzzle pressed against her head.

She responded to his last statement. "They're here! My God, Skip we've only postponed the inevitable…war."

He sighed, "Yeah, I wonder if they were here when we killed President Mantle?"

She nodded. "Perhaps that's why my father and the Russian Secret Service lost them."

Skip was oblivious to his immediate surroundings. His focus was now on his quarry, and the game—the fox and the hound, and the game had just taken on an immediacy of great importance. He felt his heart beating against his chest and the adrenaline rush. This is what he had been born and bred for…his purpose—his mission in life. What was it Bryanna, his ex-fiancée had said just before he had left for Vietnam? Oh yeah! "You were born OD green and you will die OD green, Skip Daggard, but come home to me. Don't be a hero. I can't take medals to bed."

But he didn't come home to her because of who he had become. Bryanna didn't get any medals, just a flag on behalf of a grateful nation, and a chance at life and happiness, courtesy of himself.

Skip shook his head to clear out haunting images of his past. "Yeah, while the Russians were looking for them in Europe, they were slipping in *our* back door."

Kristine looked at him. To her surprise, Skip was smiling.

Skip slowly turned his head and stared at her through his blank, blue eyes. "They almost got away with it."

She smiled back at him as she placed a gentle hand on his right thigh. She felt her pride for her husband mount. This was another aspect of her husband which made him a dangerous adversary; the enemy could never know when or where he would appear.

He looked at her again. This time sadness was permeating from his eyes. "I hope I'm wrong, and they're not soldiers, just tourists."

Terra Alta, West Virginia
Thursday, September 30ᵗʰ
1345 hours

Colonel Chin Lee knew that she and her fellow comrades were being followed. She had noticed the man in the dark green Chevy TrailBlazer trying to be too inconspicuous when they were at the traffic light in Oakland. She had been more inconspicuous stealing glances through her outside rearview mirror while she allowed this cat and mouse game to continue. Colonel Lee also knew who the driver of the TrailBlazer was: NSA's infamous Skip Daggard, their notorious spy killer.

"Chin, you must be very careful," her father had warned her. "You will be hiding in the back yard of our most dangerous adversary."

She smiled now at the question she had asked her father before leaving North Korea three months ago. "Father, why do you fear an adversary that no longer poses a threat?"

And yet, here he was shadowing them like a hawk shadows its prey before swooping down and snatching it from the earth. Chin Lee let a deep sigh escape from her lungs. Lieutenant Wong, their driver, glanced at her. "Is something troubling you, Colonel Lee?"

"What do we know of the moles? They are Soviet. Our leaders were told to join a Communist Coalition force. That soon, all Soviet mole key players would be in control.

What has happened so far? Nothing!"

"Much has happened," Lieutenant Wong began to correct her. "Twenty US Military bases have been closed. US forces have been diminished even though they are fighting a war in the Middle East. And the Second Amendment to the U.S. Constitution will soon be a thing of the past. The vote is already before Congress, and many of them are spies."

"Yes and our leaders have been informed not to worry about Military Intelligence Officer Skip Daggard because he has been retired."

"Yes, Colonel Lee. How do the Americans say? Oh, he is out of the loop."

"Then carefully look into your rearview mirror, Lieutenant Wong, and tell me what you see."

Wong did as he had been ordered. Then he almost lost control of his vehicle. "It cannot be…"

The two officers in the back seat were about to turn around when Colonel Chin Lee shouted out an order. The men sat frozen.

"The one person we had been assured that, as you say, Lieutenant Wong was out of the loop is playing cat and mouse with us right now."

"I do not understand, Colonel Lee…"

"Before we left home, my father warned me to be careful because we would be in our most dangerous adversary's back yard.

"Why he is dogging us, I cannot say. Yet, he is, which leaves me with a dilemma."

Without warning, Colonel Lee grabbed the steering wheel forcing the car right into the parking lot of a bar. She had Wong drive around to the rear and park. Her diversion worked, Skip continued past the bar. He had not observed her action because of the curve in the road, and he had not been paying attention.

Colonel Lee sat still for five minutes trying to think what she should do. Maybe she should do nothing. Or, maybe she should now become the cat stalking the mouse. She knew one thing for certain—they could not return to their hideout while Skip Daggard was prowling the highway.

She thought that a small diversion would help her think more clearly. Perhaps a cold beer would taste most pleasurable at this moment, but she realized the danger of that folly.

Lieutenant Wong looked at his wristwatch for the twentieth time. "Fifteen minutes has elapsed, Colonel Lee."

"Thank you for that piece of information, Lieutenant!"

Colonel Lee slowly opened the passenger door, slid out of the vehicle, stood up next to the Geo, stretching, still pondering their dilemma. She strolled over to the white building near the rear corner when she saw the dark green TrailBlazer drive by in the direction of Oakland. She smiled. "So, the eagle has lost his quarry."

Colonel Chin Lee was plotting a plan of action as she marched back to her vehicle. It was quite simple actually, and she would be a hero. Yes, she thought as she slid onto the front passenger seat. "He is driving back toward Oakland. Follow him."

As Lieutenant Wong did as he had been ordered, Colonel Lee derailed the idea of shooting Daggard as quickly as she had conceived the thought. She leaned back against her seat with the thumb of her right hand pressing against her lower lip. "Why not," she said out loud. Lieutenant Wong stared at her for six ticks of the second hand of his wristwatch as Colonel Lee removed a 9mm semi-auto handgun from the glove box.

Pizza Hut
Oakland, Maryland
Thursday, September 30th
1415 hours

Skip drove back into Oakland adhering to the speed law of forty-five miles per hour while puzzling over the disappearance of the Geo. He made the left turn before the bridge. He drove slowly over the railroad tracks and made the right onto Alder Street. He sat straight with his back pressed against his seat, contemplating the sudden disappearance of the Geo while waiting for the red light at Alder Street and Route 219 to change to green.

Kristine studied his face. His facial muscles were taut. She could see that he was lost deep in thought, but she could not understand what it was about the occupants of the Geo, which had arrested his attention so much that he had felt compelled to follow. Was he correct in his assumption? Yet, she could see that he was still in his analytic mode. She had learned that that was one thing, which made him such a dangerous adversary during the Cold War. He could see things that other agents failed to recognize. She looked out her window, praying that he was wrong about the Orientals being soldiers.

Skip sat quiet, contemplating possible ramifications of his statement about the Orientals: Why are they here? Are they really soldiers? Could they be part of the Communist forces?

When the light turned green, Skip made a left onto Route 219. He drove past the firehouse and Ace Hardware store, and then turned right into Pizza Hut's parking lot.

They sat quietly in their Chevy. Kristine gave Skip space. She knew he had to have time to contemplate. Yet the words were there, so she said them as she looked at him. "I pray you are wrong, and that the puzzle you are trying to create pans out to be absolutely nothing at all."

He was studying the license plate number. He looked at her. He released a short, quiet sigh. "I don't think I am. There's something I cannot fathom yet. Something remains elusive. Besides that, this number isn't right. It's a DC plate, but these letters and numbers don't jive." He said it more to himself, so Kristine did not reply.

Skip reached over and opened the glove box. He took out his cell phone, punched several buttons, and waited while the phone rang.

Five rings and someone picked up on the other end. "519th Military Police Station NCIC Operator Roberts, this line is not secure. How may I help you?"

"Hey, you old dirt-bag, how ya' hangin'?"

"Hmmm, Skip Daggard, how come you don't stop by any more?" "Didn't your mother ever teach you not to answer a question with a question?"

"Yeah, except when it comes to Skip Daggard. She warned me to stay away from you because you're trouble!"

Both men laughed. Kristine sat rigid. She saw the maroon Geo pull into the parking lot twenty yards behind them. When she looked at Skip to try and get his attention, Kristine knew he had seen the Geo because of his stiff posture, and he was drawing his .45 from his shoulder holster with his right hand. He looked at Kristine.

They stared at each other for several seconds. Finally, he breathed. "They left!"

Kristine turned around slowly, and saw that the Geo was gone. "Where did they go?"

Skip shrugged his shoulders. "The front passenger started to get out of the vehicle, you *know*, that oriental wench, and then she got back in. They just drove off."

"Leon, you still with me?"

"Absolutely, what's going on?"

"I have a plate number I would appreciate you running for me…"

"No."

Skip took his phone away from his ear glaring at it then he placed it against his ear again. "What's your problem, not gettin' any?"

Skip could hear Leon's soft breathing.

After five seconds, Leon broke the silence. "You're retired, remember? I have five months to go, and I sure as *hell* do not want to get mixed up in some damn off-the-wall spook shit that you think you need to be poking your nose in—got it?"

"Listen nigger, I don't want to hear…you gonna run the plate or not?"

"Honky, you already knew the answer to that before you rung me down."

Both men broke out into hysterical laughter.

Kristine stared at him, reached over and began caressing Skip's thigh as she smiled. This was one of those rare occasions when Skip actually allowed himself to crack-up.

Skip gently placed his right hand on hers. Realizing that he still held his handgun, he placed his weapon back into his holster, and then laid his hand back on Kristine's.

"Hold on Leon. You never met Leon, Kristine. He and I have a crazy history together. I guess you have figured it out that Leon is black."

"Yes, when you called him nigger."

Skip stiffened at the word but smiled. "Leon and I were stationed together with the 143rd Signal Battalion in Frankfurt, Germany in 1975. I had been called over to hunt down some spies. Leon is a character. During that timeframe there was racial tension brewing. Trouble looked imminent."

Skip shifted around in his seat looking at Kristine. "I had just left the company, turned right moseying up the company-street heading back to the maintenance shop. Leon had come from the Stars and Stripes store, turned right and was heading in my direction.

"I hadn't seen him yet, but he shouted, for all he was worth, 'Hey nigger!'

"It was noon. There were about 300 soldiers moving around the square. His shouting nigger froze our world, Kristine. Time stopped. The air was sucked up into Heaven as Hell began to open its gates. No one moved. I mean no one. I found the source screaming out the derogatory remarks, and then I shouted back, "Hey honky, how's it hangin?"

"As we continued to advance on each other, the look on the faces of the other soldiers was priceless. I mean analyze it—here was a black soldier strutting down the street calling a white soldier nigger, and a white soldier matching the other's swagger calling the black soldier honky. You could see the confusion in their eyes. Awesome; their minds could not comprehend what their ears were hearing."

He took a shallow breath then continued. "As we closed, the troops close to us began to move. Then Leon and I just grabbed each other in a big bear hug. He shouted, 'Ain't nothin' hangin' nigger, what's up?'

I said, "Whatcha' buy me, honky," and we both began to laugh as we strutted off arm-in-arm."

Skip smiled again and gently squeezed Kristine's hand. "That charade ended racial tension in our little corner of the world. When those soldiers finally realized what had just happened, they all began to laugh and the black and white soldiers started patting each other's backs. Leon and I developed a genuine friendship."

Kristine frowned as beads of perspiration began to ooze out from her pores along her forehead. She held on to Skip's hand as she watched him begin to disappear. His face became taut as his eyes closed to narrow slits. Now, she knew where he was going…back to 'Nam. She learned this when they were down in the tunnels under Washington three years ago, when they had plotted to terminate President Mantle. The two years they had lived together prior to that, she never knew, but was always frightened of him when he had left her mentally to what she had come to call his "private hell." She knew that this was going to be a bad trip because Skip's face had become solemn and sad. Tears began to form at the corners of his sky-blue eyes.

The battle was raging about five miles due east from his position. He was perched high in a tree located five kilometers from the Cambodian border. He had just capped his three intended targets: three North Vietnamese snipers.

Kristine jumped. She had been so intent on holding Skip's hand…

"Sometimes…sometimes the heart has bled so much it aches for human contact and friendship," Skip was saying. He broke down and cried. Three seconds and it was over. He sucked down his pain while wiping the tears from his face.

Then, without warning, he was gone again, but this time it was different because he was staring at her...through her, as he began to speak. "It was 0300 hours. The battle had been raging for two hours. I had terminated my quarry yet I did not get down from my hiding place.

"To the east, bombs continued to burst, creating a false sense of daylight. It was like watching Fourth of July fireworks only these fireworks were killing soldiers. My internal instinct was to get down and run to the battle, but my survival instincts wouldn't hear of that stupidity. So I listened to the roar of thunder, automatic weapons fire, screams, and shouts from the wounded and dying soldiers. I sat with my back pressed against the upper trunk of the tree as lightning flashed across the horizon from the bombs."

Kristine held his hand softly in both of hers. She tried not to move so she would not disturb him.

"There was a song that had a line: "the darkest hour is just before dawn," I think it was the Mamas and the Papas. They were right. By 0430 hours the battle was over. Darkness had engulfed me with its protective veil of blackness. Silently I slid down the tree going from limb to limb until I quietly dropped to the earth."

He paused again to take in some air and exhale.

"I moved in shadows letting the shroud of blackness cover my advance toward the battlefield. I arrived just as the sun was kissing the treetops, chasing away the dark things, yet casting light over the horrors of man's making."

Kristine tried to pull Skip to her breasts, but he held firm his position. She watched as tears rolled down his face. She knew that he was taking her into his war. A war, that after forty years; still lives and bleeds inside of him.

"My God, Kristine, the earth was littered with bodies."

Once again Skip broke down into a gut wrenching, can't-catch-your breath body-trembling outburst. And just as always, in three seconds it was as if he had never had his tear-jerking fit.

"*How does he do that*", she wondered in amazement.

"I stood limp at the edge of the jungle stunned by the carnage. There had been a substantial sized village here only yesterday. Last night, and early in the morning it lay between two massive opposing forces. Fire and smoke filtered up from the ruins with the screams and cries of the wounded and dying.

"I saw a soldier raise his arm about ten yards from my position. As I approached him, I saw that he was wearing a 1st Signal Brigade patch on his left shoulder sleeve. It was Haggerdy, a lineman from my unit. We were getting to know each other. During breaks, we would sit in my hooch drinking Pabst Blue Ribbon beer and eating mustard sardines.

"I held him cradled in my arms while sitting in his blood, guts, and body parts. A North Vietnamese Corpsman came over and squatted in front of us. We looked at each other. He slowly reached over and gently closed Haggerdy's eyes.

"How did this start?" I asked the corpsman as I waved my arm. "Accident," he said, "we come down from north off of Ho Chi Minh Trail. Americans and South Vietnamese soldiers come up from south; bump into each other."

"How many villagers escaped?"

"Five hundred villagers: All dead."

I laid Haggerdy down. "Guess you got a one-way ride back to Hoeboken, Hag."

"As I disappeared into the jungle, I swore I'd never, ever let anyone in again. Then along came Leonardo da Vinci Roberts." As he gently squeezed her right hand, he emphasized, "And you!"

Skip smiled again as he retrieved his cell phone from his lap, "Hey, honky, you with me?"

"Yeah, nigger, I'm still here. Give me the damn number. And you better *not* be getting me into any of that spook shit, white boy."

"Once Leon gives me the information, we can go into Pizza Hut... Leonardo?"

"Yeah, I'm here! Nothing has come up in the normal system. I'm checking the diplomatic listings now."

Skip chuckled.

Eilis began to fuss. "She's been sitting too long, Skip."

"I know," he said turning to look at their daughter. "You've been a trooper, Eilis, just hold on a few more minutes. Then we will get something to eat. You have a bottle you can give her, honey?"

"Yes, but I wanted to wait."

Skip glared at Kristine.

"*Fine*, I'll give it to her now."

Kristine took out a bottle from Eilis' baby bag. She turned around and handed their daughter the bottle. She turned back in time to witness his worried expression.

"Skip, get the hell out of there, someone just wiped out my computer!"

Chapter Two—Indecision

Oakland, Maryland
Route 39 West
Thursday, September 30th
1436 hours

Oakland, Maryland lay quiet under a dog-day afternoon as Lieutenant Wong drove the maroon Geo out of Oakland on Route 39 heading west toward Terra Alta and Kingwood, West Virginia. Colonel Chin Lee sat stiff-backed analyzing her actions at Pizza Hut. She had her weapon ready, was getting out of the vehicle to shoot the Daggards, but some warning mechanism went off in her head. A warning that her actions were ill fated; she had slipped back into the car and ordered Lieutenant Wong to drive.

Colonel Chin Lee stood five feet three inches tall. Her skin was smooth and blemish-free. She had spent her whole life as a devout member of the Communist Party.

Four months ago she turned thirty-nine, was not married, had no prospects, and was completely devoted to the communistic idea of world domination. "So," she asked herself, "why didn't I eliminate the one person who could derail the Communist Coalition forces' opportunity for victory?" She had no answer, but her mind kept screaming at her heart, or was it her heart screaming at her mind? "Be still damn you, be still," she scalded her heart in silent admonishment. Disturbed, she wiggled in her seat, smoothed out her black, pleated, ankle length skirt, and feathered her raven, short- cropped hair.

Lieutenant Wong was thirty-five, married with one daughter, and moved around the world on a slight frame, which achieved the total height of five feet six inches. He too was devoted to the Communist Party, but he loved the American western attire. He was dressed in a sky-blue western cut shirt, Levis, and brown suede cowboy boots.

And he too was wondering, as he steered the Geo around bends and along straight-aways in the road, why Colonel Lee had not killed their nemesis. But Lieutenant Wong knew better than to challenge a superior officer's decision.

Colonel Lee broke the silence. "I will have to contact my father. He will know how we should proceed, and what we should do."

She feared that the position of their forces may be in jeopardy, or worse, that the quick take-over of the US may turn into a long, bloody, and costly conflict.

Pizza Hut parking lot
Oakland, Maryland
Thursday, September 30th
1437 hours

Oakland's afternoon traffic was heavy at this time of day. The one phrase newcomers to the community had to understand was when people from the north end said, "I'm goin' up to Oakland," they literally meant just that. Although Oakland is in the south part of the county, it is situated in the higher elevations of a mountain range.

"Shit!" Skip blurted out without thinking.

"Watch your language, lover. Our daughter is present. What's wrong?"

Skip Daggard sat in silence for a few minutes.

A large flock of crows flew overhead dropping their bombs on people, vehicles, sidewalks and roadways.

"Skip."

"Yeah!"

"What's wrong?"

Skip took a deep breath as he shot windshield washer fluid onto the glass and turned on the wiper blades to clean off the fresh droppings.

"I got Leon into some deep trouble. I think NSA is involved."

"Isn't that a good thing?"

Daggard wet his lips by running his tongue over them, contemplating Kristine's question. "Under normal conditions I would agree, but Leon said someone wiped out his computer. That's not a good thing, sweetheart, especially since Leon had gone into the diplomatic files in search of the identity of who has registered that Geo."

Skip sat in silence for five minutes studying the situation and the people at Sheetz gas station and convenience store across the street. Kristine maintained a surveillance of the parking lot, fearing the Geo would return.

Skip took out a small notepad and pencil. "Normal, what's that," he questioned out loud. He placed his right hand thumb across his lips. "Normal," he said again, "what's normal?" He wrote down questions he was asking himself.

Kristine turned in her seat to study her husband. She had witnessed his puzzle-plotting modes several times, and she knew not to disturb him.

"Normal! What is normal? I've been hunting down and terminating spies within the walls of NSA, the intelligence community, and around the world since 1975." He paused for thirty-five long seconds. "I guess normal is combating enemy spies within our own infrastructure."

Kristine looked at Skip as he continued to speak out loud as he continued to write.

"Who are they? And what are they doing here? And just what was it that had arrested my attention in the first place? Oh yeah, it was their military bearing."

This is what Skip Daggard did best when he had been an active operative—figuring out puzzles by gathering pieces of information and creating a puzzle to answer his questions. Then, based on his findings, he would devise his plan of attack.

"Yes lover, that's exactly what I want to know. What made you become obsessed with that Oriental female?"

Kristine shifted in her seat as she watched Skip become pale. She straightened her gray skirt, which had ridden up her stocking-sheathed thighs.

He shifted his body to the right staring at her noticing her actions—he smiled. Then, without warning, his smile turned cold; he blurted out, "Soldiers. They *are* soldiers."

As they stared at each other, a frigid ripple of fear traveled up and down her spine.

Skip reached out and pulled her close. "If I'm right, Kristine they must be part of the Communist Coalition Force."

She sat frozen.

Skip witnessed her fear. He understood the implications of his statement. "They are here, Kristine! They're here in the United States. I know now what it was that got my attention. It was their haircuts and posture…their military bearing."

"Damn you, Skip Daggard! Damn you for the creature you are! Damn you to hell…you've killed us…and your friend, Leon," she whispered"

Kristine began to cry. Her tears fell unchecked. "Why? Why couldn't you have left well enough alone? We're retired! My God, Skip, my God, they're here!"

They sat rigid, staring at each other. Eilis began to fuss trying to dislodge herself from her safety seat.

"Skip if that's true then killing President Mantle did not resolve anything. We only postponed the inevitable…World War Three."

NSA
Fort George G. Meade, Maryland
Tango-Echo Group
Thursday, September 30th
1438 Hours

Deputy Director of the National Security Agency, General Ashford Bardolph stood close to the I-Spy intercept communications system for ten minutes glaring at the blinking cursor on the monitor screen.

He knew the plate numbers that the NCIC operator at the 519th was researching. He did nothing but glare until the operator accessed the diplomatic listings. He had given the order, "Pull the plug on that son of a bitch."

"Yes, sir."

In a flash it was done…the virus sent and delivered.

General Bardolph proceeded to his office on the third floor of the original building of NSA.

NSA had come into existence in 1952 stemming from a need, after WWII, for a unified military intelligence organization. By the 21st century it had grown to be the parent of intelligence gathering within the intelligence community. NSA and the military intelligence units encompassed a huge section of the south sector of Fort Meade. MI units, especially those of the army, had been restructured and reorganized as NSA began sponging up other MI organizations such as ASA (Army Security Agency) and USASTRATCOM (United States Army Strategic Communications Command).

General Bardolph leaned back in his cushy, black leathered executive's chair contemplating his move, studying his options like a master chess player. After rubbing his jaw for three minutes, he picked up the receiver of a special in-house phone.

"This is Captain Harding, sir!"

"Captain, I want you to take two men with you, and go to the NCIC Office at the 519th Military Police Provost Marshall's Office and give Mr. Roberts his walking papers."

Captain Harding had been with the General in Tango-Echo during the NCIC search of the secret numbers. He was also associated with the General because they had both been planted at NSA for one purpose.

As Captain Harding drove away from NSA heading toward the Provost Office, he gave grave consideration to what authority, or regulation, gave him the power to authorize the retirement of a civilian in another military organization. A broad smile moved across his face. The catchall authority that allows NSA to do almost everything in which NSA operates: "In the interest of national security."

NCIC Office
519th MP Provost Marshall
Fort Meade, Maryland
Thursday, September 30th
1500 hours

The building housing the 519th Provost ran parallel to Mapes Road. The entrance was in the rear parking lot side of the building. The MP desk was on the left side of a small entranceway running lengthways to the room.

Another set of doors led into the first floor corridor. The holding cell was right oblique across from the doors. Mr. Roberts' office was left oblique from the doors at the end of an inverted "L" shaped corridor.

Leonardo da Vinci Roberts sat with his back straight up in his gray cushioned chair. He had typed in the plate number Skip had given him, but the regular listings provided no clue. Now, he was beginning to worry because that meant either it was a diplomatic plate, or it was a special issue plate, which meant he could be infringing into territories where he did not wish to tread or belong.

"That damn Skip," he said to his monitor screen, "he's always getting me into crap."

As Leon typed the numbers, he allowed a small smile to spread across his face. He thought back to Germany when he and Skip first met.

They were stationed with the 3rd Armored Division, and both wanted to be Military Police. It was near the end of May 1975 when he learned Skip's true identity. Back then, Skip was posing as Sergeant Derry Batair, a damn spook rooting out spies during the Cold War.

When he typed in the last number, Leon pushed away from his desk in astonished bewilderment. His computer screen had gone blank. Leon tried to reboot to no avail. "A virus?" he asked himself. Then it hit him. NSA! Shit! "I've got to warn Skip."

Just as Leon hung up his phone, three NSA agents came bursting into his office.

"Damned if I do, and damned if I don't," Leon spoke softly to himself as he rocked in his chair. He had given Skip the warning. He knew that Skip would decipher its meaning.

Colonel Beard, the Provost Marshall, and three men stood rock-steady inside of his office near the closed door. "Leon, these men are from NSA. They say you have breached national security, and that you are to retire immediately."

"Sir, if I had breached national security, it was damn sure unintentional. And how in the hell did I manage to do that?"

Captain Harding approached Leon's desk. He snatched up a notepad. "By trying to identify this diplomatic plate number, that's how."

Of course he had destroyed the paper with the number on it, but Leon cursed himself for a fool. He had forgotten the page underneath the one he had written the numbers. It became visible after Harding had used a pencil by lightly shading in the near invisible numbers.

"What I want to know, Mr. Roberts, is how you came by this number?"

Leon began to stoke his pipe. He took his time filling the bowl with tobacco and lighting his pipe. He began drawing on it, blowing ringlets into the air. While doing so, he considered his position. Should he give them the information?

He remembered something Skip had told him once. "MI has a devoted satellite. Its sole mission is to scan world wide telephone conversations, honing in on key words that had been programmed into the system's listening devices."

"So, if that's true," Leon thought, "then these ass-wipes already know who provided him with the number."

Leon asked himself, "What would Skip want me to do?"

After he drew three times on his pipe, Leon said, "You already know. It was Skip Daggard."

Captain Harding smiled. "Pack up your belongings. As of this moment you are retired. Put in your papers immediately."

"So, that's how it is?"

"That's how it is, and you can be thankful that we are not arresting you for interfering in our business."

Leon wanted to…oh, how he wanted to tell them to "fuck off and die", but his satisfaction would come from Skip's actions because there was definitely something *wrong* with this picture. And he knew that somewhere, somehow, Skip would be forced to fix whatever was broken.

Pizza Hut parking lot
Oakland, Maryland
Thursday, September 30th
1515 hours

Skip placed the hot pizza box on the back seat. "Eilis don't get into our pizza. It's very hot. Wait until we get home." He smiled at his auburn haired daughter Eilis, who was almost three. She sat complacent in her car seat. Eilis was named after Skip's mother by strict orders from Kristine.

Kristine finally met Mrs. Daggard three months after Skip and Kristine's previous actions in Washington. One month later, Eilis Daggard passed away of cancer.

As Skip slipped in behind the steering wheel, Kristine said, "I am glad that I had met your mom before she…"

Skip looked at her through his soft, blue eyes. "So am I, honey. Mom really took to you. I didn't have the heart to tell her that you're a Russian spy."

Kristine threw a playful punch at his right shoulder. "What are we going to do, darling?" she asked as they headed north on 219 out of Oakland towards Deep Creek Lake and Friendsville.

"I've been giving that some thought, Kristine. Your father was in the hierarchy of the Soviet KGB, right?"

She nodded her head.

"He is now one of the Deputy Directors of Russia's Federal Secret Service; the KGB's successor."

Again, Kristine nodded her head trying to figure out where Skip was going.

As they drove past Taco Bell, Skip sighed taking a quick look at Kristine. She looked back at him. She stretched out her left arm and began to massage his right shoulder.

Skip looked back at the road, enjoying the soothing sensation of her hand.

"Before they had gone off radar, Skip, the Communist Coalition force consisted of thirty million soldiers. The Soviets were forming paramilitary units within the hard line Communist countries. They wanted back what they had lost in 1989.

"The wall had been constructed by the U.S.S.R in 1961, dividing East and West Germany. When the wall came down and Germany united, that action caused the destruction of the Communist bloc countries and their restructuring as independent countries.

"The KGB was not disbanded, honey. They simply…vanished along with the Soviet military and most of the munitions. My father helped to establish Russia's Federal Secret Service. Their first order of business was to locate and arrest all members of the defunct KGB."

Skip took a stern glance at her, and then resumed his surveillance of the highway.

"From documents and interrogations, the Federal Secret Service learned of the Communist plot to seize world control." She paused and studied him for any reaction. "Skip, my people had no idea where that force had gone. They had disappeared."

Skip glared at her again. "I hope, h-o-n-e-y, that I'm not going to find out that you and your friends have been plotting this military coup."

"You will never fully trust me, will you?"

"Perhaps; I don't know. But I just can't fathom it, darlin', me, of all people, that I'd fall in love with a commie spy, and that she had been in love with me almost her whole life."

Kristine cringed at his words. She gently placed her head on his right shoulder, then looked at him with sensual eyes, "And you *do* love me, don't you, lover?"

A smile spread over his face, "Yeah! Darnedest thing I ever heard of. Yeah, honey, I love you," he said softly as he placed his right hand on her left thigh.

They were driving on the bridge over Deep Creek Lake. Vacationers and local people filled the waterways with various sizes of motor boats. Some courageous adventurers were enjoying the lake in canoes and kayaks along the shorelines.

Skip sat bolt up in the driver's seat. "Damn," he blurted out, "I know why they're here."

"*What?*"

Skip pulled over to the shoulder of the road once they had crossed the bridge. He put his vehicle in park and turned toward Kristine. "I know why they're here. Look at history, honey. For instance: World War One. Europe was holding its own. But when the US entered the war, we made the difference.

"During World War Two, Europe was barely holding its own. Japan was beginning to gobble up Asia. Again, when America entered the war, we made the difference.

"The Communist Coalition force is going to hit the US first; take out the dragon while the commie forces are at full strength."

They held hands looking at each other. "Skip, I think you're right. What do we do?"

Skip rubbed his chin with his right hand while puzzling over an answer.

"Well," he smiled catching her off guard, "we're going to go home and eat our pizza."

He began to laugh, which made Kristine and Eilis laugh.

"Then," he added, "We're going to get down and dirty. I'll contact Hanalin, and you, my lovely...you will contact your father."

Now Skip understood why the North Koreans had been testing missiles. The UN and the US went ballistic on them back in 2007/'08 for conducting their nuclear missile testing. Then North Korea did not have long range capabilities, but their tests continued through 2009. But if they had long range capabilities now...

Chapter Three—Spies in NSA

NSA
General Bardolph's Office
Fort Meade, Maryland
Thursday, September 30th
1800 Hours

Captain Brand Harding sat quietly at the huge oak conference table sipping fresh, black coffee from a stout mug ornamented with a leg and claw of a bald eagle clutching two lightning bolts, the emblem of the defunct ASA (Army Security Agency).

He walked straight-backed on muscular calved legs, stood six feet in his stocking feet, and carried the two scars on his evil looking face with pride. He had won the scars during the Soviet invasion of Afghanistan. His black eyes accented the evil permeating from his cruel stare and sinister smile.

General Bardolph had a map laid out on the table. He was studying specific locations marked with blue dots. "What did this fellow, Roberts have to say?"

"That it was Daggard who had called him with the plate number."

General Bardolph looked up from the map that pinpointed the locations of the Communist Coalition forces. "We already knew that, Captain. What I want to know is, does Roberts pose a threat?"

Captain Harding gave some thought to his commanding officer's question while he took three sips of his coffee. "No, sir, he does not."

"Then," General Bardolph said, "We have to eliminate Daggard." His words caused an uncontrolled tremor to shake his huge frame.

"Perhaps the best solution would be to discredit him…"

General Bardolph leaned across the conference table, his face alive with rage. "*Discredit him!*" he shouted with indignation in his tone. "Captain, we will do just that. However, this man has no scruples when dealing with his enemies. And we have to go on the assumption that Agent Daggard has already figured out that his enemies are within the intelligence community and seated within the government.

"To think otherwise could lead to disaster. No! We must conclude that Daggard is on to us, and that he knows there is a large enemy force within the borders of the US. So this leaves us with no alternative, Captain. We *must* terminate that threat."

General Bardolph fell back into his chair allowing a deep, foreboding exhale of breath to escape from his lungs. His skin began to feel the ripples of defeat, as his round face became rigid with determination. "Daggard must be terminated immediately, Captain."

He went back to studying the map as he lighted up a Cuban cigar. Once his cigar was lit, the general puffed on it vigorously as a gray cloud of smoke surrounded his head. He sat complacent, as Cold War images kept resurrecting themselves in his mind.

Captain Harding finished his coffee. He got up from his seat and went to the small table, which was against the inner wall five feet from the entrance door. He refilled his cup. As he turned back towards the conference table, he said, "Coffee is one American luxury I enjoy the most."

When he was seated, Captain Harding spoke again, "He is only one man, sir…"

General Bardolph shot up from his chair. He reached over his desk and slapped the coffee cup from his subordinate's hand. "You idiot!" he spit out his words, "You stupid, stupid idiot!"

Captain Harding pressed himself against the back of his chair. He had never seen such viciousness in his leader before.

"Tonight," General Bardolph declared, "you go out to Friendsville and wipe them out." He noticed the sinister smile on Captain Harding's face.

"Do not play games with this man, Captain Harding," he chastised. "No torture or lechery. No assassination. Make it appear an accident. Understood?"

"Yes sir."

"It is a three hour drive; why are you still here?"

NSA
Sierra-Gulf Group
Fort Meade, Maryland
Thursday, September 30th
1820 hours

Captain Harding began to breathe heavily as he thought about tonight's escapade. He made his way down the corridor to his office. He punched in the key code on the silver wall-mounted keypad. Once inside, he pointed to Lieutenants' John Pearl and Tim Hamstead. They followed him into his small office.

Captain Harding's section was a 20 by 50 foot rectangular room. There were fifteen desks in this room sectioned off by gray colored metal partitions. Captain Harding was in charge of 45 analysts, working three 8-hour shifts and alternating weekends, a 24/7 operation. The analysts' roster consisted of thirty senior army sergeants, seven senior Marine sergeants, and five senior air force sergeants, with a master sergeant in charge of each group. Their mission was to analyze and catalog all military correspondence of enemy and friendly countries and military forces in the Middle East.

Captain Harding fixed himself a cup of coffee, using another mug with the old ASA insignia. He did not use any milk or cream derivatives, but he liked two heaping spoonfuls of sugar.

Once he had fixed his coffee, he offered his subordinates the opportunity to fill cups—both declined.

He sat down at his gray metal desk sipping his coffee thinking how he was going to molest Kristine Daggard. He had wanted her ever since the first time that they had met during their training in "Little America" in Georgia, Russia, which now was a starving free country.

He turned his attention back to the present as he explained, "We have been tasked with a vital mission." He took three sips studying the reaction of his subordinates.

"We have been offered the distinct honor of terminating the bad-ass."

Lieutenant Pearl leaned forward and whispered, "*Agent Daggard?*"

Captain Harding took two sips of his coffee before nodding his head.

The two Lieutenants stared at each other for four seconds before they turned back to their leader. Lieutenant Hamstead spoke, "When do we do this, and how many others will be joining us?"

Captain Harding was enjoying this moment of toying with his two subordinates, so he drank his coffee until he had finished the black, steaming brew. He rose from his chair and fixed another cup. When he turned back and began walking to his chair, he could see the realization spreading over his men's faces.

He sat down, took four sips of his drink then said, "No one else. Just we three…"

Lieutenant Pearl jumped to his feet leaning over the desk, "Are you insane, Captain?" Pearl dribbled spittle down his chin.

Captain Harding jumped to his feet. "Sit down, Lieutenant. We do not need anyone else"

Lieutenant Hamstead rose in a slow steady movement. "Sir, twenty men would not be enough. Maybe even one hundred would not be enough…"

Captain Harding waved his left hand, "Enough! He is only one man. We leave in thirty minutes. Get ready."

"You do realize that we are going to our deaths, don't you, sir?" said Lieutenant Pearl. "Who gave the order?" he asked. Of course he did not need to ask; he had known that his captain had been with General Bardolph.

Lieutenant Pearl began to fidget. He was trying to express his feelings and knowledge without offending his superior.

"Go ask our general," Lieutenant Pearl stated, "He had Daggard once—in chains. Go ask him, Captain. Ask him what he thinks about Daggard being *just one man*."

Captain Harding's face flushed red with anger. He issued his order to his Lieutenants in a harsh voice. "We are leaving in twenty-five minutes."

Daggard residence
Buffalo Run Road
Friendsville, Maryland
Thursday, September 30th
1835 hours

Skip stood on their front porch listening to the gurgle of the water in Buffalo Creek as the water followed its course to the Yough Lake. He faced east, lost in the brilliance of the fire in the sky, as the layers of bright oranges and reds accented the autumn colors of the leaves swaying in rhythm from a gentle breeze.

Nine robins bobbed their heads in unison penetrating the rich, green grass with their black beaks pulling out worms then flying up to their nests.

Skip turned as the screen door squeaked and Kristine stepped out next to him. She put her right arm around his waist as he laid his left arm over her shoulders. "My God," she exclaimed, "the sky is beautiful."

"Yeah, a golden crimson fire in the sky."

They stood together for five minutes lost in the serenity of the valley.

Kristine broke the silence. "What are we going to do, darling?"

Skip turned his head and stared at her. She looked back at him. "There you go with questions again." He smiled at her. She smiled back at him. Right now at this moment, there was no time, only peace in their paradise!

"I've been contemplating that issue, darling, but so far I haven't come up with a solution. I know what has to be done…"

Kristine interrupted him. "Do you truly believe that they are here? They could be tourists from the Korean Embassy."

Five robins returned for more worms, while six crows began chasing each other around the tops of eight sixty-foot pine trees

Skip exhaled a deep, remorseful sigh. "I would agree with you, Kristine, if it had not been for Leon's warning. I'm sure that they are Korean soldiers not diplomats."

He studied the colors in the sky. They began to fade as the earth rotated on its axis giving the false impression that it was the sun moving west. The sky began to cloud over.

Images began to invade his conscience; there was nothing he could do to stop them. For some unknown reason he decided to share them with Kristine.

"I was standing on a platform one morning with John. It was our turn to burn top secret documents and traffic-tapes that had no more purpose. It was 6 a.m., Kristine. We stood there on that cement platform marveling at the huge size of the morning sun hanging over the rice-paddies.

"It was as if we could reach out and touch it. We tried. The sky was a golden hue of several shades of orange."

Skip shivered. His face went blank. His blue eyes narrowed to vertical slits on his face as amber fire exploded from those slits.

Kristine had witnessed this transformation many times. He was gone—back to Vietnam. She had to pee but held her water. She knew something horrible was coming. She had been down this road with Skip before.

Six seconds later, Skip exhaled. He was back. "It hadn't been an autumn sky, Kristine; it had been a September sky, 1968. It had been the dawn of my death."

He turned to face her as she turned and faced him. She could see the sadness in his eyes.

"That dawn was a burning fire in the sky just as this sunset has been."

His breathing became labored and his voice hoarse. He was choking on his words. "They came that night, Kristine. They came from the jungle across the rice-paddies in boats. They came and we had not been issued weapons in order to defend ourselves."

Skip turned away from her. Sadness overtook his face. She believed that he had stopped breathing. He turned back to her, wrapping his arms around her. She could feel the water from his eyes running down her neck as she too began to cry. His whispered words echoing in her ear, "I had faced the enemy. I died."

She squeezed him, hugged him, held him, and then she whispered to him, "I love you, Skip Daggard."

Eilis' crying interrupted the moment. They went inside to tend to their daughter.

Daggard residence
Buffalo Run Road
Friendsville, Maryland
Thursday, September 30th
2215 hours

Skip Daggard paced the great room of their cabin. It was the type of place he had always dreamed of, the log cabin that he and Bryanna had spoken about during their senior year in high school.

The cabin was 28 feet wide by 48 feet long situated on ten acres fronting the creek. The white-painted steel front door faced the creek and the road. The great room was a living room, kitchen combination. The bathroom was off the kitchen and part of the utility room.

The living room area was to the left and the kitchen was to the right of the front door, when entering the house. The huge hearth and chimney was part of the outside wall four feet left of the front door. To maximize a heat source from the hearth, they had a cast iron wood-burning stove inserted into the hearth with a glass window in the door, so they could enjoy watching a fire burning.

Two bedrooms and a study were in line directly across from the front door. All three rooms were ten by ten. The center room was Eilis' dorm. Their bedroom was off of the kitchen area, while the study was off of the far side of the living room.

He had just put three logs in the cast iron wood burner when Kristine came from Eilis' room. "She's asleep; now what?"

Kristine knew from experience not to prod him while Skip was in his analytic mode. This was his puzzle-solving attitude. She had learned that this process is what made Skip different from almost every operative in the world. While many operatives took information at face value, he would stop and take the time necessary to put the pieces together. The pieces of information he had gathered which would help him reach a plan of attack.

Ten minutes had elapsed. Skip turned to add fuel to the fire. A slight smile formed around his lips. It was his indication that he had come to some resolution.

Skip turned from his task to look at her. While taking in her beauty, he expressed his solution.

"I am going down the road to contact General Hanalin. The small white building on the corner of Old Morgantown West and Route 42 is a repeater station…"

Kristine stared at him. Skip smiled. "The hooch houses a main frame and a dedicated secure military land line…"

Kristine stared at him incredulous. "Out here in the middle of nowhere?"

Skip cracked up, and then collected himself when he saw her angry glare. "This area is rich in history, Kristine. Friendsville was the first white settlement in these parts in the seventeen hundreds; seventeen sixty-two to be exact, by John Friend. He and his brothers came over the mountains from Virginia.

"During the Indian uprising, Friendsville was the only white settlement in the region not attacked because the Friends had not lied to or tried to cheat the Shawnee, and the Indians were always welcomed.

"Civil War battles had been fought around the area, and Braddock was killed just thirty miles from here up in Farmington, PA., during the French and Indian Wars. The place there called Fort Necessity was where George Washington incurred his first defeat at the hands of the French and their Indian allies. "

She stood with her legs spread and her hands on her hips, while her eyes threw daggers at him. "That's one thing which infuriates me about you, Skip Daggard."

"What's that, my lovely?"

She took in a deep breath, staring him down. "When I ask you what time it is, you tell me how to build a watch."

He glared at her for two seconds. "Oh yeah?"

He could see that she was formulating a reply.

"Yeah, and you better not say, fuck-off, or I'll punch you right in the face."

"Okay, okay, so what does history have to do with the building? No one knows the future, honey, so precautions have been taken. We have National Guard and reserve units all over the country. So in order to allow for whatever comes down the pike, those units have communications with each other by utilizing mainframes housed in buildings like the one I just mentioned.

"There are repeater stations, thousands of them, in out of the way places just like the one up the road."

He strolled across the floor, took her in his arms and kissed her. "Remember the last time you tried to punch me?"

She stepped back smiling. "I guess you're the one who has forgotten."

Skip rubbed his jaw. They laughed.

The only light in the great room came from a sixty-watt light bulb over the kitchen sink. Glowing, blue-orange flames from the fire danced in front of the window of the cast iron stove.

"While I'm gone, contact your father. Use that handy-dandy scramble device you have stowed away."

Kristine spun around staring at him. "*You know?*"

"Sure! After what we had been through, and knowing where you had come from, the device just didn't seem important enough to start anything over."

She went into his arms planting kisses all over his face. "Skip, since we are all packed, why don't we leave right now? I can use the scrambler on any phone. Call it woman's intuition if you want, but I have this clawing sensation all over my body that we need to leave... now."

He squeezed her tight, kissed her passionately, and then whispered in her ear, "When I get back we'll leave."

Skip turned around to look at her as he stepped off the front porch. The night was black with stars twinkling. He was contemplating the idea of taking them with him.

"I wish we had a dog," she said.

They stared at each other studying each other's physique, committing the moment and looks to memory. "Remember what I had told you once about dogs being in my food chain?"

She swiveled her hips a few times then said, "*I don't believe you.*"

Skip came to her as Kristine closed the front door behind her. He gently kneaded her firm buttocks pressing his body against her slender, tall frame. They French kissed as Skip glided his fingers of both hands up her back causing shivers of excitement to ripple along her spine.

She could tell from experience what his passionate kisses and his husky breathing meant. She spread her legs as his left arm curled around her waist. His right hand drifted down from feathering her shoulder length blonde hair to her right breast. Her nipple responded as he toyed with her flesh. She reached down and unfastened his belt then unzipped his zipper.

Skip dropped his right arm down and worked his hand up and under her skirt and along her long, slender legs up over the top of her black thigh-high stockings to her crotch.

Twenty minutes later she whispered in his ear. "See, I have learned something."

"Yeah, what's that?"

"The idea of danger makes you horny."

They laughed. "Turn off the porch light when I leave, honey. I won't be gone long."

As Skip drove out of the driveway heading up Buffalo Run Road toward Route 42 there was something about the shadows that disturbed him.

Captain Harding had watched the scene unfolding on the porch from the group of pine trees twenty yards from Daggard's home. The scene had so excited him that he had to mentally restrain himself until the sound of Daggard's vehicle was swallowed up by the night.

He charged forward. His two men could hardly keep up with him. Captain Harding kicked in the front door, raced across the twenty feet of floor space and punched Kristine in her Germanic face. He grabbed the baby from her arms as she began to fall and threw Eilis towards Lieutenant Pearl then knocked Kristine to the floor. He stepped over her, bent down yanking her by her shoulder length, blonde hair and dragged her up onto the bed ripping off her clothes. He had forgotten everything his superior officer had said.

Repeater Station #10
Old Morgantown Road
Thursday, September 30th
2230 hours

Skip had parked his truck ten yards down the hill from the repeater station. As he slipped the key into the lock, he took a quick survey of the surrounding area, unlocked the door, removed the key from the lock, stepped inside, and closed the door behind him. Once the door was secure, he slid his left hand up the wall until he felt the light switch.

The white building was eight feet long and six feet wide. A mainframe occupied the center of the floor. A repeater station is strategically located in order to enhance voice and telephone signals over many miles.

Skip moved swiftly to the left back corner of the building. The green box was one foot wide, two feet in length, and six inches deep. The writing on the panel door declared in bold, black letters: **AUTHORIZED PERSONNEL ONLY-PROPERTY OF THE US GOVERNMENT**.

Skip used a special key to unlock the box. The box contained a series of jacks connected to distant ends via fiber-optic cables and one black in color handset with a cord attached so the other end could be plugged into any jack port an operator wished to use. He plugged the end into the Pentagon circuit and dialed up General Hanalin's specific code and numbers to ring up his cell phone.

As the phone rang, Skip heard the wailing of sirens as fire engines sped past the building down Route 42. A cold, penetrating chill created a series of trembling shivers of his body.

"Sally, how many times have I told you *not* to call me at this hour when I cannot *leave* my office?"

The phone went dead. Skip disconnected the jack immediately. "Shit! General Hanalin is a prisoner inside the Pentagon?"

Another siren went past wailing in the night. Skip knew, with the wailing of that siren, he should have listened to Kristine as a cold shiver rippled along his spine. The night air was cool, yet perspiration exploded from his pores as he ran to his vehicle.

Remains of the Daggard residence
Buffalo Run Road
Friendsville, Maryland
Thursday, September 30ᵗʰ
2300 hours

Skip Daggard fell to his knees near the body bags. Firefighters were rolling up hoses and putting equipment away. Three small fires still burned. Smoke filtered up his nostrils causing a burning sensation to his eyes.

Skip attributed it was the irritation from the smoke, which was causing the water buildup and tears to fall from his eyes.

He rested his butt against his heels taking in the scene before him; the charred ruins of his house, the two body bags, and firefighters cleaning up, while two men with shovels doused the small fires with dirt. Skip took all of this in as his mind continued to process events.

The Friendsville Fire Chief, Steve Olson, stood near his right shoulder. Two state troopers from the McHenry Barracks stood close by.

"It was completely engulfed by the time we arrived, Skip," Olson stated. "I'm sorry, Skip, but this was no accident."

Skip Daggard barely heard Olson's words because he was already beginning his transformation process as he unzipped the child's body bag. He had to force himself to look. Slowly he allowed the rage to seep through him allowing the demon to begin its ascent.

He stared at the two index fingers resting on Eilis' bare belly. He began to emit grunting sounds from his mouth. Sounds that were forming from deep down in the pit of his stomach where the demon was beginning to awaken as it felt the restraints being removed.

Skip slowly moved his head staring at Eilis' hands. Unable… unwilling to control his demon any more, Skip Daggard shattered the midnight air with a piercing, Celtic war cry that held everyone frozen in their positions, staring at him.

Chief Olson leaned forward. "Rodeheaver and Sampson pulled them out."

Skip acknowledged this piece of information by nodding his head at the two firefighters. He leaned down as his tears fell on her charred face. He kissed her burned, swollen lips. Gently, Skip lifted her head. The bullet had entered the left side of her head just above her ear. As if not wishing to awaken Eilis, Skip carefully laid her head down.

His rage was taking hold now. His demon was stirring, shifting, and beginning to rise.

He scooted along the damp grass on his knees. With trembling hands, Skip unzipped the adult body bag. Ridden with guilt, Skip could not look at Kristine's face right away. Instead, he stared out into the blackness of the night listening to the moans of the pines, firs, and locust trees as they swayed in the strong breeze. He spoke out into that blackness, words that were coherent to no one but himself. "I should have listened to her. *I* should have understood her intuition." He forced his head to tilt downward. He forced his eyes to look upon her face.

Skip broke down with an outpouring of gut-wrenching tears and sobs as he lifted her up and held her close to him. "Forgive me! Please… please forgive me," he cried.

He laid her down softly, then leaned over and gently kissed her cold, dead lips. Her right breast had been hacked off. The fire had fused it to her belly as had happened with Eilis' fingers.

Skip zipped the bag closed. He rose to his feet wiping away his tears, sucking down his sorrow. As Skip turned, the two state troopers stepped forward. The sergeant said, "Mr. Daggard, we are sorry for your loss, but you will have to come with us. There are some questions."

Skip stared at them through rage-filled, blank eyes. A look that sent shivers of fear rippling throughout both troopers' bodies.

"This is war. You're not involved yet…but soon."

Skip turned to Chief Olson. "Steve, please put them on ice for me at the morgue. When this is over…I will bury them."

The state troopers maneuvered themselves in order to intercept Skip. Chief Olson stepped in front of them. "Let him go. There's something going on here and he is the one who can handle the situation."

Emergency vehicles began leaving. Skip leaned against his Chevy SUV while observing the bodies of Kristine and Eilis being placed on gurneys then lifted into an ambulance.

"This is why, Kristine, why I had never gotten married. Now we are retired, but you and our baby are the first casualties of the coming crisis."

As the ambulance drove away, Skip climbed into his vehicle. He leaned back against the seat resting his head against the headrest. He settled into the seat and closed his eyes and placed his hands on his thighs. He gave in to his rage allowing the demon free reign. The rage surged through his body releasing the demon. The demon surged up from its dormant hiding place free of its restraints.

When Skip Daggard opened his eyes five minutes later, he was what war and the army had made him, a cold, calculating, killing machine. Skip Daggard was gone, replaced by the demon.

It was the demon who drove out of Buffalo Run Valley intent upon a rampage of carnage. He turned left onto Route 42 heading south toward Friendsville, Interstate 68 and NSA.

Friendsville, Maryland
Friday, October 1
0025 hours

He drove out of the valley leaving the destruction behind. Skip was hell-bent on his own path of destruction, but his intuition screamed at him. "What are you doing? Pick your position. Let the enemy come to you. You know the drill."

He listened to the lambasting for five miles into Friendsville. Just before the entrance ramp to I-68 East he turned around at the Marathon service station, drove back to his place, and parked his TrailBlazer in his driveway.

Skip Daggard watched smoldering ringlets of smoke rising from the ashes of his home. He slid out of his vehicle viewing the destruction through hard, cold, penetrating eyes. His heart, like ice, felt no emotion. "This is war," he said out loud, "and you and Eilis are its first casualties. But I promise you this, Kristine there will be many more before this war is won."

A light rain began to fall. The warm temperature moved on a gentle breeze. Skip Daggard let the water soak his face as he drank in the cool liquid. He turned and marched to the rear of his vehicle, raising the hatch door. He lifted a piece of the carpet, pulled on a small, black colored ring, and pulled up the false decking.

As he stared out over his land, Skip cried, "They are going to pay, Kristine. They are going to pay dearly. I promise you and Eilis."

Skip Daggard reached into the belly of his SUV and retrieved his war bag, which consisted of a large backpack, a Colt .45 and his sniper rifle. As he saddled up, he gave no thought to any plan. He would leave his vehicle in his driveway, pick a location and wait.

He walked across his yard into the woods. He crossed over a small runoff creek in back of his house, then up the hill to Bud Frantz's barn.

The slight drizzle had stopped. A gusty wind had blown the clouds away, and a full moon lighted his way. Stars winked at him as he stood in shadows near the old barn.

He studied the area for five minutes before crossing Meyers Road. Skip walked up the hill past Bud's farmhouse into the woods. He commanded a large view of the valley from the position he had chosen twenty yards into the woods.

Skip built a temporary shelter of downed tree limbs, branches, and leaves. Once he was satisfied, he wrapped up in his poncho and then went to sleep while visions of Kristine and Eilis invaded his dreams.

Chapter Four—The Enemy Strikes

NSA
General Ashford Bardolph's Office
Friday, October 1
0930 hours

Fort Meade lay quiet and serene, warming up with the aid of a bright sun, after an early morning shower. One hundred twenty soldiers of the 704th MI Brigade were preparing to complete their annual training in soldier skills. Their knowledge would be tested in compass, chemical warfare, map reading, disassembling and reassembling of the M-16 A-4 and 204 assault rifles, and setting clamor mines.

General Bardolph paced behind his oak desk wearing out the plush, deep blue carpet. He lit one of his Cuban cigars, took two long drags, blew smoke into the air, and then smashed the stogie into tiny fragments in his brown colored, glass ashtray. He responded to the knock on his door. "COME IN," he shouted.

Captain Harding and his two lieutenants entered, looking curiously at their leader.

General Bardolph said sarcastically, "Sit down at the table, gentlemen."

The officers took up seats around the small, round table in the center of the room left oblique from the general's desk. "Did all go well?" he demanded in a pleasant tone.

Captain Harding swiveled around in his chair to the left and right in a back and forth motion as he faced his leader remembering how good Kristine had felt. "Is something troubling you, sir?"

General Bardolph slammed a file down on the table before Harding. "You tell me, *Captain*."

Captain Harding flipped the cover of the light tan, manila file folder over. He scrutinized the four pictures for thirty seconds. "So, this is the ruins of Daggard's house. I think we did a splendid job of it."

General Bardolph leaned down going nose to nose with Harding. "You blundering idiot! Don't you see it?"

Captain Harding looked again, and then passed the folder over to his men for a look-see. "I don't see the problem, General. They're all dead."

General Bardolph threw a chair across the room. "Look again you blind, bungling fool."

Captain Harding took another glance at the photos. "You mean the vehicle?"

General Bardolph threw up his arms. "If we were back in our own country, I would shoot you where you sit. LOOK AT THE PICTURES... Captain. I had I-Spy satellite take photos of the Daggard's house just before you torched it. Now look at the after photos again.

"Do you know whose vehicle that is? It belongs to the most notorious son of a bitch in the US arsenal. You raped the woman, didn't you? Then you tortured them, didn't you? After I gave you explicit orders not to play games with this man...just to kill them."

"He was not at home. And the fire got out of control. Besides, he is only one man. What can he do?"

General Bardolph became exasperated. "Do! What can he doooo? Oh, I have forgotten! You do not hunt; therefore, you have never been in the woods with a wounded animal."

Captain Harding showed his confusion in his eyes, and canting his head, he said, "Sir, I do not understand. What is..."

"You idiot! It's quite simple. It's a message. He left his vehicle there on purpose. Now, take your other two idiots, and this time, Captain, *kill* him. Get out!"

A Secret Bunker
5 miles south of
Kingwood, West Virginia
Friday, October 1
1100 hours

Colonel Chin Lee slammed the phone receiver down on its cradle. She stomped around the operations room for three minutes before she could get her anger under control. "I knew in my gut that we should never have trusted those idiot Soviets," she spit her words out as a cobra would its venom.

Her operations personnel had learned the hard way that when their colonel was in this state of rage the best thing to do was to listen and not move or utter a word.

She turned to Lieutenant Wong. "Those moles in NSA were supposed to terminate the Daggards. Those idiots bungled the job. They killed his wife and daughter but left him alive." Colonel Lee went into a rage. She flipped the conference table over then began throwing chairs against the wall. Her soldiers ran from one corner of the confined space to another to avoid being struck by flying objects.

Exhausted, she fell into one of the few chairs that she had not smashed against the wall during her rampage.

"Colonel, your father," her radio operator said in a trembling voice.

"Father, I have been trying to reach you."

"I have received distressing news, Chin. We have been discussing options."

"Father, Daggard is on to us…"

"I know!"

She took the receiver away from her left ear looking at it as if the receiver was her father's face. She stared quizzically at the handset.

"Father, we did nothing wrong! Three comrades went with me for supplies to a place the Americans call Wal-Mart. We were at a traffic light. And like magic, father, he was there. I was going to shoot him but there were police close by."

Silence, but she could hear her father's heavy breathing.

Colonel Chin Lee waited.

Her father whispered, "We are doomed."

"Father, those Soviet idiots had an opportunity to kill him but bungled their mission. General Bardolph has just informed me that he has sent those same idiots back to Friendsville to terminate Agent Daggard."

"Perhaps we should pull our troops out," he said. "Unfortunately, President Huong is determined to destroy the US and unify Korea.

"Chin," her father began to whisper, "*you* must find him…kill him."

Colonel Lee squeezed the handset. Her long nails punctured the skin of her left hand drawing blood. She whispered to her father, "Agent Daggard will be dead before the sun sets tonight."

Colonel Chin Lee hung up the receiver, wiped blood from her hand, and then wrapped a white handkerchief around her hand. She looked over at Lieutenant Wong. He was staring at her. "I had to tell him something. I will allow the Soviets one more attempt."

Buffalo Run Valley
Frantz farm
Friday, October 1
1200 hours

Skip Daggard sat with his back against a large locust tree. He surveyed the valley below looking for any movement but there was none. Some of the local inhabitants of the valley had driven along Buffalo Run Road viewing the destruction of his house. He had counted seven vehicles in an hour and a half. No one had stopped to take longer looks.

He peeled off his poncho so the sun could penetrate his skin and warm up his chilled bones. He ate cold C-Rations of beans, hot dogs, and peaches, and washed his food down with a few swallows of water from his canteen. His legs were stretched out with his rifle lying across his lap. He knew they'd come. It was only a matter of time.

Friendsville, Maryland
Friday, October 1
1430 hours

The sky was clear with only a scattering of cotton ball shaped clouds dotting the blue canvas. The Youghiogheny River made lapping sounds as it splashed against the cement supports of the bridge leading into the town of Friendsville. It had taken an hour to coordinate the assault against Skip Daggard. The two teams would rendezvous on Maple Street, the main thoroughfare into Friendsville. They would meet in the parking area near the liquor store at the corner of Water Street just before the bridge leading into the town.

The small, quiet community of farmers and loggers lay quiet and peaceful in a valley of protruding peaks. The town consisted of one grocery store, a gas station, bank, auto repair garage, post office, one bar, three hotels, liquor store, boat manufacturing plant, pharmacy, and a few eating establishments. Recreation could be found by enjoying rafting on the Yough with the rafting company housed near the Youghiogheny River and the bridge. The one beauty and barbershop was closed. All of the establishments are within a few minutes walking distance of each other.

The six hundred and ten inhabitants of the quiet hamlet went about their daily routines clueless of the events taking place within their realm. What most of them knew was what Chief Olson had told them, "Arsonists had torched Skip Daggard's home and murdered his wife and daughter."

The dark colored Ford Expedition SUV drove off of I-68 at the Friendsville exit. At the end of the ramp, the vehicle turned left onto Friendsville Road heading north. The vehicle went eighty yards then turned right onto Maple Street. The driver drove a quarter mile, then steered her vehicle into the parking area between the bridge and the liquor store and parked with the vehicle facing Maple Street.

Agent Mark Stough, FBI Field Operations Officer out of Morgantown, West Virginia, sat straight-backed in the front passenger seat. He was forty-five with wavy brown hair and a fair complexion. He viewed the world out of clear, green eyes. He had no illusions about his organization's role in the world. He was a devout communist and had been trained as an American in Georgia, Russia. He was Soviet and believed, without doubt, that the Soviet's manifest destiny was to rule the world.

Mark Stough had infiltrated into the US twenty-five years ago by joining the navy and Naval Intelligence. He retired five years ago from the navy after serving his last three years with Naval Intelligence at NSA at Fort Meade, Maryland. He went right into the FBI. Now he was operations officer at the Morgantown headquarters.

There were four of his agents with him. He had been ordered by General Bardolph to assist NSA agents to hunt down and terminate Agent Daggard.

Bardolph said, "I have alerted higher authorities that Agent Daggard is a communist spy. I have forwarded documents proving my allegations throughout the intelligence community. You will not be hindered in your mission."

Agent Stough looked over at his driver, Agent Samantha Bell. "It seems that some things never change, Agent Bell. Three years ago President Mantle had declared Agent Daggard a traitor and had set the CIA, ATF, and FBI on Daggard with orders to kill him."

Stough chuckled, "Now, its Daggard's own people who are declaring him a traitor...a spy. Do you see the irony of the situation, Agent Bell?"

He observed, through the driver's window, the black GMC Yukon SUV slow down. It pulled in alongside of his vehicle and parked.

As the NSA and FBI agents disembarked from their vehicles, Agent Bell asked without moving, "Do you *really* believe his people will be that naïve...comrade?"

It took Agent Stough a few seconds to process her question before he answered. "It doesn't matter what I believe. I have my orders. And I told you before; *do not* use that word any more."

A tall and muscular man walked forward. Stough and Harding greeted each other. "I'm Captain Harding with NSA," he said reaching out his right hand.

"I am Agent Stough, FBI." He accepted Harding's hand in a hardy handshake.

Both men scrutinized their surroundings taking notice that there were not many people around and those who drove by did not pay them any attention.

"Shall we go kill a spy?" Captain Harding asked. Both men laughed.

As Stough began to get into his vehicle, he noticed Agent Bell's stern stare directed at him. He got in and closed the vehicle door. "What is your problem?"

She glared at him. "You are an idiot just like that fool." She nodded her head toward Harding.

She sat complacent. Comrade Bell stared straight-ahead looking out through the windshield. Sadness washed over her because she understood that pending doom had reached into the vehicle choking her.

The Soviets were attempting to achieve their ultimate goal…world domination. "You *fool*!" She could not hold back her contempt, her anger, or her fear any longer. "Do you not understand, comrade? We have lost! Three hundred agents tried in vain to hunt this man down. *Three hundred*! He eluded them and completed his mission."

Tears began to form at the corners of her brown eyes. They continued to spillover and roll down her cheeks. "We are eight soldiers, comrade. What, in the labyrinth of your heart and mind makes you believe we will prevail where so many others have failed? We are doomed!"

Agent Stough glared at her.

Agent Bell turned her head. She stared down Agent Stough as contempt shot out from her brown eyes. She exhaled a deep, heavy sigh. "What, in your wildest imagination makes you believe we will be victorious today?"

He began to speak. She raised her right hand.

"Do you not understand, comrade? Does your arrogance penetrate that deep into your tiny brain? Can you not fathom our dilemma?"

Agent Bell glared at her counterpart.

"Comrade," she began in a soft tone, "the KGB had tried to terminate him for thirty-five years. Yet, Agent Daggard has continued to fight the Cold War, killing many of our best agents."

She stopped to breathe, staring at Agent Stough.

"And Bardolph, that bungling fool, had him in chains." Her rage and hate for Bardolph exploded. "That incompetent had Agent Daggard in chains." She exhaled with an exasperated sigh. "In chains…Bardolph had managed to capture and imprison our notorious nemesis. Instead of killing him, shooting him dead, Bardolph indulged himself with torturing Daggard."

Agent Bell threw up her arms. "So, comrade, what happened? *What happened*? Agent Daggard escaped."

She glared out of her door window and saw the NSA Agents get out of their vehicle and start walking towards theirs. "So tell me, *comrade*, what in your arrogant thought process makes you believe that the eight of us are going to be victorious where so many others have failed?"

Captain Harding tapped on the passenger window, waving to the agents inside to come out. They huddled around the hood of the FBI SUV as Harding unfolded a satellite topographical printout of the Buffalo Run Valley area.

"We'll leave here and drive north on Route 42 toward Markleysburg. We will turn right onto Buffalo Run Road. There is a driveway near the second bridge that goes in about fifty yards to a garage and a house. We will…"

"How do you know this?" Agent Stough asked.

Agent Bell threw up her arms. "As I have said; idiots! They were here last night, *remember?*"

Captain Harding stared at Agent Bell. He turned his attention to Agent Stough. Stough waved off her comments and Harding's questioning eyes with his left hand.

"We will park our vehicle between the house and the garage as we did last night. There is a path through the woods along the watercourse that leads to a huge tree house. We will take up our position in the tree house seventy yards in the woods."

Captain Harding followed the route with his index finger of his left hand during his explanation. "You and your agents will continue on Route 42 until you come into the town of Markleysburg. You will make the right at the "T" intersection, and drive out to Route 40. Then you will turn right onto 40 and proceed for a few miles, then turn into Caney Valley.

"Drive past the boat shop about three miles, park, and then proceed on foot until we combine our forces once you have flushed out our quarry.

"Spread your agents out and proceed through the woods and these fields driving Daggard."

Agent Bell turned away. She walked a few yards from the vehicles, crossed Water Street, and stood on a grassy area looking down at the river. She took a pack of Marlboros from her purse as Agent Harding glared at Agent Stough. "What is her problem?"

"She is convinced that we are doomed; not only the eight of us, but the war as well."

As she lit her cigarette and took a long, deep drag, inhaling the smoke then exhaling the gray cloud into the atmosphere, she turned around mocking her male counterparts with her demeaning eyes. "Yes, comrades, we are doomed. We are in his back yard, as the Americans would say. But all of you seem to be acting in accordance with selective memory." She took another long drag of her cigarette, taking her time to exhale the smoke through her nose.

The sky began to cloud over.

Agent Bell taunted her comrades by taking three more long drags of her cigarette. "You seem to forget," she began with slow, accusing words, "that Agent Daggard thwarted our war plans three years ago within one second and with one bullet. And now, with our submarines jockeying into position and our military in its hiding positions across this country, here we are with our resources devoted to the termination of one damn American." She could not hold back her anger further as she looked around making sure that there weren't any citizens within hearing distance.

She threw her cigarette down, crushing it with several vicious twists of her left foot. She marched up to Harding jamming her nose against his, screaming accusations in his face while showering him with spittle. "You raped her, didn't you? You tortured her, didn't you? Both you and Bardolph had the opportunity to kill him, but you both reveled in toying with him.

"You wanted to see him quake, to tremble, to plead for mercy, but all you have done is to fuel his rage."

Agent Bell backed off a few steps. She began to cry. "All you have done, Harding, is to unleash the only weapon in the American's arsenal that can kill us; the one antagonist who can unite the Americans, and destroy us. We are doomed," she cried burying her face in her hands.

She cried for several minutes while they stared at her. She raised her head and glared at Harding. "I only hope that I can live long enough to watch you die."

She turned from her comrades. Agent Bell sat on the curb of the bridge and took out her cigarettes. "I am going to enjoy three more cigarettes and several deep breaths of free air."

Agent Bell drew deep of the tobacco tastes of three Marlboros for fifteen minutes. She smoked them to the filters. Once she had done so, she stood up and sucked down ten healthy gulps of free, crisp air. As she marched to her vehicle, she hissed out her orders, "Comrades, it is time to go to our deaths."

The enemy spies drove out of Friendsville. They turned right onto Route 42 toward their rendezvous with destiny. They were going to try and flush the lion from his den...pluck the eagle from his nest.

Buffalo Run Valley
Friday, October 1
1505 hours

Skip Daggard witnessed, in amazed wonder, the subtle movement of the strange, but familiar vehicle keeping a slow pace along Buffalo Run Road. He studied the vehicle and the driver from his hiding place in the woods. "So, they got my message," he said out loud while grinding his teeth.

Skip Daggard viewed the vehicle on Buffalo Run Road through his binoculars. The vehicle drove to the intersection of Buffalo and Meyers, turned around and drove past the burned ruins of his house.

"Dumb-shits," Skip said, "nothing like announcing your presence."

Finally, the vehicle drove into the driveway on Sarah Joy's property from Buffalo Run Road near the second bridge coming in from 42. Once the occupants finished slamming doors and made their way into the woods, the forest began to settle down.

A gentle rain had cleansed the valley. Once it had stopped birds began chirping. The forest began to breathe as the wind picked up, playing a game of hopscotch across the leaves and from treetop to treetop. When the natural sounds of nature were normal, Skip eased himself up from his hiding place.

He had two weapons with him; two old friends that had never failed him: his .45 and his M-14/M25 sniper rifle. He also had his survivor pack in which he carried four days' rations, water, and three days' change of clothes, a compass, an extra knife, medical kit, and fuel to start a fire. He had learned to keep such things handy at all times—lessons learned in the army—hard lessons.

Skip began to modify his position. He had not developed a specific plan. He left his mind open to opportunities as they might present themselves. This ability to act without orders, and take the initiative is the most problematic difference with the US military and all other military organizations. While officers in other countries' forces will wait for orders to act, a private in the US military will simply attack. He will take the initiative when opportunity is there without waiting for orders.

Foreign strategists have lost many hours of sleep since 1776 pondering what they have called "lack of disciple" of the US military. And it is due to the initiative of the individual American soldier that has led US leaders not to allow foreign military leaders to take charge, or be in authority over US forces in the field.

Skip used terrain features and deadfalls for cover and concealment. He had studied this procedure under an extremist named Staff Sergeant Jacob Madden, a snake eater extraordinaire, one of the Green Berets' top snipers.

Skip's initial training took place in the jungles of Thailand. Every time he made an error, Madden shot him with a pellet gun.

"Cover and concealment," Madden had said, "is your best chance for survival. Don't just walk through an area, but commit it to memory. Observe, feel, and taste it. Know the smells and habits of the indigenous creatures. Let the surroundings live in your mind."

Buffalo Run Valley
Friday, October 1
1730 hours

Six point eight miles northeast of Friendsville a huge hawk glided on the uplift of the wind. His wings were extended. His call went echoing down the valley as he soared above the field in front of Skip.

Skip Daggard took up a sitting position behind a huge pile of dead falls. The forest had been harvested two years ago. A dirt logging road dotted with large, gray stones snaked its way from the bottom left corner of the wood line toward the top right corner of the hill. He inhaled the fresh fragrance of wet, cut grass.

He shifted slightly in his position. He was looking from a ridge on Bud Frantz's property over the farm fields and down onto his property. Something was wrong. Something was out of place on Sarah Joy's property, which was the forested property on the south side of Buffalo Run Creek across from his. He knew that four people had been in the Yukon that had driven up her driveway. He had tried, in vain, to observe the movements of those men because the October forest was still overgrown with foliage.

Skip used short, quick looks through his camouflaged, self-focusing, small pocket-sized Tasco binoculars. He made four slow movements swiveling left then right, finally focusing on a dark shadow.

Several times he swiveled his binoculars left then right then back again avoiding staring too long at the spot which concerned him. Finally, after five minutes of searching, Skip remembered the fortified tree stand that Sarah's husband and two of his friends had constructed five years ago.

Skip saw a brief movement where he figured the tree house should be. "Gotcha!" Too many covert operations and Vietnam had trained him to be wary and never take any observation at face value. He focused on the spot watching the movement of his quarry.

The depression he had chosen behind the clump of deadfalls was just deep enough to hide his body. Knowing where his enemy was, Skip rolled into the depression. The dark earth had a musty odor to it. He felt as if he had rolled into an old root cellar.

He took out a camouflaged poncho from his pack. Using slow and deliberate movements, he covered his position with the poncho. He snaked out of the hole and covered the poncho with natural debris.

As he lay behind the barricade, safe in his hole, Skip dug out a small amount of dirt under the dead falls for a firing port. When everything was accomplished to his satisfaction, Skip thought back to another time, another place...Vietnam, November 1969.

"No damn way in hell! I'm not going. Send Hill or Benjamin...I have thirty days left, and I ain't goin' north for no damn body no way... no how."

"Sergeant Daggard," Lieutenant Hanalin said, "you're going. Study this picture. This is the spy. He's posing as a Thai Soldier. Find him. Terminate him. But before you do, have a friendly chat with him. Prove to him that it would be in his best interest to surrender his cohorts in Kharot."

A misty, light rain began to fall. This was the time of year in Garrett County where the seasons change from summer to autumn, painting the landscape in brilliant colors of oranges, gold, reds, and greens. It was a time of celebration of Autumn Glory. Schools closed on Friday so families could enjoy the Firemen's Parade and festivities Thursday evening, and the Autumn Glory Festival that weekend.

Skip studied the trees dressed up in their autumn glory robes and pondered his situation. He knew that the weather could change any day now that it was October. Temperatures could plummet in a few hours bringing snow to the county and be gone by the next day.

The mountains and valleys in Garrett County play a huge part in the weather patterns. It could be a light, short rainfall as before, or turn into a raging blizzard dumping inches or several feet of snow by midnight.

Skip allowed a smile to take shape at the corners of his lips, but the smile never reached his eyes. His smile was due in part because he was prepared for the weather. He figured that those dumb-shit city agents would not be dressed for the changing weather. However, he never took anything for granted, so he would consider the fact that his enemies would have made proper preparations for the quickly changing weather patterns.

Cover and concealment were skimpy because of the logging, but due to his training and experience, Skip knew how to make do.

His training field had been Vietnam so it was only natural for Skip to dig his fortification between two groups of deadfalls; one for frontal action, and one to protect his rear.

By 1800 hours the rain had stopped, but the temperature had dropped from sixty to forty degrees. Skip witnessed slight movement in the tree house. He lifted his rifle, adjusted his scope, and placed the crosshairs on the forehead of a man with a muscular build. Just as he was pushing the safety button forward and began to squeeze the trigger he whispered, "This one's for my daughter". He froze. A twig had snapped behind him.

Friend Farm
Friday, October 1
1731 hours

Agent Mark Stough sat quietly in the front passenger seat looking over the countryside of rolling fields, houses, and pine trees. They had kept going past Buffalo Run Road where Captain Harding had turned. Agent Bell continued on Route 42 pointing their vehicle west toward Markelysburg.

A topographical map lay on his lap. "I don't like this,' he said out loud to the three agents in the vehicle. "No sir! I don't like it at all," said Mark Stough.

Gram Link, who was sitting in the back behind Stough, said, "What don't you like?"

"Make this right onto Frazee Ridge Road, Bell," Stough said.

"This isn't Route Forty," she began to argue.

"Just make the friggin' right turn, and pull over to the side of the road." Stough shouted at her.

Agent Bell slammed on the brakes because she had passed the road. Stough's right hand shot out stopping him from slamming against the dashboard. Link banged his head against Stough's seat. Agent Burnham collided with the back of Bell's seat.

"What the hell is your problem?" Stough shouted.

Bell did not answer as she backed up, made the turn, and pulled over as ordered. She kept her eyes looking forward out of the windshield.

"Is everyone all right?" Stough asked

Agent Stough retrieved his map from the floor. He rested the open map on his lap as he studied terrain and roads. He looked up trying to see what lay behind the crest of the hill before them. His heavy sigh made his fellow agents shift uncomfortably in their seats.

"Have any of you been to war?" Stough's question caught them off guard.

Gram bit on the question. "What does that have to do with this?"

"I haven't either," Stough shared, "but Agent Daggard has: Vietnam,

Granada, and the Middle East. And he fought the Cold War with a vengeance no one ever understood. Plus, he was one of the best operatives at NSA.

He paused, placing the palm of his left hand under his chin contemplating about the mission, when Agent Bell broke into his thoughts.

She had shifted in the driver's seat so she could look at him straight on. "Now, comrade, I believe you are beginning to comprehend my earlier comments." She stared at Stough, watching him as he processed her words.

"S-h-hut u-up!"

She turned back around in a quick, easy motion, and faced forward.

The gray had gone and a blue sky had taken charge, clouds lingered in the west.

"Drive!"

They drove up a hill and then the road went into a slight downhill slope and dead-ended at a farmhouse.

Agent Bell parked the vehicle in the driveway twenty feet from the house at the end of the road. As they got out of the vehicle they noticed the high weeds growing where grass used to be. The wind played with a screen door.

"All right, this is what I was studying when *someone* grew a lead foot."

Agent Bell adopted an arrogant posture and feathered her auburn hair with her fingers.

"See? We're just above the valley. Down over the hill to our right is Meyers Road. If we walk through the fields in front of us for approximately five hundred yards we'll be above the Frantz farm.

Before Bell had a chance to speak, Stough continued, "The farm overlooks Daggard's place. I'd say that he's between us and Harding's group right now."

Agent Bell lit up a Marlboro. She inhaled the smoke deep into her lungs before exhaling the gray smoke out through her nose.

Her three comrades stared at her. "What is your plan, Comrade Stough?"

"How many times do I have to tell you, Bell, not to call me that?

Sometime—somewhere the wrong person will hear you. But to answer your question, this is my plan.

"We'll stay in the middle of the fields. We have to go about five hundred yards due east, which should put us in the center of the second pasture."

"Then we'll fan out in a line about ten yards apart and start over the hill towards Harding's position. He opened the hatch door, "Choose your weapons." Stough closed the door. Each agent locked a thirty round magazine in their new AK-47's. "You know our orders! If you see Daggard…shoot!"

Chapter Five—Enemy Casualties

Buffalo Run Valley
Friday, October 1
1800 hours

The elite of the elite of all operatives, Skip Daggard froze. With utmost care, he released his pressure on the trigger. To make any movement now would be suicidal. He slowed his breathing. The roof of his hideout was constructed using strong limbs and branches. If an intruder would happen to step on his roof, they would not fall through.

The sun was in the west to his right. The clouds had moved on leaving behind a clear, early-evening sky. There was plenty of light, but dusk would be settling in bringing nightfall to the valley within the next few hours.

Someone stopped nine inches to the left of his position. He heard another person walk up to the one who had stopped. "Why have you stopped, comrade?"

Skip overheard the man chastise the woman in a harsh, severe tone as he corrected at her. "Do not use that term again. If you cannot control your language, I will have you sent back to Siberia immediately."

They began to move downhill. Skip fought the demon for control as he choked down his rage. He wanted to jump up from his hiding place and slice them up like slivers of bacon. But he had been too well trained to allow his emotions to cause him to act in a heedless manner.

As the four agents moved out of the woods across a small alcove clearing into a small section of woods, Skip waited. He had shifted his rifle from his target in the tree house to the back of the head of the man the woman had referred to as comrade.

Skip had shut everything out. Nothing existed but the targets to his front. There was no hate or rage, or the dead, lifeless faces of Kristine and Eilis. Nothing! He applied his entire concentration on the four targets before him.

To Skip Daggard, there was no other world, only the world he now occupied. The world soldiers had come to know as…the killing fields.

He observed his quarry as they crossed Meyers Road. He watched and began to count yardage as the four agents moved across the meadow heading towards his property.

"Two hundred and ten…two hundred and twenty…two hundred and forty…two hundred and…"

He squeezed the trigger. Working the bolt of his M-14/M25 rifle, he fired his weapon making it shoot as if it was a semi-automatic. Before the man the woman had called comrade had pitched forward, the fourth bullet had hit its target.

Skip moved swiftly, maneuvering the muzzle of his rifle to his right, while working the bolt, plunging another cartridge into the breach. He witnessed the horror in the eyes of his target through the man's binoculars and his scope as he squeezed the trigger watching the man's head explode.

The agent who had been standing next to the one Skip had just killed dropped to the floor of the tree house. Skip estimated his target's position. He counted to three…held his breath… exhaled slowly, and then placed two bullets through the front wall of the tree house.

Out of his peripheral vision, Skip detected movement. He shifted his rifle further to the right. His first bullet severed the spine of a man who was running causing him to drop immediately. Two more bullets fractured both knees of the second man who was running passed the man who had just fallen. Both men lay bleeding and incapacitated on the deer trail.

Quickly, Skip came out of his hole flinging the roof aside. He charged down the hill through the woods and across the fields passing the barn and bodies of the man called comrade and his compatriots. Skip went down the bank onto his property and across the two-foot wide watercourse. He rushed from the woods across his manicured yard and through a section of woods ten yards wide. He stumbled out onto Buffalo Run Road. He caught his momentum as he made four long strides across Buffalo Creek and up the incline onto Sarah Joy's place close to the tree house.

Skip squatted on his heels gasping for breath as he studied the two men who lay on the trail bleeding. No one spoke for five minutes. Skip reached behind himself. He produced a K-Bar knife. Then he took a wet stone, spit on it, and began sharpening his already razor-sharp weapon.

As Skip tested the sharpness of his knife with a blade of grass, he directed his question towards his knife as he continued to grate the blade back and forth across the wet stone. "Who ordered the hit on my family?" his face a piece of stone.

The agent with the severed spine was about to speak when the other one ordered him silent. Skip's strike was sudden and fast. It took the man's brain one minute to receive the pain-waves that the right ear had been severed from his head.

The man screamed out in agonizing pain clasping his right hand over the place where his ear used to reside. Now it lay in the dirt near the man's shoulder, a useless piece of flesh. Blood flowed out between the man's fingers and down the back of his hand.

"Who ordered the hit on my family?" he asked the man with the severed spine again.

"General Bardolph…"

"Shut up you idiot!"

Skip reached over and grabbed a handful of jet-black hair. He jerked the man's head back. In one even stroke of his knife, Skip scalped his enemy.

As the man lay whimpering in excruciating pain, Skip turned his attention back to the agent with the severed spine. The fear in the spy's eyes ripped buried memories from hiding places in Skip's mind, slamming images against the wall of his conscious mind.

Before the chopper touched down, Skip burst from the jungle dragging his charges behind him. He threw the three spies into the gaping hole in the right side of the gun ship, jumped in and ordered the pilot to liftoff.

As the co-pilot began to turn, Skip saw the pilot grab the man's helmet forcing the co-pilot's face forward. Skip studied the faces of the three Vietnamese girls for several seconds before he spoke in Vietnamese, "Where is this man?" he demanded showing them a picture of a suspected Vietnamese spy.

The first girl refused to answer. He grabbed her by her long, raven hair. She screamed and tried to struggle. Skip held firm his hold then yanked her from the deck of the chopper sending her airborne at five hundred feet.

"My God," the co-pilot shouted, "did you see that?"

The pilot, a Chief Warrant office Fourth Class glared at his friend. "I didn't see anything and neither did you. Furthermore, we're not even on this mission. And, I had warned you before not to look back there. The cabin's empty."

The Huey had one door-gunner. He stood behind his .50 caliber machine gun fastened in his safety harness, giving the countryside his full attention, oblivious to the interrogation that was taking place behind him.

Skip pulled down a seat from the back wall and sat down. He studied the third girl for a full minute. He guessed her age to be twenty-five. The first girl, the one he had disposed of, was sixteen. The second girl looked to be eighteen. She was huddled in a corner, whimpering.

He asked her, "Where is this man?"

The girl's mouth became a torrential river of information…all useless. So he grabbed the struggling, screaming, snapping girl by her hair and neck and threw her out.

He looked over at the oldest woman after he had sat down. "Don't suppose your goin' to say anything, huh?"

She glared at him through two black portals mirrored with hatred.

Skip shook his head as the man near him moaned. "If you give over the info, I promise to make it quick and painless."

The man talked for fifteen minutes without being prompted. "General Bardolph had ordered your family's termination because of your meddling. The two in the tree house were Captain Harding and Lieutenant Hamstead. It had been Harding who had tortured your wife and daughter."

Without warning, Skip rose and walked over to the tree house. He climbed the wooden ladder fastened to three trees. When he reached the top of the platform, he opened the door. He grabbed the collars of both men and threw their bodies to the ground.

When Skip's feet touched the ground, he turned to the wounded man, "And you are?"

The man could no longer control his bladder. "Lieutenant Pearl"

Skip squatted. "Which one is Harding?"

"The muscular one!"

Skip cut out Harding's heart shoving it into the dead man's mouth. He looked back at the wounded man, "Your real name?"

Lieutenant Pearl could not move to look at Daggard. He was lying face down in the dirt facing away from the tree house along the trail. "Alex Gorbachev...no relation."

Skip studied the sky. Soon night would take over and the sky was threatening snow. But this is Garrett County; the sky could dump two feet of snow tonight with temperatures in the teens, and tomorrow it could be sixty degrees with the snow only a memory. Or, it could warm up and it would rain.

He studied the dead men. He had lost his chance to torture the bastard who had killed his girls, but one still lived.

"You're the enemy," he said to Alex Gorbachev as he picked up a thirteen-inch stick that was two inches round. He moved back over near Gorbachev and the agent he had scalped. He began whittling a point at one end. "So, what else do you have to say, Gorbachev?"

"There are thirty-five Soviet agents strategically placed in the hierarchy at NSA and twenty-five in the FBI. The people you killed here today are field operatives. There are six in the CIA at Langley, five in Homeland security, and three on the general's staff at Fort Devens.

"General Motly, the Air Force Joint Chief of Staff in the Pentagon, and Admiral Hinkly of the Navy Joint are moles. There are thirty-one moles in the Senate, and seventy-six in the House. Two are on the Presidential Advisory Cabinet, and three in the Secret Service."

The man he had scalped choked and spit up blood. Skip leaned over him placing the point of the stake he had just whittled against the man's left eye. Skip picked up a huge rock, raised it in the air—slam, he drove the stake home. The enemy's scream was short-lived. Skip focused his attention back to Gorbachev, "The Orientals?"

The spy's voice began to fade. He coughed looking at Skip. "That would be Colonel Lee of the North Korean Communist Army. She is in charge of the North Korean interests in the invasion."

Skip took out a small memo pad and pen. He gave his writing material to the spy. "Write down their names."

Through gasps of pain the spy wrote names in the memo pad for twenty-five minutes. He had to stop periodically due to his pain. He finally dropped his left arm to the ground wheezing and crying out from his pain. Skip rummaged through Gorbachev's coat pockets.

"Here, he snapped," call your general."

"Y-oo-u pp-u-nn-c-h in nn-u-mm-b-e-r—s."

The spy cried out the numbers as Skip typed keys on the pad of the cell phone.

The phone rang.

"Harding?"

"General Bardolph, this is Daggard. Your people are dead and I'm coming for you."

Skip turned off the phone. He slipped the cell phone into his own coat pocket while looking at his enemy. "What invasion? What's your game plan?"

Skip jerked the man up by the fleece collar of his coat. He let him fall back to the ground. He was dead.

Skip rose retrieving his rifle. He sauntered down the recently worn deer trail to the creek just bellow the tree house. Buffalo Run Creek gurgled over obstacles and rippled around rocks creating whirlpools of white foam.

He stepped out onto a flat rock and squatted. He removed his knife from its sheath and began cleaning the blood and flesh from it in the clear, cold water. He bent down scooping up cold water with his right hand, sipping water from his cupped hand. He stood up once his thirst had been quenched.

Skip wiped his blade and hand on his pants leg, returned the knife to its home as he looked across the creek at the smoldering remains of his house.

Once again, Skip Daggard stood alone at some water's edge. This time it was in his own front yard, and the struggle he found himself engaged in would be fought across the American continent, and truly for his own people. This is what he believed from the information he had gathered.

His mind began to meander. Memories came screaming forth from his subconscious like banshees from hell.

Skip shifted in his seat as the warbling sounds of the chopper blades filled the stifling afternoon air.

"What you do with me?" the girl queried.

"I could torture you, but your eyes have already revealed that any torture would be a waste of time. I have a special surprise for you. I'm going to turn you over to CI."

Her eyes widened with fear. "I talk…"

Skip held up his right hand, "Stop! You had your chance. I'll let the counterintelligence goons have you. They have more time than I do."

Without warning, she launched herself from the chopper.

Skip Daggard stood on the south bank of Buffalo Run Creek as tears welled up in his eyes. "You were right, Kristine! You were right." He shouted across the creek, "My meddling was what got you and Eilis killed." Then he fell to his knees crying and screaming and punching at the dirt. Thirty-five seconds later, he rose to his six-foot height sucking down his grief.

As he splashed through the creek and walked across his yard past the remains of his home, he turned his head looking back and said, "I made you a promise, Kristine. These kills were only the beginning."

NSA
General Bardolph's Office
Friday, October 1
2000 hours

General Bardolph placed his cell phone down on his desk. He reached over his desk with his right hand, raised the lid of his box of Cubans, and took out a cigar. General Ashford Bardolph clipped the tip of his cigar then put it into his mouth lighting the end. As he puffed on his cigar and blew ringlets of smoke into the air, he began to analyze the immediate crisis. And he knew, instinctively, that the situation *was* a crisis.

General Ashford Bardolph was sixty-seven years old. He was

completely bald only because that was his preference. He viewed the world from a communistic point of view through hazel colored eyes. His grizzled face was dotted with pox marks.

He had been a spy in the US Intel Community for the Soviets since 1974. During that year, he had helped in providing the Warsaw Pact Forces with vital information. And in November of that year the Warsaw Pact Forces called a war only to have that conflict snatched from them because…because…because of interference from that detestable Agent Daggard.

General Bardolph pushed away from his oak desk, slowly gaining his feet. Then he turned around and went to a window behind his desk. He pushed back the heavy green curtains and raised the white venetian blinds. He took two steps backwards as he puffed on his cigar and stared westward.

"West," he said to himself. "West; two hundred miles away to the west is where the thorn, who is prickling our efforts for a swift take over of this damnable country, is in hiding, and he has just killed eight of my best agents."

He sighed with heavy breaths of hot air as he puffed on his cigar calculating his next move. There was no question that Daggard had to be killed…but how? West! West lay the enemy. "One damn American," he said out loud. "The same son of a bitch, who had spoiled our nice little war three years ago," Bardolph exhaled a heavy sigh. "Why can't you die you son of a bitch, why can't you die," Bardolph screamed around his cigar.

His people couldn't believe it when Secretary of State Kelly had made contact with Schmirnoff at the Russian Embassy in Washington requesting their help in plotting the assassination of President Mantle. The assassination would have started World War Three. This would have given back to the Soviets all the territory that they had lost with the destruction of the Berlin Wall. For the Soviets it was the catapult, which would launch them into complete world domination.

For the second time in construction of historical events there stood a monumental antagonist…Military Intelligence Chief Warrant Officer Skip Daggard. Again, he had been underestimated, and again, he was at a place where he should not have been, the White House

Communications Center, when he should have been in Morristown, New Jersey.

He intercepted the message from Kelly to Schmirnoff, and for the second time in thirty-five years, he, Agent Daggard, foiled the Soviets plans for world domination.

General Bardolph sat back down at his desk. He took out a pad of lined paper and a pen, and wrote Agent Skip Daggard at the top of the page. He underlined the name three times. He spoke at the name as if the man was standing before him. "We now stand on the threshold of victory preparing to take over your country and the world, and here you are again, standing in the doorway thwarting our efforts to acquire our birth-right."

General Bardolph, who had dreamed of fulfilling the Communist Doctrine, placed his pen on his desktop and picked up his cell phone. He punched in a code-specific set of numbers and sat back waiting.

"This is Colonel Lee."

"Kill him! Kill him now, and do not fail. But before you do, you must go and retrieve the bodies of my agents"

General Bardolph hung up his phone.

Colonel Chin Lee's Headquarters
Kingwood, West Virginia
Friday, October 1
2015 hours

Colonel Chin Lee dropped the receiver into its cradle and mumbled, "We are doomed," she said to no one. Then she looked at Lieutenant Wong, seated across the table, which contained a topographical map of West Virginia, Maryland, Pennsylvania, Washington, D.C., and Delaware. "The Soviet idiots have bungled their mission. Now they want us to retrieve their fallen comrades and complete their mission," she spat out venomously.

Colonel Chin Lee scrutinized the topography of the five states, paying special attention to the mountains and their elevations because these were the states that had been assigned to the North Korean Armies. Not out of antagonism by the Soviets, but more from necessity—the

North Koreans were better mountain fighters. Washington, Oregon and California were going to be destroyed by missiles.

While she studied the terrain, Colonel Lee agonized over the fact that the one who could usurp their efforts for a swift victory was roaming free in his home range, killing her allies at his discretion. And now the bungling fools wanted her to clean up their incompetence.

She let an exasperating sigh escape from her mouth. She said to her officers, "I hope this is not an omen of things to come, and that these incompetent fools *can* carry their weight in the upcoming war. These Americans are not to be trifled with, nor taken lightly.

"Once they have been demoralized and many captured or killed, they will follow like sheep, but to think they will fall like dominoes, is absurd…"

Colonel Lee stopped so abruptly; her officers stared at her. "Unless… unless the Soviets have their own agenda regarding our future and that of the Red Chinese forces."

Buffalo Run Valley
Saturday, October 2
1235 hours

Lieutenant Wong drove the black Ford van down Good Hope Road then turned left onto Buffalo Run Road. As the vehicle made the turn, Colonel Lee stared out of the passenger window. She sat straight up then relaxed.

"Is there something wrong, Colonel Lee?"

"*What?*"

"I asked you if there is something wrong."

She was lost in the serenity and beauty of the valley, but there had been something…what?

As the van continued toward Meyers Road, she could sense why Daggard had settled here. It was peaceful and serene until *they* had invaded his home. A shiver rippled up her spine. It was her words, invaded his home and killed his family. She became somber with her thoughts. "Perhaps it is an omen," she stated out loud. "After all, the Soviets have had two opportunities during the past thirty-five years to deal a death-blow to the US.

"Two weeks before the American Thanksgiving holiday in 1974, then, three years ago, with the aid of President Mantle, the Soviets were handed a prime opportunity for sure victory, but once again Agent Daggard proved to be the catalyst in destroying those endeavors by terminating his own president.

"And now, Lieutenant, who is it that stands before us and has just killed eight Soviet agents, and, in all probability, has been provided vital information regarding our mission?"

She paused to admire the autumn splendor of colored foliage. A sigh escaped from her mouth. "This is a beautiful place and we have brought death to this paradise."

As they started up Meyers Road, she screamed, "*This...this!*" she slammed her left fist against the dashboard of her vehicle several times. "Who is *this* damn soldier who will not die or go away?"

Colonel Lee glared at Lieutenant Wong. He had maneuvered the van through a recently mowed field and passed an old dilapidated barn when he stopped so suddenly that Chin Lee slammed her head against the door window.

They both stared in awe and sheer amazement at the positions of the bodies. There was a single bullet hole in the center of each of their heads.

"I do not understand..." began Lieutenant Wong.

"He knew who they were," she responded. "He knew exactly who they were."

Lieutenant Wong began to fidget in his seat as he tried to look around and out of the back door windows. "D-doo y-o-u th-ink he is still here?"

"He is still close." She hid her teasing smile. "He may be lying close waiting for whoever comes to retrieve these bodies." She laughed hysterically when Wong jumped.

"That is not humorous, Colonel Lee!"

This task of loading bodies in her van was no task for a colonel in the North Korean Army. She had puzzled over General Bardolph's request that she collect his dead. Perhaps he did not want fear to begin weaving its way into the ranks of his soldiers. Whatever the reason, she had agreed to gather up the bodies of the dead Soviets.

When she and Wong stood over the bodies looking around, a

feeling began to creep through her being. She knew why she had come. It was to be near *him*. Colonel Lee studied the landscape: the autumn foliage, the dark green grass, and the blue open sky. Once the four bodies had been loaded into the back of the van, they drove to the other location. There, they found the one whom had been tortured and the other one who had not been molested.

Colonel Lee squatted near the bodies studying how both men had died. When she rose, she tried to avoid Lieutenant Wong's eyes, but she had been too slow in turning away from him. He must have seen the fear in her eyes.

"Colonel Lee, what is it?"

She hesitated. She stared off towards the woods where the other bodies should be located. She pointed to the bodies when she turned back to look at Wong. "This one had been tortured, but not for information…as a warning. You see the disfigurations? Swift and meaningful! A warning, Lieutenant Wong! But this one; this one had not been disfigured. He had been given mercy. This means Agent Daggard knows. This one talked."

It took them two hours in order to get the four bodies out to the van and loaded.

At 1645 the snow from last night had vanished and the Indian summer was back with a vengeance. Skip sat just inside his cave. The heat from his small cooking fire reflected off of the walls, keeping him warm as the flames danced in the fire pit and provided eerie dancing figures which twisted and wiggled along the cave ceiling.

He had seen the van earlier but it had not left the valley along Good Hope Road, so Skip pondered the idea that it might have gone out to Route 42. He knew why they had come, yet, he was puzzled as to why the Orientals, and not Soviets, were sent to retrieve the bodies.

He had been waiting, rifle at the ready, but when he saw the occupants of the van, he moved the butt of his rifle from his shoulder to the ground. He cursed himself because a quick flash of sunlight reflected off of the muzzle of the barrel.

As he sipped coffee, Skip began to chuckle. He could still see the wide, white eyes of the startled black bear as he had fast-crawled into the cave, slamming into her last night.

He had backed up against the right wall just as fast. "All right, momma," he said quiet-like, "we can share the comforts, or you'll have to go."

She moved like Jell-O up from the ground, but once she gained her feet, the dancing began. After throwing each other around the cave for fifteen minutes, the bear left shaking her head and giving long, backward glances at the new occupant.

He studied the flames dancing along the ceiling. His eyes began to water as tears rolled down his face. "Well, Kristine my darling, I bet I can tell you where that Communist Coalition force is now!"

Skip Daggard's nightmare came charging out from the depths of long ago forests.

The VC boats kept coming across the rice-paddies from the jungle, docking at the perimeters of the US site. It was after midnight and he stood just outside the realm of the flood lights' glow. They came out of the boats pointed AK-47's at him, laughed, walked the perimeter, and departed as quick as they had arrived. He was the only one who had seen them because the Thai guards had already fled the AO. He knew that he was going to die. He had surrendered himself to all of Death's sensations.

Skip shook his head trying to clear out old memories. He could not stop the invasion of new ones. The charred remains of Kristine and Eilis were before his eyes. "I promise, darling, I promise you and Eilis that they will all pay."

Skip wiped tears from his face. He began to formulate a plan of attack before he turned to go back into the warmth of his sanctuary. He had learned that there were one hundred and seven spies in the House and Senate. That meant there were too many to take out separately.

"I guess the world is in for another shock," he mumbled to himself as he prepared for another cold and lonely night.

Chapter Six—Enemies Collide

Buffalo Run Valley
Corps of Engineers
Sunday, October 3
1200 hours

Skip Daggard sat on a three legged, camouflaged canvas campstool just inside the cave wiping tears from his eyes. He swore viciously and pledged his revenge. "They'll pay dearly for what they have done, Kristine. I swear it! I will hunt them down and kill everyone involved."

He watched the maroon Geo come down Good Hope Road. The driver maneuvered her vehicle off the graveled road next to the rust-brown colored bar gate, and stop. He studied the Oriental female as she got out of the Geo. His position was good. The cave was small but well concealed by mountain laurel bushes and pine trees.

From his hideout, Skip had an excellent view of the junction of Good Hope and Buffalo Run Roads. As he observed the movements of the girl dressed in the brown uniform of the North Korean Army, he began a study of the past several days.

Had it only been four days since he got involved in this mess? And Kristine and Eilis—both gone. So what in the *hell* is that Korean bitch doing here?

Skip kept his eyes on her as Colonel Chin Lee strolled to the edge of Buffalo Run. The water was down. In some places it was one to two feet deep. In other places, one could walk across the creek by stepping on exposed stones.

Colonel Chin Lee had no idea what she was doing here or what she would or could accomplish, but she knew that, once again, those bungling Soviet idiots had botched their mission. It was now up to her to terminate the adversary and keep her promise to her father. She paced back and forth in front of her vehicle without looking across the water at the spot where she had seen a flash of light yesterday.

She wasn't sure if it had been the reflection of light, or something else pulling at her, drawing her toward her enemy. She knew that he was not far away. She could feel him; sense him. He was close—just across the watercourse.

October seemed mild to her in this country compared to her home. By now, the ground in Korea would be frozen and covered with snow.

It would be in the low twenties in Pyongyang. She would have to wear a mask in the evening so her lungs would not freeze. "Yet," she asked herself, "what had drawn me to this spot?"

She looked out across the creek at the tall pine and locust trees and what appeared to be a dark shadow where she felt such a shadow should not exist. She smiled. She had found him.

Colonel Lee guided her index finger of her left hand over her lips. "I did not put on lipstick. Now, I wish I had. But what would it matter?"

Skip Daggard was her enemy and for the Communist plan to work, it was necessary for him to be killed.

The subversive moles at NSA believed this; that is why they burned down his home in an attempt to kill him and his family.

Skip sat in his chair watching her. He sat straight up. "No way!" he said to himself. But sure enough, there was the slight gesture from her again, that ever so slight wave of her hand.

"Now how the…! Oh well, if she knows I'm here, I'll just go down and shoot her," he spoke to the cave walls.

Skip rose from his chair taking up his rifle in his right hand. He walked out and down the hill.

Colonel Chin Lee studied his movements. She smiled because her adversary was coming to her by a weaving pattern around trees and shrubs using as much cover as possible.

Her heart began to pound against her breast as Skip came closer. "No! No!" she said scolding herself. "This could never be. We are sworn enemies and soon the war will begin. He *must* die…now."

Skip approached like a cat advancing on its prey but with one distinct difference; he scanned their entire surroundings, where a cat's attention is completely focused on its quarry. When he got within seven feet of the female, he stopped with the muzzle of his rifle pointing at her chest.

"How did you know I was here?"

"I am Colonel Chin Lee..."

"I don't give a shit who the fuck you are."

A warm breeze took flight tickling golden leaves adorning the trees.

She raised her hand. "I want you to know that I, nor my people, had anything to do with killing your family."

"Son of a bitch," he said while studying her eyes.

"I am not a bitch!"

Skip smiled. He took in her form, dress, and arrow-straight posture. She didn't wear any makeup over her smooth, brown skin. Her face was round but not quite moon-shaped. Her hair was shiny and black like raven feathers, and her brown eyes were dark and penetrating. Yet, she stood with her arms along her sides breathing heavily.

"Listen, colonel, we can have a romp in the grass, but you can forget anything else."

"*What!*"

"If you want to get laid, fine, but you can forget about any long-term relationship."

She stared at him in disbelieve. Chin could not fathom the arrogance of this capitalist pig. "You flatter yourself, Agent Daggard," she said laughing as she sat down on a large bolder that had been placed near the brown-painted metal post barrier. "You are conceited. I did not come for sex." She studied his blue eyes, pox marks and scars on his face. A shiver rippled along her spine, and for the first time in her life, Colonel Chin Lee looked upon the face of death. She maintained her composure while returning his stare. "After all," she said to her self, "he will be dead in a few minutes."

Skip wanted to caress her face to see if her skin was as smooth as it looked, instead he sat on the ground still maintaining his distance. "Why are you here Colonel Lee? I don't mean here in this spot. I mean here in my country."

Colonel Lee sighed as she looked around. Two roads merged close to where they sat. Good Hope was a dirt road paved with crush and run stone, whereas, this section of Buffalo Run Road had been topped with asphalt. She could hear Buffalo Run giggle as it flowed not twenty yards from their position.

"So," Skip accused, "you're part of that Communist Coalition force the Russian Secret Service lost back about three years ago."

Colonel Chin Lee sat up staring at him. "How..." She realized the question she was about to ask him was ridiculous. After all, she was face to face with one of America's best operatives. The world's best operative to be precise.

She meshed her fingers together then said, "Yes."

Skip smiled. "Well, at least you're honest." Then he broke out in uncontrolled laughter.

Colonel Lee sat staring at him, puzzled. "You find this situation humorous?"

Skip collected himself. "Absolutely; once again we have an enemy on our soil who has no idea or concept that they are about to step ankle-deep in *shit*. Have you studied world history, Colonel Lee?"

"Of course!"

Skip shook his head. "Go home, Colonel Lee. Take your soldiers and go home."

He rose to his feet in one slow, easy movement so he would not cause her alarm. "Colonel..." What analogies could he give her? What associations could he use? "Did you study *our* history? American history?"

She nodded her head but was confused.

The wind began to blow, shaking treetops providing information that the weather was once again going to change.

Skip studied her posture and the beauty of her face for a long minute before he spoke again. "This country was founded on one basic, simple principle "no taxation without representation." In other words, don't come here to enslave us and tell us what to do. King George tried and was sent packing...not once, but twice."

"Agent Daggard..."

"I'm retired!"

She stared at him as if she was trying to understand his last statement.

"Agent Daggard, we have given much thought and planning to this war, and how we will relieve your people of their freedom. Our agents have been deeply imbedded in your agencies and government for many years."

Skip backed up towards Good Hope. He started pacing back and forth ten feet in front of her clutching his rifle with both hands. He turned to face her after pacing for four minutes.

"Yes, I know." He padded his left vest pocket of his coat. That pocket contained the names he acquired from Lieutenant Pearl—Alex Gorbachev. "And I know the Communist philosophy, "world domination no matter how long it takes." So, now you think the time is ripe?"

She rose in animated movement and exhaled a small amount of air.

"It is. We now have control of your government. In one week, the vote to delete the Second Amendment will be ratified by our controlled Congress and all Americans will be forced to turn in their weapons. Your military forces will be depleted. The only force remaining will be in the Middle East. Your forces in South Korea will be dealt with... swiftly."

Skip shook his head in disbelief. "You *did not* study our history, Colonel Lee. No ma'am, you did not because you and your leaders failed to read between the lines.

"What do you know about our Revolutionary War? For instance, did you know that George Washington's Continental Army consisted of only three thousand regulars? Sometimes those ranks swelled to five thousand. The bulk of his military strength, of his army, was the militia, which consisted of farmers, men, women, children, and Indians who hated the French and British."

He began pacing once again. He took off his wool, black watch cap and rubbed his head.

"There was no government, Colonel Lee, no president or Congress, only a document, a Declaration of Independence. In reality, that document was a declaration of war against the greatest military force in the world at that time.

"Three thousand soldiers were all Washington had to engage the best equipped army and navy in the known world. What saved the 'American Experiment,' Colonel Lee, wasn't the Continental Army. It was the people who came down from the hills and mountains and plains. It was the men and women and children who came with their own weapons, shot, powder, and a determination to live free."

Skip stopped to take in air.

"You, just like all of our enemies, do not know us. *Hell,* half the time *we* don't know ourselves. And our Civil War—every country has had one or more, but *we* Americans, Colonel Lee, we Americans are the only people who have fought against ourselves only to reunite under the same doctrine and reaffirm our way of life to include recognizing two distinct flags."

Skip had to stop and catch his breath. He sniffed at the air and felt the coming change on his face. He studied her small physique. She had to tilt her head back in order to look at his face. He took in her uniform.

"Damn, woman! You have balls to wear that uniform."

Her back stiffened. "I do not."

They smiled at each other.

"I didn't mean literally—I meant figuratively."

Skip inhaled a large amount of air then he exhaled it in a slow and deliberate manner trying to infuriate his adversary.

"Colonel, you came here like the British did thinking that if you sever the head, the body will fall. No ma'am! You didn't study our history at all. The British came here twice and we sent them home… both times. And the French, they helped us fight the Brits and figured they'd take over once the British were run out of the country. They, too, underestimated us.

"Once Lieutenant General Lord Cornwallis surrendered at Yorktown, thanks to help of the French Armada, Washington had his guns trained on them and told them to leave with a hardy thank you for their help.

"Now, we have been fighting a war in the Middle East; a war that we didn't want. We've been labeled crusaders, which we're not, but we are fighting a war that was declared against us on 9/11/01. But to the dismay of the Muslim world, we have followed and attacked our enemy throughout five countries causing their barbaric downfall."

He paused once again to catch his breath. Then, he had to turn from her. He looked off towards the Ross farm. He began to struggle against his desires as his need surged forward. He could...why not...*hell* no!

He turned back to face her. "And now, here you are with a large military force believing that once you usurp our government and delete portions of our Constitution that you will be able to march over us with little *resistance*? No ma'am, you and your leaders haven't a clue what's about to happen to you."

Colonel Lee listened. As she listened to the passion in his words, she felt an icy chill begin to seep into her being; a cold, penetrating chill that began to shake her confidence in a swift victory over the capitalistic, overbearing, egotistical Americans.

"We're not perfect. We've committed crimes against races too, like the American Indian, but we're only two hundred years young and still learning. We are a free people and each generation has made sacrifices to insure our freedom is preserved.

"And take the Native Americans. Do you think they fought in wars to help the white man? No, colonel, they fought for *their* people. But they provided the US forces with intelligence that the enemy could not decode—their native language. And they will fight again."

She jumped due to his swift movement as Skip shifted his position. "Go home Colonel Lee while you still can. Once the battle begins, none of you will leave."

Colonel Lee had believed that she had come to understand the Americans: That they were money-hungry, greedy, sexual deviates who thought of no one but themselves. She also thought that she understood the killer now standing before her because she had spent ten years studying his operations.

Chin Lee, a colonel in the North Korean Communist Army, had believed, as did her leaders, that once the US Government was destroyed, its military rendered useless, the US Constitution amended out of existence, and all the personal weapons confiscated, America would be ripe for take-over. Now, here in this remote country setting, she had just received a crash course in American history. Not the kind of history you can read about, but what Daggard had said, "What one reads between the lines."

Colonel Chin Lee did not like what she just heard. She knew that the Americans would fight, but the fact that they would never surrender hadn't entered her thought process. A cold shiver rippled up and down her spine. A premonition began to take shape in her mind that the coalition leaders had made a grave mistake by sending only twelve million soldiers into hiding in the US.

They believed that a small force would be able to mop-up the small band of malcontents after the missiles and bombs had been used. She, nor her leaders, had any idea that those malcontents would number seventy-five million or more. And that each one would be armed because they would refuse to surrender their personal arsenals.

The sun felt warm on her face. Colonel Chin Lee watched Daggard as he strolled down the overgrown dirt road parallel with Buffalo Run. Both man and water meandered in an easterly direction.

Skip Daggard traveled ten yards before he stopped. He stood with his back straight listening to the gurgle of the water in the creek. A minute passed. Then he turned to face Colonel Lee. "You believe that our situation is hopeless, don't you?"

She nodded her head.

"Well, it's not!"

Without warning, Skip turned and began to walk away. He took seven steps, and then turned to face her again. "I'm going to share something with you, Colonel Lee! It's a phrase we have in the army... *don't start no shit, and there won't be no shit*. Go home, Colonel...go home."

Colonel Chin Lee went face to face with her inner self. Deep in her heart she knew that she did not want a war—she only wanted...what did he mean by his last statement?

With a strong resignation, Colonel Lee withdrew her weapon from her coat pocket and forced the slide rail to the rear. She allowed the slide action to slam forward charging a cartridge into the chamber. She raised her arms steadying her aim, and began to apply pressure to the trigger.

Skip Daggard took three more long strides then stopped. He did not look back, nor did he speak. Sweat began to form on his brow.

Tense seconds ticked away. He waited. Colonel Lee finally dropped her arms to her sides. She released the trigger on her weapon. Then she returned it to her coat pocket and stepped off toward her vehicle.

Skip Daggard stepped off with his left foot and began to sing cadence to himself. "Left, right, left, right...I don't want no more of army life, gee ma' I wanna go, gee ma,' I wanna go home."

As she walked to her vehicle, Chin Lee began to recall some of the history she had learned about the US. Many governments called the Americans 'war-mongers.' Yet, they did not want any part of Europe's war until Pearl Harbor. Then the pacifist, isolationists reared up like an ancient dragon spewing fire and destruction, devouring its enemies.

Colonel Chin Lee was a soldier. She did not fight for glory or communist expansion. She fought for her people's survival. Korea's population was out of control and had been for thirty decades. When the officers of the North Korean Communist Army had been approached by the Soviets who wanted to take back control of all they had lost with the destruction of the Berlin Wall, to share world domination, her leaders accepted their offer without hesitation. Now, as she leaned against her vehicle, Colonel Chin Lee began to realize, like the Japanese must have done too late, that perhaps they should have let the sleeping dragon lie dormant while they conquered the rest of the world. Then the Communist Coalition could ask for the surrender of the US. But all of that was mute now. The wheels of war were already turning. Colonel Lee shivered again because deep down she had a premonition—a dreadful foreboding—that once again a powerful war machine had made a grave error in its judgment of these Americans.

Buffalo Run Valley
Corps of Engineers
Sunday, October 3
1225 hours

Skip Daggard followed the dirt road until it ran into Buffalo Run Creek. He stood at the water's edge listening to crows cawing and the gurgle of the creek as it splashed over rocks and cement slabs of an old bridge. He scolded himself. "Damn, Skip, you sure overloaded your mouth back there. What was that all about anyhow? You'd think you were running for some office or something!"

The slide action of Colonel Lee's weapon was still ringing in his ears. "Boy, you came a squeeze of the trigger closer to a piece of *that* farm. I wonder why she hadn't fired?

"Oh yeah, it was there in her eyes…she loves me." He slapped his face with his right hand. "Skip Daggard, you are one conceited SOB."

This quiet and peaceful area was rich in history. In the eighteenth and nineteenth centuries this dirt trail had linked the area to Route 40, the National Highway that George Washington had surveyed and helped construct for General Braddock during the French and Indian Wars. Who could have guessed back in 1755, that twenty years later, George Washington would be leading the American Revolution and be the first elected president of a newly formed country?

During the Indian trouble, Friendsville was the only white settlement that had not come under attack within the vicinity of the fighting. Some say it was due to its defensive position, but the truth is that when John Friend first came to the area, he made friends with the Indians. Instead of trying to steal from the Shawnee, he purchased the land from them. He gave his hand in friendship, and a promise that the Indians would always be welcomed.

John Friend's word has been kept throughout the centuries, and a piece of land overlooking the town of Friendsville has been given back to the Shawnee so they have a place to stay during their yearly visits.

As he crossed the seven yards of the creek, he began thinking about her. She was beautiful. Her black, pageboy styled hair shined even though the sun was hidden behind a gray sky that threatened rain.

The creek was knee-deep at this spot because of the rains. However, he could cross by stepping on rocks that were submerged between three and five inches below the waterline.

Buffalo Run Creek ran from west to east, and married up with the Youghiogheny. Its tributary, Laurel Run merged with Buffalo Run under the second bridge on Buffalo Run Road about a quarter mile from Route 42, which was also known as Friendsville Road.

Skip sat on a rock once he reached the northern bank. He was now on the Corps of Engineer property. He looked off towards the west. Although he could not see Colonel Lee, her image was imbedded in his mind.

He tightened his bootlaces staring out over the terrain.

Skip took in a deep breath of fresh, crisp, clear mountain air, allowing the air to escape from his lungs on its own accord.

This is not where he wanted to be at the age of sixty-two. He wanted peace, easy living and lots of loving. His heart began to ache. He stared off towards the west looking over the creek and through the forest as if he could see Kristine and Eilis standing on their front porch greeting him as he crossed the yard.

No! At age sixty-two his plans did not include fighting a war for his country's right to exist. He wondered just how much he had to sacrifice for his people. He had given up one woman for his country, Bryanna, his high school sweetheart. Three days ago his wife and daughter had died for their country, and he had just discovered that an enemy now rested in the womb of America waiting for the order to erupt from the earth to enslave his people.

In an instant, he became cold and hateful. He jumped to his feet clutching his rifle, giving great consideration on running back and shooting Colonel Lee. Tears began to roll down his face. He stopped. He sat back down on the rock lost in his past.

He had had a good childhood. It wasn't anything to write home about, but he and his sister, Mary always had what they needed, sometimes with frills. Then, one day when he was ten, Skip discovered a huge bag hidden away in the back corner of his parents' closet. He had pulled on this white silky material until he had several yards of the silk out and on the floor. His mother, Eilis, had walked in and gasped in horror. "Hurry, Skipper! Put that away before your father comes home."

"What is this, Mom?"

There was no time for questions. Mom hurried to repack the silk when Dad had shouted from the front door, "Anybody home?"

Mom began to tremble as we heard his footsteps on the stairs. We were just pushing the pack back into the closed when Dad came in.

He filled the doorway with his enormous body. Fire shot out from his hazel eyes.

Mom stood defiant. Without warning, she turned and went back into the closet. I stood frozen as Dad stepped into their bedroom. We could hear mom rummaging through boxes on the top self. She emerged with her prize. She dropped a Prince Edwards cigar box on their bed.

She turned on Dad. "Tell him! Tell him now!" She shouted and stormed out of the room.

Dad stood by the bed, like Andre the Giant, staring at the cigar box. It seemed like forever before he lifted the lid. He began sifting through ribbons and medals.

Wow! My dad was a war hero.

He took out a German Iron Cross and laid it down on the bed with gentle hands.

"You know there is German blood on your mother's side," he said choking on his words.

I stood there with my mouth open. It was the only time I had ever seen him cry.

He smoothed out the medal with soft touches of his huge fingers.

He never turned to look at me as he stood there that day crying and caressing the Iron Cross. "She had a brother. We became close friends."

He did not elaborate.

"I was in the 101st Air Borne. We were part of the Normandy Invasion..."

My mouth gaped open.

"We were fighting the Germans in a small village. It was door-to-door and vicious. I went down in a basement searching for hideouts. The Germans would hide soldiers in cellars. When we passed through, they would come out and open up on our rear."

He stopped to wipe tears from his face and eyes. He lifted the medal and laid it gently back in the box as if it were a sleeping baby. Then, he turned around to face me. He burst out into tears. "He took off his Iron Cross. 'Hitler,' he said, 'had placed this around my neck. Keep it for our family.'"

Dad placed his huge hands on my shoulders, staring into my eyes. "He wouldn't surrender. I killed him."

Dad seemed to have disappeared into another world. Then he looked at me again. "I pray that *you* will never know or learn about war, Skipper. Let's go find Mother."

Skip slowly gained his feet. He could still see the anger in his father's eyes. "What was it that you had said after ten minutes of cussing me out after I had joined? Oh, yeah! 'You'll learn.'"

He bowed his head as tears spattered on the damp ground. "I learned, Dad. It took me awhile, but I learned. Whoever thought that they could make up rules for war is a fool. War is man's insanity against himself."

Reality seeped in slowly against his will. He knew he could not stay here any longer, yet, he resisted the idea of leaving. Colonel Lee could not shoot him, but she may send someone else.

He knew why he had lingered in his valley. As long he was here Kristine and Eilis were close.

But now he had been discovered. "How in the *hell* did Colonel Lee do that? How could she have known where I was...that I was here?" Then Skip remembered her eyes. It was all there in her eyes. "Fuck you, bitch! Some place—sometime soon, one of us will have to die."

He moved back into the cave and began to pack. He had warned her. "Go home, Colonel Lee," he had said. "Go home and raise a family."

He stood in the entrance to the cave watching the dust settle back down on the road as he got a glimpse of her vehicle disappearing around a bend in Good Hope Road. He gave long consideration to his motor mouth, and why he had talked so much. "Perhaps," he said out loud, "to avoid another useless war."

With all the people starving to death in the world...if only all the countries could settle down and pool their resources. "Yeah, wouldn't that be something; a world at peace." But he knew that he was not the only one who dreamed of that utopia.

He slipped his backpack on and retrieved his rifle.

Skip Daggard stood at the entrance of the cave staring off to the west. There was no more smoke rising from the ruins. Still, he was reluctant to leave Buffalo Run Valley.

He had left his SUV in the driveway...a warning to those who had perpetrated the crime. Just a subtle note to let them know that they had fucked up and that he would be coming for them. "Give the bastards something to worry over," he said to himself.

"What was it Colonel Lee had said? Oh yeah! 'It wasn't my people. They were Soviet moles.' So much for the end of the Cold War!

"Which way to go? Canada maybe? No. Retreat or withdrawal was not an option. It's time to gather a fighting force so when those commies pop up out of the ground they will be staring down the barrels of our armies' weapons. Yeah! Right! So how am I supposed to put an army together in a month? Do I have a month?"

What did Colonel Lee say? "'That the Second Amendment would be deleted and the collecting of guns would all begin in less than two weeks.'"

So, he didn't have a month. He didn't even have two weeks because all the ammo and guns and war surplus from army and navy stores had to be collected within seven days. "Damn, another cluster-fuck." But he had become a master at dealing with those situations in the army. "What was the phrase? Oh yeah! SNAFU—situation normal, all fucked up!"

Skip Daggard began to think as he walked north through the forest following a deer trail through stands of oak, locust, and around highland laurel bushes with the Youghiogheny River and lake on his right. A hawk called as it sailed through the gray sky in search of food.

He wasn't concerned about covering his trail at this time. That would come later when he finally decided on his destination and plan of action. But he knew that he had to make contact with his local VFW 10077 in Deer Park, and then contact the commander of the Vietnam Veterans Association in Cumberland.

Each organization could spread the word along to all of their respective organizations. Next, he would have to acquire a copy of *Soldier of Fortune Magazine* so he could contact an officer of one of the survivalist groups that he hoped were still advertising in the magazine.

But where can they go? He had to figure that out before making any contacts. And how would they communicate with each other without NSA or CIA intercepting their transmissions? Hmmm! Why not use NSA's systems? That would teach them not to screw with him.

Skip had covered fifteen miles before he took a break. He was at Route 40, the Historical National Pike. Skip stayed in the forest until he had reached the Yough Dam.

He was now on the run again. Only a few years had passed since he and Kristine had taken to the underground tunnels under Washington to keep America and the world from a catastrophic world war. Now, as then, it was mostly his own people he had to elude.

Skip decided to take to the forests in and around the OhioPyle Recreation area. He would have to follow Route 40 west, and then turn north toward Confluence on Mae West Road. Local legend states that the road was so named after Mae West because of all the curves in the road.

As he walked on the gravel shoulder of the asphalt highway, Skip began to put a plan together, but his thoughts kept wandering back to his conversation with Colonel Lee.

Why had she come seeking him out? That's exactly what she had done…sought him out. "How in the *hell* did she know I was there?"

Skip knew that she most likely had seen the reflection of sunlight off the barrel of his rifle.

It was hard for him to determine whether she had grasped the concept that he had tried to get across to her. What had he told her? Oh yeah! "Colonel Lee it isn't about governments but about freedom. During our Civil War some yanks asked a group of rebel prisoners where they were from. They were told the hill-country of Tennessee. A Union sergeant responded, "'Hell boy, you don't have any slaves!'"

"'No, Sah,'" the prisoner responded, "'we'a fightin' 'cause we don't like nobody tellin' us how to live or what to do.'"

"Freedom, Colonel! We started fighting for it in 1775, and we've fought to hold onto it for two hundred and twenty-eight years. So, what in the hell makes you think that you're going to come here with your army and take our freedom from us? Not yesterday! Not today! And damn sure not tomorrow!"

"But you will have no military. You will all be ordered to turn in your weapons."

And that was when he had simply turned and walked away. Now he had to put action where he had put his mouth. He had to build an army. "Skip Daggard," he mumbled to himself, "this is how George Washington must have felt when Congress made him Commander of a non-existing military that had to fight and defeat the greatest military power of the known world at that time."

He stopped for a breather. As he surveyed his surroundings, he began to chastise himself again, "Skip Daggard, you sure stepped into the dog poop this time."

Skip began to formulate a plan as he drank from his canteen. He would let the VFW's, American Legions, Vietnam Vet organizations, and survivalist groups form the armies while he did what Skip Daggard did best…go hunting…hunting for spies.

Chapter Seven—A Decision

OhioPyle, Pennsylvania
Monday, October 4
0700 hours

A gentle, light rain had fallen during the night. Skip huddled over his small fire one-quarter mile in the woods from the OhioPyle State Park sign off of Sugar Loaf Road. He had an olive drab wool blanket draped over his shoulders, covering his back. He sipped on scalding hot coffee wondering how many British, Americans, French, and Indians had sat here, or close to his position, during the French and Indian Wars.

Nemacolin's Trail was about five miles south of his position. The area was abundant with history. It was this type of history he had tried to convey to Colonel Lee.

George Washington was a surveyor for General Braddock. It was Washington who was responsible for widening the Indian chief's trail so the British could move their supply trains over the Laurel Highlands. That trail became Route 40, also known as the National Highway.

Braddock was killed and buried in the road during one of those struggles about twenty miles southwest of Skip's campsite. He had been buried in the road so the Indians would not dig him up and mutilate his body. His body was later exhumed and buried off the road. A monument now marks his grave not far from the original place in the road.

A combined force of French and Indians defeated Washington at Fort Necessity. The battlefield is now a historical site located on Route 40 in Farmington, Pennsylvania.

Skip Daggard finished his second cup of coffee. A sadistic smile took shape around his mouth as he took out Gorbachev's cell phone from his backpack and dialed in a code-specific set of numbers. He broke the yolks of two eggs that he was frying while the ring tone began.

Colonel Chin Lee's Headquarters
Kingwood, West Virginia
Monday, October 4
0705 hours

The Bunker system the North Koreans were occupying was part of an elaborate maze of tunnels and bunkers linked together across the United States. This system was constructed during the 1950s when the Cold War had begun, and the human race had learned the destructive nature of the atomic bomb.

The system was built to house the US government and its entire military force; at least those forces that could take refuge in the system.

Bunkers like the one Colonel Lee and her staff occupied were strategically constructed and stocked with food rations, water, and weapons. The weapons had been systematically removed during the mid-seventies but the food and water rations had been maintained.

Each bunker complex consisted of a war room twenty feet by twenty feet. Two small offices were connected to the war room with a large window and a door. Each room opened into the war room. A large map of the world occupied the south wall of the war room. Three, three-foot brass wall-mounted lamps provided light to the map. The lighting from these lamps provided an eerie atmosphere in the room when the overhead lights were turned off.

There were quarters to house five hundred male soldiers and three hundred female personnel. This particular complex had three latrines with shower facilities. One facility was for enlisted males; one for females to include female officers; and one for the male officers.

Colonel Lee came out of a stall. She jumped when she noticed Lieutenant Wong standing just inside the door.

They stared at each other for a few seconds. "Are you going to contact General Bardolph?"

Colonel Lee walked to the washbasins and began washing her hands. She puzzled over his question. "I will make my report this morning, why?"

"Which report; the one that you *too* had failed to kill Agent Daggard, or the one affirming your love for our enemy?"

Colonel Lee spun around glaring at Wong. She stepped backward one pace. His smile was unexpected.

"Everyone seems to be preoccupied with preparing for battle. I do not believe that they have noticed. But I have been with you for several years, Colonel Lee; therefore, I know your likes and dislikes. I know your dreams and wishes. And I know the moment when you gave your heart to our enemy."

She listened to him, intrigued.

"What is your plan of action…now?"

She studied the gray painted walls and floor. She could hear the air filtration system humming as fresh air was blown into the bunker system through a maze of filters and water purification devices.

"I am not in love with him." Yet, as she spoke the words, her heart shouted, "*Liar!*"

She stood tall with her arms folded staring at the gray painted cement floor. Slowly, she lifted her head staring into the smiling face of her best friend. She smiled back at him. "I do not know what I am going to do."

"If you abandon this mission, Colonel Lee, take me with you."

Lieutenant Wong turned, leaving the latrine to his leader.

She stood alone in the room with its twelve stalls, nine sinks, and locker room that included one large shower with fifteen showerheads. She stood still counting everything in the room. Colonel Lee admired her reflection in a mirror over one sink. She feathered her raven hair with her fingers. Her smooth face was not round but not quite oval. She stared into her eyes looking deep into herself. Her soul shared its secret with her. Colonel Lee smiled. Her heart filled with sadness. "How could love come to me now? Why did life have to be so cruel by giving me a lover who is my enemy? But *is he* my enemy?"

Colonel Lee shook her head as if to clear the nonsense of love from her mind. She had a phone call to make.

NSA, Fort Meade
General Bardolph's Office
Monday, October 4
0707 hours

Within the arena of human events man has tried to buck destiny with no real outcome. Individuals throughout history have tried to alter a predetermined course and chart their own paths, either for good or evil, only to be swallowed up by that destiny which they had tried to undermine.

These were the thoughts that invaded General Ashford Bardolph's mind as he sat at his mahogany desk. His plush office was situated on the third floor of the original building at NSA.

The building had been constructed and manned in 1952 when all of the military branches' intelligence and counterintelligence organizations were formed into one intelligence-gathering force of military and civilian personnel.

Its purpose was to create a central location for a unified military intelligence organization. Although civilians are part of the organization, its director is a general, usually two stars, rotating from each of the four branches of the military with the Deputy Director a one star.

General Bardolph was a realist. He knew the implications of allowing a nemesis such as Agent Daggard to live. He rose in an easy motion, pushing back his chair. He turned and waddled to a window.

Bardolph stared off toward the west, pondering the future. Daggard had been the cause of two Soviet debaucheries. In 1975 he had terminated several Soviet moles in the 3rd Armored Division. Three years ago he assassinated his president when he had discovered that President Mantle had conceived a secret war arrangement with the displaced Soviets.

"Damn," Bardolph explained to his image in the windowpane, "I had him 1975 chained, tortured and trussed up for killing. Yet, that son of a bitch managed to escape."

General Bardolph clasped his hands behind his back as he began to pace the carpet behind his desk, allowing his mind to wander. Now the Soviets were in striking position—their armies entrenched in the US. And of all disasters to occur, Skip Daggard has killed several of his men and the bastard had, again, managed to survive and is out there, ready to retaliate. Once again they had him, and once again that slippery eel had managed to escape.

How many times during the course of the Cold War had his people tried? Too many to even consider. Now that world domination was in their grasp…

General Bardolph fell into his chair. "Oh well! Colonel Lee will put an end to this Daggard issue," Bardolph said as he sat rigid and scowling.

Captain Harding was dead. So were seven others…people who were to be placed into key positions when time called for their placement. Now, because of that damn meddling fool… "Well," he said out loud, "Colonel Lee will be calling me soon with wonderful news." He had learned in the past two years that he could trust her to accomplish a mission.

General Ahford Bardolph smiled as he leaned over his desk for a cigar. He leaned back in his chair, bit off the tip of his Cuban, spit the end in a wastebasket to the left corner of his desk, and then lit his cigar as a satisfactory smile spread across his clean-shaven face. His world turned to shit with the ringing of his code-specific cell phone.

"I'm coming for your scalp, you commie spy!"

The line went dead.

General Bardolph almost fell over backwards as he chomped down on his cigar splitting it in half, his arms flailing trying to grasp the edge of his desk before his chair careened over backwards. After twenty years as a Soviet spy in the United States Army Intelligence Command, he had learned one fact: Skip Daggard did not waste his time making idol threats. A huge smile overtook the general's face as he got up from the carpeted floor. "Taunt me all you like, you bastard. Soon Colonel Lee will pluck you from my side when she shoots bullets into your antagonistic body."

OhioPyle, Pennsylvania
Monday, October 4
0730 hours

Skip Daggard danced around his small fire laughing. He looked like Kevin Cosner in that scene from *Dances with Wolves*. He had heard General Bardolph crash to the floor before he hung up. Skip was dancing and laughing because he knew that Bardolph probably had wet himself when he heard his voice.

It wasn't because of Bardolph that Skip danced. He danced for himself, because in dancing he could release the demon and the tension, and he could get lost in his thoughts.

The faster he danced around the fire, the more tension was released. He gave himself over to the dance so he could think. His mind was bombarded by many images of war, spies, death, and destruction.

Images of his mother, father, Mary, and Bryanna standing at his grave burst forward. Next came a series of scenes with him hunting down and terminating spies within the US infrastructure, all for this moment in history: the destruction of the United States.

He danced around the fire spinning and turning for twenty minutes before he finally fell to the ground exhausted. His mind was alive and replenished. He sat up and studied his surroundings. He regained his feet after sitting on the ground for five minutes. He put his coat on and sat on his stool near the fire. He poured himself a cup of scalding black coffee wishing for some evaporated milk and sugar, while he inhaled the fragrance of wet leaves.

His plans had been shaped and finalized during his dance. He took out the cell phone and made a call. Skip had learned that a tracer block had been established for Gorbachev's cell phone so NSA could not isolate his location when he had called General Bardolph.

"General Hanalin!"

"Hey, Mac…you alone?"

"Of course I can't deal with that issue right now! I can't believe you even bothered me with it."

Skip hung up immediately. "So, they're keeping tabs on old Mac, huh? And so they should."

Skip Daggard sat staring off beyond his fire. This was not a position new to him. One difference was that his present camp was on his own soil, and the enemy was here, not in some remote country or outpost.

The purpose of his call to Hanalin was to affirm that he was a prisoner at the Pentagon.

He allowed his mind to wander. Three years ago he had killed the president and secretary of state for preparing to perpetrate treason against the American people. In 1999 he boldly strolled into NSA during the Director's monthly meeting of high-ranking Intel personnel and capped eight spies who he had been hunting down for twenty years.

"Man, did the proverbial shit hit the fan that day," he said out loud.

Now, it wasn't a case of a few spies or a rogue president. Now the entire nation and freedom of his people was at stake. And he wasn't young anymore. He was sixty-two and the old football injury to his left knee was slowing him down. The cold did not help.

"All right, Skipper," he said to himself as he stood up while his bones complained. "What do I know?"

Skip studied his surroundings while he thought about his life and the state of affairs of man and the role spies have played in the course of history. In his case, when he had announced to his mother and fiancée about his decision to go into the army after graduation, and the military police, his mother threw a fit. He had tried to explain to her that once he separated from the service, he could get a job with the Morristown Police Force.

She stood her ground, so he went into communications, which ultimately led him into a life of lies, deceit, and killing, which in turn led him to an ultimate sacrifice: giving up his fiancée, a normal life, being buried at Arlington Cemetery, and operating under a new identity, Sergeant Derry Batair from January 1970 thru August 2000.

"Your whole premise was to keep me safe, mom. You wanted me in something that was not too dangerous. Well, mom, I haven't been safe since June 1968."

Skip shook his head to clear out past events. Now he would have to modify his plan of attack. First, he would have to free General Hanalin and kill a few spies in the Pentagon. While he packed, Skip put the final touches to his up-coming operation.

As he stepped out, he shuddered at the thought of going down into the tunnels of Washington again; back to his secret room where he and Kristine had shared secrets of their own on their way to save the world from another world war. His tears were spent now, but his heart still sat heavy in its cradle transmitting its sadness throughout his body. He spoke out to the gray dawn. "It seems that all we did, Kristine, was to postpone the inevitable."

Skip Daggard walked, a soldier with a purpose, and as he walked, he checked his weapons. Once again while the human race moved through its turbulent existence, man was oblivious to its destruction as Chief Warrant Officer Retired Skip Daggard marched toward an unknown future.

Colonel Chin Lee's Headquarters
Kingwood, West Virginia
Monday, October 4
0835 hours

Colonel Chin Lee had piddled around the war room studying the topographical map, sidestepping the issue of calling General Bardolph. Time was of the essence. She had to make her report. She also knew that *her* people were going to be furious, but she really did not care about them. After all, they had just killed her father. What had she been told? "Your father was going to betray us. We are watching you. Conduct yourself properly."

She looked across the table and noticed that Lieutenant Wong was studying her intently. They stared at each other for several seconds. She knew in her heart that she could trust her old friend, just as she knew that if she went to Agent Daggard's side, she was not taking Wong with her. It would mean immediate death for his entire family. Just as quickly as she had thought those words, her heart shouted out to her mind the precise information her psyche needed to know.

Lieutenant Wong watched her retrieve her cell phone from her left pocket. Their eyes locked together as she pushed the speed dial button. The bustle of activity within the confines of the war room drowned out the ringing of her phone. She had to walk into a corner in order to hear.

"General Bardolph, the issue will be resolved by this evening."

"Excellent, Colonel Lee, excellent! Thank you!"

"We have buried your agents outside our bunker within the woods so the mounds would not be visible."

She heard a heavy sigh come from General Bardolph.

She closed her phone then returned it to her pocket. She jumped because she had not noticed that Lieutenant Wong had come up to her. "You will always be my big sister," he whispered close to her right ear. "I am saddened that you are going over to the losing side. Yet, I am happy for you because you have finally found that which has eluded you for so long." He released a long sigh then said to her, "Love him well, Chin. Love him well." Then he turned and left her standing in the corner gasping for breath.

Ten minutes later, Colonel Chin Lee of the Korean Communist Army opened the trunk of her maroon Geo and dropped her war bag inside. When she moved to the driver's door she saw Wong standing by the door to the bunker. She threw him a kiss. He saluted. She bowed. Chin Lee left the hidden area driving off into an unknown future and to an enemy she had fallen in love with.

OhioPyle, Pennsylvania
Monday, October 4
1100 hours

Skip Daggard had decided on one immediate plan of action as the morning marched on towards the mid-day period. He was going to terminate Bardolph. What he needed was a vehicle. He had formulated a plan to rectify that problem while he had packed and cleaned up his camp area.

He knew that he could not rent a vehicle because that would alert his enemies to his location. He couldn't midnight requisition a vehicle either because the local authorities would be alerted to the theft, which meant that his enemies within NSA would also be alerted. So, his only option was to borrow a vehicle from a friend.

Skip analyzed and worried over which should come first: free General Hanalin, or kill the Deputy Director of NSA. He laughed as the idea of flipping a coin raced through his mind.

He left the forest, turned left onto the shoulder of Sugar Loaf Road, and began to walk east. At 1.6 miles, he turned right onto Taylor Road heading south. This route would shorten his walk back to Route 40 by 2 miles. Approximately 1.7 miles, Skip turned right onto Mae West Road, Route 281 heading south.

Mae West Road snaked its way to Route 40 over 3 miles of hills, turns and bends. Due to the steep and winding climbs of the roadway, it took Skip one and one half-hours to make the trek.

Markleysburg, Pennsylvania
Monday, October 4
1414 hours

Skip stepped out with a slight limp heading back toward Route 40. The cold weather often had an adverse affect on his left knee and the terrain he was traversing did not help matters. He had to stop several times along his route. Twice he drank from the small stream that followed along Mae West Road.

Once he got to the junction of Mae West Road and Route 40, he turned right. Just as he turned left onto Main Street in Markleysburg and came abreast of the elementary school, he collided with Colonel Chin Lee.

She immediately pulled over to the right shoulder of the road staring at him.

Skip stood on the graveled shoulder of the roadway staring at Colonel Lee in complete disbelief. He shook his head. "Are you stalking me, Colonel Lee? We have laws against that in this country." Then he laughed.

Colonel Chin Lee sat in her vehicle staring at Skip. She thought, "This man is insane. His country is about to be destroyed and he stands there on the side of a road making jokes."

The sun was out and the sky clear. Once again the temperature had rebounded to a comfortable sixty-one degrees.

"I have decided," she said with a tremor in her voice, "I am going to stay."

Skip studied her facial expression. There was humor, sadness, and sincerity etched in her smooth, olive skin.

"Sorry to hear that! I guess you've come to kill me? After all, this is our…what, third encounter?"

She allowed her mind to make a permanent image of his face.

"I have been ordered to kill you. I have decided to join you." Her statement was so matter of fact, that her words caught Skip by surprise.

Her head fell against the top of the steering wheel. She began to cry. Skip shifted in place while a torrent of tears spilled out from her eyes and down her face.

After a few minutes, Colonel Lee lifted her head, wiped the tears from her eyes and face, and looked at Skip Daggard. "I am thirty-nine years old. I have devoted my life to the communist party." Her face went stone cold. "They murdered my father because he voiced his opposition to this war."

This was something he could understand...revenge. "So?"

"You are one man. Yet, you will face an army of seventy million. Your wife and daughter have been sacrificed. Yet, you do not run and hide."

He thought about a reply for several seconds. "Yeah, we Americans are crazy in that respect. We'll take a little slappin' around. Some butt kickin', but when we're attacked and our people murdered...then...its war."

"Your situation is hopeless, yet you refuse to surrender!"

Skip turned his head left towards Route 40, trying to formulate his words. He looked back at her.

"A hopeless situation, Colonel Lee?"

"Chin."

"What?"

"Chin. My name is Chin Lee."

Skip studied her body language, her face, and her eyes for a few minutes in order to read the woman's truthfulness.

"All right, Chin Lee. A hopeless situation is what George Washington faced when he was made commander of an army that did not exist and was expected to beat the army and navy of King George the Third.

"Hopeless is watching your men freeze to death at a place called Valley Forge wondering what the spring would bring, then, loading your half frozen soldiers into long boats, crossing a partially frozen river in a blizzard, and attacking a formidable enemy at a place called Trenton... and kicking ass.

"Hopeless is watching the twin towers crash to the ground killing our people, and realizing war has just been declared against us and wondering why."

Skip stopped to catch his breath and admire Chin's beauty. He continued as he stared at her. "Our soldiers are dying in the Middle East but they're dying on battlefields. And what our enemies always seem to forget, that ever since this 'American Experiment'—freedom, every generation of Americans have taken, in their hands, the Declaration of Independence and have fought to preserve it.

"You say that I am one man who refuses to surrender but that's not true. There are about three hundred million Americans who will refuse to surrender. So, you see, I'm not alone."

Skip studied Chin as she slipped out from her vehicle. He chastised himself once again for diarrhea of the mouth. He had noticed she was now wearing a black mini skirt, white blouse, sheer stockings and black pumps.

The sun was toward the west. The sky was painted in shades of blues, gold, and pinks, and dotted with small grey clouds. He studied her face allowing his eyes to drink in her figure "Damn," he thought, "she's beautiful."

Chin Lee invaded his thoughts. "So, now what, do we shoot it out?"

She leaned her back against the car with her arms crossed under her ample breasts, all the while studying the features of this man her people and the Communists have hunted and tried to destroy for thirty-five years, or has it been forty years?

Chin Lee could see the sadness in his eyes as Skip looked off toward the southeast—his home. When he looked back at her, his sadness was gone, replaced with a cold, steel stare. "Reckon not!"

As a Chinook wind began to blow, they scrutinized each other through defiant eyes.

Skip began to inhale long gulps of the warm air.

Chin Lee stared in amazement and wonder.

"Indian summer," he said. "I believe that's what it's called when warm weather returns for a while before winter sets in."

She tilted her head. "I do not understand."

"The warm wind is what we call a Chinook. We will have warm temperatures and no more snow for the next few weeks."

She nodded her head while kicking at the gravel with her left foot as she leaned against her vehicle. Chin Lee lowered her head to stare at her feet then she looked back at Skip. "My government killed my father. They killed him because he voiced his disapproval of this war."

She lowered her head again but she didn't cry. Instead, an angry hatred began to manifest itself within her heart.

Skip's comment was cruel. "And that's the kind of people *you* want to fight for, huh?"

Their eyes locked for ten seconds before she responded. "I am thirty-nine. I have been a member of the Communist party since my twelfth birthday. I have been a soldier since I was sixteen. My father was all I had left of my family.

"My government has taken him from me. *I hate them*!" She paused for a deep breath of air as her eyes turned cold.

"I have given great consideration to what you said earlier. I am defecting. I have vital information that you will need."

Skip almost fell over. His stumbling brought laughter lines to her face as she broke out in hysterical uproar.

How could he soften her loss? Why should he even try?

"I gave up one fiancée for my country, and my wife and daughter gave up their lives. I can't make you any promises, Chin but if you want to take the walk, I'll go with you and we'll see where the trail takes us."

Chin Lee sighed. Her breasts heaved and fell several times. She watched the clouds roll across the sky. "There is a Lieutenant Wong. He is my best and only friend…"

Skip let air escape from his lungs in two short bursts. His eyes softened just a little. "I am not going to be in charge of the army, Chin Lee. My mission is to terminate the moles and everyone associated with the spies. Once that's done, then we will join the battle."

She stood up straight.

"Yeah, that's what I said—we. I need a vehicle to get around, and I just thought of an idea. You can be my driver so your vehicle doesn't have to stay somewhere and perhaps be noticed."

Skip studied the cars and occupants as they passed by.

"You can be my get-a-way driver. Plus, you can point some of the spies out to me."

Chin nodded her agreement as Skip crossed the road. As he passed behind the vehicle he stopped and looked over at her. "If this Lieutenant

Wong can be saved, it means we will have to let others live so as not to cast any suspicion on him. That may not be possible. You understand?"

She nodded. She opened the trunk so Skip could drop his burden. They both slipped into the vehicle. As Chin turned the key, Skip whispered, "Take me to Washington. I have an old friend to free."

Chin Lee turned right at the stop sign at Main Street and Route 40. They drove over a route steep in history heading east toward Washington and…war.

Chapter Eight—Invading the Pentagon

Pentagon
Arlington County, Virginia
Tuesday, October 5
0900 hours

General Hanalin sat behind his oak desk in his office on the first floor, a prisoner. Although he could conduct routine business as the Army Joint Chief of Staff, his movements and phone calls were being monitored.

He had been able to reveal startling information to Skip during their last brief contact. The most important piece of information being that he was a prisoner inside the Pentagon. Now, he was given limited access and mobility within its walls.

General Hanalin leaned back in his executive-style black leather chair with his hands clasped behind his head, smiling. Whatever was shaping up beyond his walls was a variable he could do nothing about. Yet, he knew one variable that he could count on. He would bide his time.

General Mac Arthur Hanalin knew that come high tide or the end of the world, Skip Daggard would come for him, and those moving through the halls of the Pentagon, the enemies of the state, were going to pay for their treachery.

Georgetown
Tuesday, October 5
0910 hours

President George Washington had been nobody's fool. When southern representatives approached him in 1792 to move the capital from New York closer to the south, he saw an opportunity to protect the new government from attack. It had been Washington who had selected the new site and he had been involved with private landowners to sell parcels to the government. Under his guidance, specific subterranean passageways had been constructed, just in case the new government would have to abandon the capital. His wisdom had been validated several times.

In a secret written accord, Alexandria, which Washington annexed from Virginia, would be returned to Virginia in 1847. However, Georgetown would become a suburb of D.C. in 1878.

Because this area was not a state, but land donated or sold by private landowners, or by the states of Maryland and Virginia, the new capital of the United States was simply a territory and has remained so until today. Although the issue of statehood for the capital has been voted on several times, Washington still remains a territory. The capital bears George Washington's name, but D.C., meaning District of Columbia, (actually, Dedicated to Columbus) was so named by President Washington due to his respect and admiration for Christopher Columbus.

Like spokes of a wheel, tunnel systems branch out of Washington in all directions. Some lead to dead ends, while others are escape routes. Four such systems run under Georgetown. One tunnel branches out from the Lincoln Tunnel near the White House. Another one runs under the Capitol Building and ends at a bunker system east of the center of Georgetown. One starts at a vault in the subterranean basement of the Federal Building, stretching out all the way to the Catoctin Mountain Range in Thurmont, Maryland, and ending at Fort Ritchie. This tunnel also has a trunk line from the White House. A fourth tunnel taps into the Washington tunnel under the US Mint and ends at the CIA Headquarters at Langley. The one that interested Skip now was the tunnel system with a massive bunker system and underground tunnel under the Potomac River, which was tied into the original Washington tunnel. This system is a maze of false lines with one that dead-ends at the Pentagon.

Skip sat at an old oak table sipping coffee as steam filtered around his brow. "If I get as much as a slight inkling that you're playing me, Chin, I will shoot you."

Chin sat on a cot near the south corner of the bunker. She stared at Skip. "I do not understand!"

Skip sat silent for two minutes drinking his coffee while watching her over the rim of his cup. "You have learned more in the past fifteen hours about our secret passageways than most intelligence people learn during their careers, and you will learn more.

"So, if I get a whiff on the wind that you've lied to me, I will kill you...immediately."

She smiled. "I understand. Where are we?"

"You commies, always with the questions; Kristine was the same damn way, always asking questions."

Chin rose in disbelief. *"She was a Communist?"*

"Soviet," he said with a hint of pride in his tone. "During our last mission together, she informed me that her father had been some headcheese in the KGB. He moved over to the new Federal Secret Service when the Soviets lost power."

Skip poured a cup of coffee for Chin as she approached the table and handed the cup to her. "I almost shot her, and we were engaged. So I guess you can figure out where that leaves you.

"I mean I had the muzzle of my weapon in her face with the hammer cocked. Damn good thing I was in love with her!"

Skip was not going to explain the intricacies of the bunker, or answer the curious questionable looks in Chin's brown eyes. She was still the enemy.

As he began sipping at his second cup of coffee, Skip studied the well-stocked bunker. The food consisted of military C-Rations, bottled water, and MRE's (Meals Ready to Eat). The communications systems were up-to-date so the members of the Pentagon could still conduct war from this position. Each bunker along this subterranean system could house a small group of Pentagon officials and two Joint Chiefs of Staff. The rest could make their way to the "Little Pentagon" at Fort Ritchie.

Skip closed his eyes. He studied his situation. He knew that he could not access the Pentagon unless he was in disguise. And his disguises were in the secret room in the Lincoln tunnel.

The plan that was formulating in his mind was simple. However, two ideas were working in parallel. That was normal for him because this system of analysis usually provided Skip with the best alternative or plan of action.

The two possibilities were: go through the tunnel system he was now in and access the Pentagon through the subterranean compartment, or walk through the front doors as an officer to see General Hanalin. As Skip was contemplating his choices, a third scenario cropped up, slowly taking root. That plan was to go through the front doors as an officer to see the spies, terminate them, then grab Hanalin and escape through the underground system before anyone knew what had happened. In his final analysis, he decided to combine plans two and three. He would go through the front doors, free Hanalin, and then, they would terminate the spies.

"I'm going to leave you here, Chin. If I'm not back within twenty-four hours, go back to your people letting them know you had set me up for capture."

Chin listened but refused his plan. "If you are not back, I will find a way to free this General Hanalin."

He wasn't going to argue with her because he had learned from Kristine that arguing was often futile. Instead, he stared at her for several seconds before he spoke. "Why are you doing this? Is it just for revenge, or are there other underlying issues?"

The bunker smelled of musty cardboard boxes and stale, damp, trapped air. Lighting was adequate, but a dripping sound of water was prominent in the quietness of the moment. Chin could hear the beating of her heart and wondered if Skip could hear its pulsating pounding as well.

She had to tilt her head up to look into his eyes even though they were five feet apart. "I know that you have just suffered a great loss," she said not averting her eyes. "I cannot expect you to feel anything for me, but I have powerful feelings for you. My father's murder was the emotional shove I needed to help me decide."

Skip did not smile. He stood his ground looking down at her

absorbing her radiant beauty with his eyes—her raven hair, silky smooth olive skin, pert breasts, and her military posture.

"What is it about me that sparks the hearts of you Communists?" he inquired without sarcasm.

He let a long breath of air escape, and then he moved forward towards her. "Listen, Chin…"

"No! You listen before you go."

Skip stepped back. "You have something to say?"

"Yes, information you must have."

Skip sat down in his chair at the table. As Chin began to speak, his mind had already left the bunker. It traveled down the tunnel system until it came to another room—a secret room in the Lincoln Tunnel. A room where not long ago, another Communist, his Kristine, had vital information he needed in order to act on behalf of the American people.

"Maybe your target is not the Secretary of State but the president. We've known about his condition for a year…he has terminal cancer. He has set up his own assassination plot so he can die a martyr."

Now, three years later, another Communist female is informing him that, she too has vital information, information that he must have in order to protect the American people. Skip rose to his feet in animated movement. "The Fates can play havoc on us humans," he spoke softy, "I served through most of the Cold War constantly battling you commies, and in two of the most darkest hours in American history, it is Communists who provide crucial information…go figure."

Chin wanted to go to him. She ached to hold him and shower him with her kisses. Instead, she remained steadfast.

Skip released a short sigh. "What is the information?"

Chin studied him for three seconds then she spoke in a whisper. "You only have two weeks to activate your forces…"

"*TWO WEEKS!*"

"Yes! Because of you, the Soviets have decided to move up their time-schedule. How do you Americans say…fear…fear factor."

Skip chuckled. "Then I better get my ass in gear. I mean I better get going."

As he stood by the bunker door prepared to leave, Skip turned, "Chin, if I go under, you do what is best for you."

"If you should die, Agent Daggard, then I will fight in your stead. Go!"

He studied her face, looking into her eyes as if he was trying to look into her soul. Chin returned his stare with her own, looking into the blue eyes of the man she had fallen in love with—her heart pounding against her chest. "Go, do what must be done."

Then she kissed him. "Go, now!"

Skip stepped out into the tunnel system touching his lips where she had kissed him as Chin Lee secured the door behind him.

Down the long, dark tunnel reeking of stagnate stench and cast in haunting shadows, Skip walked alone towards the unknown. But he wasn't alone—dancing in a circle around his head, danced the three Fates who controlled humans' destinies.

Secret room off the Lincoln Tunnel
Washington, D.C.
Tuesday, October 5
1300 hours

Skip hadn't gone through the tunnel systems pell-mell. Instead, he took his time, allowing himself the opportunity to analyze events, his plans, and the information Chin had given him.

"You have two weeks before the Communist forces attack, but only one week before the forced gun collection begins. In five days, your Second Amendment will no longer be valid.

"The Soviet moles are acting quickly as to derail your efforts. So whatever you had planned to do, you must achieve that now, or lose your country," she had told.

Skip Daggard stood before the stone wall of his secret hideout. His hand rested on the stone lever. He fought against his will to activate his hand into action. He stood with his shoulders slumped down. His head hung forward with his chin resting against his chest as if it was too heavy for his neck muscles to support.

His tears splashed on the ancient stone floor at his feet. It had been here, just beyond this stone wall, about thirty-eight months ago, that Kristine had dropped her bomb, and they had set-off together to terminate a traitor in the White House. He sucked down his pain and worked the lever. The wall grated as it moved inward.

Georgetown
Tuesday, October 5
1310 hours

Chin Lee conducted a tour of her surroundings. She ripped open the top lids of a case of C-Rations, taking out one box of foodstuff. She placed a can of pork and beans, peaches, and cheese and crackers on the table. Chin tore open a small bag containing a small pack of cigarettes; toilet paper, eating utensils, salt and pepper, and a P-38 can opener.

She used the P-38 to open the peaches, devouring them in short order. Next, she attacked the pork and beans in the same manner, then the cheese and crackers. She opened a bottle of water and drank the entire pint of fluid in one chug.

Once she was full, Chin sat at the table scrutinizing her actions. She was not the type of person who would abandon her post, nor negate to carry out orders. "So, why did I do it," she reprimanded herself. "I will not go back, Skip Daggard," she said as if he was standing next to her. "I have chosen my mate, and I have made my choice to be free," she stated her issues. Chin Lee began to question the word.

"What is it?" she asked the silence of the bunker. Down, deep inside of her something began to stir…freedom began to take root in the pit of her stomach. A sense of the word was shaking her soul. Free! A comprehension started squeezing her mind searching for understanding while attacking her communistic viewpoints—viciously attacking those views—destroying them within the moral fibers of her conscience.

This new and strange sensation that was taking hold of her was frightening, yet, she felt exhilarated because she felt the restraints of her oppression being snapped from her body, mind, and soul. Free! She was… *free*. Free to choose. Free to love. Free to die. Another realization began to grow from within her. It was an understanding… an understanding of an idea which drove the Americans to fight.

As she sipped another cup of coffee, she realized another lie—the

Americans were not warmongers. They did not seek out battles, but if battles were brought to them…they would fight. It is all there in the pages of history, and yet, she wondered how one man was going to save his people.

He had sacrificed everything for his country. In her final analysis, she knew that Skip Daggard would sacrifice himself for his people. "How strange," she thought, "his people does not know that he exists, yet, he had been fighting for them for thirty-seven years, and now at the moment the Americans need a champion, he stands. No one had ordered him to do this…strange."

She finished her coffee, placed her cup down on the table, and rose, lady-like, smoothing out her black mini skirt and straightening her stockings. Chin Lee walked over to the Army Combat Uniform (ACU) Skip had laid out for her and began to change her clothes. Her heart began to ache as she slipped her stockings off and stepped into the uniform pants. She knew what was coming—there was no hope for the Americans.

Once her country launched its first missile, Iran and Sierra would launch theirs, wiping out all US forces in the Middle East. US forces in South Korea would be dealt with in a matter of hours, and the entire Communist force would attack the US and Europe.

"One man," she said out loud as she buttoned her ACU blouse, "one man who refuses to lie down and surrender, hmmm, perhaps!"

Secret room off the Lincoln Tunnel
Washington, D.C.
Tuesday, October 5
1330 hours

Skip Daggard stood in front of the mirror, triple checking his disguise. "It is almost perfect," he said to the face in the mirror, "but nothing is ever perfect," he declared as the memories flooded out from his subconscious. He had tried to avoid the memories when he had stepped into the room just a short time ago. The first thing he had done was to salute the mass grave in the corner. "I'm back sergeant," he spoke with conviction to the grave where President Lincoln's Sergeant of the

Guard and his soldiers were buried. "Destiny has taken another turn. Another war is shaping up on our shores."

Skip broke down and allowed his sorrow to erupt as he let the tears fall. Thirty-five seconds later he had sucked it up. "I'm here alone because the enemy has killed my world. But they believe that they can walk in and take away our country and our freedom. I swear to you and our comrades who have and are serving, this will not happen on my watch."

The mirror gave up the scenes which had taken place in the room three years ago. He could see Kristine standing in front of him while pointing his weapon at her.

"I had to tell you, Skip, even if it meant my life because you are the only one who can make the shot. I love you, Skip Daggard. I have loved you since I was twelve years old."

He couldn't hold back his tears. He let them fall again as he cried. This time it took him forty seconds to suck it up. He checked himself again in the mirror, straightened his uniform, and looked around. He started to chuckle, remembering the secrets he had shared with Kristine. He never knew until then that he could share them with anyone.

As he checked the incinerator grenades he had placed back then, he reflected on their conversation while they had been in the Washington Monument before he took out the traitors.

Skip closed his eyes. They were there together in the monument when she had asked, "Skip, what secret were you never to tell?"

"It's a secret I've kept for forty years, Kristine," he had told her.

Now, he wished that he had shared with her. But here in his secret room he felt her presence. He closed his eyes so he could visualize her face. "I will tell you now, darling. MI folks can't be taken prisoners of war. When our sight at Bang Pla had come under attack for the third time in as many months, an MP company had been sent out to our location. Their mission wasn't to protect us, Kristine. Their top-secret orders were to protect the code. *We* were expendable. Do you remember that movie we saw, *The Wind Talkers*? Well, that was the situation for my entire unit."

He had to fight himself for control so he could open his eyes. When he did, Kristine's image was gone.

Once again Skip Daggard stood on the threshold of destiny with his people's freedom in jeopardy. He saluted the grave where the Civil War soldiers were buried. Skip turned and operated the lever. The stone wall opened. Skip stepped out into the tunnel. He turned facing the wall and took one last look inside as he worked the lever. The stone wall closed. Skip faced down the tunnel, and then he moved out smartly with the three Fates sitting on his right shoulder.

Pentagon
Arlington County, Virginia
Tuesday, October 5
1405 hours

The Pentagon is located in southwestern Arlington County, Virginia. Brigadier General Brehon B. Sommervell conceived the idea in July 1941. It is the headquarters of the United States Department of Defense and the nerve center command and control. Its work force consists of twenty-three thousand military and civilians, plus three thousand non-defense support personnel.

General Hanalin sat at his desk eating his lunch. He enjoyed chili even though his gastric juices rebelled. While he ate, Hanalin pondered a course of action, but dismissed each idea. He had been in worse situations, and when hope looked dim, his Snoopy, Skip Daggard, would appear. He wasn't going to try and second-guess how Skip was going to access the Pentagon. All he knew for sure was that Skip would come.

He jumped when his phone rang. Hanalin lifted the receiver from its cradle with a trembling hand. "General Hanalin!"

"Sir, this is Sergeant Peters in the main lobby. There's a General Guard to see you, sir."

Send him up, Sergeant. Thank you!"

General Hanalin went to a secret compartment in his coat closet. He turned the dial on a safe. When the tumblers clicked and the steel door swung open, Hanalin removed the Colt .45 and six loaded clips. He locked one clip into the butt of the handle and stuffed the other clips into the pockets of his dress blue uniform.

Just as he stepped back into the room and closed the door the front door to his office swung inward and his old friend stepped inside, closing the door behind him.

Hanalin spoke with amusement in his voice, "General Guard, huh?"

Skip responded, "Figured you'd get the humor, Mac, guard, like in guard dog, like in Snoopy, my code name in 'Nam" Skip said as he placed his briefcase on Hanalin's desk.

Skip removed two 9mm handguns specially designed to hold twenty-round clips. "Wait here, Mac. I have two spies…"

"Like hell!"

The old warriors stared at each other while the second hand on the brown, white-faced wall clock ticked off ten seconds. Skip inhaled the aroma of Captain Black pipe tobacco and smiled. "All right old son, let's do it. OK Corral, eat your heart out."

They made their way down a corridor towards the Defense Intelligence Agency (DIA), which had been created in August 1961 to assist in the coordination of military intelligence and to serve directly the needs of the Secretary of Defense, the Joint Chiefs of Staff, and the unified and specified commands.

As they moved with purpose through the long corridor, they passed the Secretary of Defense's office. Skip's sudden stop caused Hanalin to collide into his back.

"Back up, Mac."

When they entered Secretary Beuford's office, Skip drew one of his weapons and shot two men who had been standing before the Secretary of Defense giving a bogus report. One had been General Motly, the Marine Joint Chief of Staff. The second person was an agent in DIA.

Daggard took out two pieces of paper and pins. He pinned the papers to the lapels of both men. He looked at Secretary Beuford. "They were spies. I hope you're not."

General Hanalin and Skip left, moving down the corridor just as agents from DIA appeared in the doorway of Secretary Beuford's office. Skip pushed on a panel. A wall panel swung open. They went through closing the section behind them. It was the only section of that corridor that was not under the scrutiny of a security camera.

Chapter Nine—A Gathering of Patriots

Georgetown
Tuesday, October 5
2100 hours

Skip Daggard, Chin Lee, and General Hanalin sat at the table feasting on hot C-Rations. Skip took notice of Hanalin's glaring stares. It wasn't until they had finished eating before Skip explained. "Remember that I had told you about some Communist coalition force?

Hanalin glared at Skip but nodded his head.

"They're here and ready to take over the US. Their agents killed Kristine and Eilis five days ago. They were supposed to get me too. They failed. I got them.

"This is Chin Lee. She has defected from the North Korean Army because she says that she's in love with me..."

Skip had to jump because Chin had clobbered him in the back of his head.

General Hanalin lowered his head. "Damn, Kristine and Eilis gone under." He cried for a few minutes, and then collected his grief. "Finest spy I ever met," Hanalin said smiling.

He looked over at Chin Lee. "Let me see if I understand this," Hanalin directed his comments to Chin Lee. "You are a North Korean Communist? And you are defecting to our side?"

Chin Lee nodded her head.

General Hanalin studied her and Skip for three minutes while they finished eating.

Once they were finished eating, Skip went to the latrine to change his clothes and remove his disguise. When he returned, Chin was cleaning off the table and Hanalin was sitting, smoking his corncob pipe.

Skip sat down. Chin Lee came up to his left side, "What has happened?"

Skip wrapped his arm around her waist. "There are two less spies in the Soviet arsenal."

"Oh, hell," Hanalin exclaimed. "They were in the Secretary of Defense's office. Secretary Beuford looked up when we entered. The spies turned and Skip said, 'My code name is Snoopy, and neither of you will ever know the outcome,' as he drew his weapon and put five rounds in each spy.

"Then he looked over at the secretary as he affixed eight by ten labels on the two men, identifying them as spies. He told the secretary that he better take good care of the troops or he'd be next."

Hanalin took several puffs of his pipe allowing a gray cloud of smoke to climb out of the bowl of his pipe into the air. He blew three puffs out from the left corner of his mouth.

"Then we went to the subterranean basement of the Pentagon. Skip took me through a secret compartment that I had no idea existed. He brought me here. I know this place. I have been here before."

Chin moved closer to Skip so his head was pressed against her right side. She looked down at him as she stroked his head. "So, two down and two hundred and forty to go."

Skip gently pushed her away and rose to his feet. "I'm tired...I'm going to bed. I didn't take you out of there because of old times, Mac. I have a mission for you and we'll discuss it in the morning. Good night!"

Chin and General Hanalin watched Skip disappear down a corridor where the quarters were located. She wasn't sure if she should join him. Her heart was compelling her to go to him, but woman's intuition was telling her not to go. She obeyed her instincts.

Hanalin leaned back in his chair staring after Skip. "I knew he was crazy, Vietnam and all of the killing, but I had no idea how calculating and cold he had become. He just walked into the Secretary of Defense's office, drew his weapon and started shooting. His eyelids had narrowed to pencil lines, and his face was a piece of granite. What do you mean two hundred and forty more to go?"

Chin Lee was standing by the table still arguing with her inner self whether or not she should go after him.

"I do not know if I have the right to explain. But I do know that Agent Daggard is going to place his confidence in your abilities as a military leader." She turned and strolled out of the main bunker room and found her own sleeping quarters.

General Hanalin leaned back in his chair with his hands clasped behind his head, contemplating the day's events and conversations. He came to a frightening conclusion; the Communist coalition force that Kristine had warned Skip about must be here in the United States and spies must be at work in the government.

Hanalin finally rose and found his own sleeping quarters.

While they slept, Skip Daggard dreamed of huge snakes trying to devour him.

Chin Lee dreamed of a gentle hand caressing her body and freedom and war.

General Hanalin dreamed of his wife, Nancy, who had died of cancer, and of a soldier who had become a cold, calculating, killing machine.

While they slept safe in their sanctuary, an enemy force was preparing to attack.

Bunker System
Georgetown
Wednesday, October 6
0630 hours

At 0630 hours, Skip was in the shower. As the curtain was pushed along the bar Skip's arm shot out like a striking snake grasping the intruder by the throat. It took him ten seconds to realize it was a naked Chin Lee standing before him. He released his grip. "There are ten other stalls, Chin," he snapped at her while his eyes examined her nakedness.

Their eyes locked for a few seconds. Then she stepped into the stall allowing the warm water to beat down on her head and slender body.

As she turned around in the shower letting the warm water soak her skin she said, without looking at Skip, "Do not attempt that again, Agent Daggard, or I will break your arm." She lathered her body with Dial soap.

"Expert in martial arts, are *we*?"

She tilted her head to let the water pepper her face. "At least I am," she answered sarcastically.

They both laughed.

By 0730 hours, they all had showered and dressed, and were now sitting down to breakfast of hot C-Rations and coffee. General Hanalin broke the solitude. "I cannot figure it, Skip, for thirty something years you fought the Cold War with a vengeance, yet you marry one Communist, and somehow managed to have another one defect so she could be with you. Go figure!"

Chin Lee smiled, but Skip reprimanded his friend with a cold, hard stare.

Once breakfast was over, Skip laid it out for General Hanalin. "Remember that Communist coalition force Kristine had warned us about?"

Hanalin nodded his head, "Yeah, you already told me!"

"Sarcastic in the morning, aren't you, bub?

"The reason the Russians couldn't find them is simple…the bastards have been hiding here in the US and in the Arctic Ocean.

"So, here's the deal, Mac. They have about one hundred and seven spies in the Senate and House I have to terminate. Leaders will deal with the other one hundred and three spies in those organizations where the spies are working.

"You, my old friend, have to put together an army of militia with the aid of the VFW, Vietnam Veterans, American Legions, and survivalist groups, and as many of our National Guard units and reserve components and regular active duty units as possible."

Skip took out a map Chin had given him before they had driven away from Markleysburg.

"Oh, *is that all*?"

Skip glared at Hanalin as Chin looked on. Then Skip looked down at the map.

"This map Chin has given me is a topographical map of the US."

Skip pointed to the tip of a line, "See the red line that begins near Fort Devens in Massachusetts?" he said, looking sideways at General Hanalin as he ran his finger along the red line south through New Jersey down to Maryland via Washington, D.C.

"You see how it goes, Mac? Down through West Virginia, then the line swings west into southern California then up the West Coast intersecting with every major military facility. This is a major strategic move, Mac. The enemy has learned about most of our secret tunnel systems and strategic bunker locations, and they have occupied them."

"The moles…"

"Moles, hell Mac, these spies have been quite active. And now their activities are about to pay off for them." Skip smiled a huge genuine smile. Both General Mac Arthur Hanalin and Chin Lee stared at him.

"You find this amusing, Skip," Hanalin queried.

"Yes, sir I do because those idiots have to come up at specific locations." He let his words seep into their brains, but saw their confusion.

"Which means, old friend, that their exit points are limited; they will be bottlenecked during their deployment."

General Hanalin began to smile.

Chin Lee had not comprehended the reference.

"So, all I have to do is have our forces stationed at those locations…"

"Yes, with plenty of hand grenades and flame throwers," Skip smiled again.

Chin Lee stood next to Skip. His implication took root. She understood. A gasp of air escaped from her mouth. General Hanalin and Skip looked at her. She returned their stares.

She understood all right. The Communist forces had made another grave error. If these two men could muster an army in time, then the Communist forces may all be killed before they could exit the bunkers and take the field.

She shuttered at the thought because she could have been down in those trenches if she had not decided to defect.

She stole a glance at Skip. It took her several seconds before her mind registered the fact that he was staring at her. "What?" she demanded.

"You were leaning against me when your body trembled. Are you all right?"

She worked his question around from a Communist's perspective for a full minute before she answered him. "Remember your promise about Lieutenant Wong. I expect you to honor your word."

General Hanalin stared at Skip for a few seconds. "*What's this?*"

Skip looked down at Chin. Her brown eyes were void of emotion. He smiled because the vacancy he saw was something he had often seen in his own eyes. Skip looked over the table at Hanalin. "I told her we would do what we could to save her best friend, Lieutenant..."

"*YOU WHAT,*" Hanalin jumped to his feet. "Are you crazy? You know battle—once engaged it is complete bedlam. And you want one soldier saved? Where is this guy located?"

Skip exhaled a long, deep sigh. "He's in that White House bunker system just southeast of Kingwood, West Virginia. But I don't want one soldier saved...I want him shot..."

Chin Lee turned on him with her claws extended. Skip put up his right hand to silence her objections. "I want him and five others wounded. That way he's protected."

General Hanalin cocked his head to his left. "*What?*"

Skip released an exasperated breath of air. "She's staying," Skip declared pointing his right thumb at Chin, "but Wong will be returning to Korea. Now you get it?"

General Hanalin studied Chin Lee for three minutes.

She returned his stare.

He rubbed his jaw between the thumb and index finger of his left hand. He looked at Skip. "So, you want the militia who attack that position to take all of them prisoner, then kill them, but only wound Wong and five others—leaving them for dead?"

"Yep, you've got it just fine."

"You're out of your mind!"

Hanalin began to pace along the length of the table while analyzing this information. He paced for twenty ticks of the second hand then stopped. With his hands clasped behind his back, Hanalin asked Skip, "Have you given any consideration that she could be setting us up?"

"I have. And if it is a trap, then she will die along with all of them."

Chin Lee turned her head to her right as she stumbled backwards from the look in Skip's eyes. She had to grab hold of the corner of the table because her knees began to buckle. For the second time in her life, Chin Lee knew what Death looks like.

Skip and Hanalin stared at her. The low hum of the generator reverberating around the silence of the room was pulsating against their eardrums. Chin and Skip were locked in a trance-like scowl for several seconds before Skip's unexpected smile broke their trance.

"I don't owe you any explanation," he said to Chin. He paused, searching for words. "You came here as an enemy; part of a force with the intent to destroy our democracy and enslave us. You're Communist, Chin. And I've been fighting Communism since 1968.

"When the Berlin Wall came down, and the Soviets lost power, many of my colleagues and I knew and understood that the Cold War had only shifted to a different battlefield. And, it appears we were right because that battlefield is here in America and now."

Chin moved towards Skip to hug him. Skip put up his right hand. Chin stopped as a painful sadness squeezed her heart. "Will you ever trust me?" she whispered.

"Maybe, but perhaps your so-called defection is part of the plan and, at the right moment…Maybe!"

Skip looked back at the map. He placed his hands on the table for support as he bent over the laminated four foot by 3 foot rectangle drawing of the US. As he studied the map, Skip noticed tiny red dots and their locations. He let his eyes swing along an imaginary line connecting the dots in his own mind. He began in Alaska, shifted down along the West Coast, and then followed the dots along a line through the mid-West and Southern states. The lines ran from Fort Wainwright, home of the 1st Brigade, 6th Infantry Light, Arctic soldiers and Ladd Airbase near Fairbanks; Fort Richardson, home of the Alaska National Guard and primary elements of the 1st Battalion (Airborne) 501st Light near Anchorage, and Joint Base Lewis-McChord. His scrutiny continued to Seattle, Tacoma and the Puget Sound. Then on to San Diego, Travis Air Force Base, San Francisco, Lackland Air Force Base, Egland Air Force Base, Fort Stewart, Fort Gordon, Paris Island, and every military installation in Virginia, including Fort Detrick, Fort Ritchie and Fort Meade.

Skip's eyes stopped on Washington, D.C. There was an X over Washington with tiny red dots placed on the Pentagon, the Capitol Building, and the White House. That's when Skip's eyes focused in on New York City. Skip sighted in on the three, red X's side by side. His breath exploded from his lungs, as did his words from his mouth, "Son of a bitch! S-o-n of a bitch!" He glared at Hanalin, and then directed his hatred at Chin Lee. "We've been fighting the wrong fucking war, Mac, Siberian?" He spit his question out at her.

Chin shivered. Her body trembled with fear. She feared Skip's retaliation. Yet, she stood rock-steady. "It was a test…"

"A TEST," he shouted, "what the fuck's that mean?"

"We wanted to…" she paused. "We wanted to see how fast your planes could scramble and from what bases. We did not know about the Apaches."

Skip glared at her as he processed meaning from her response. He leaned his hands back on the table as he stared at D.C. on the map. His breathing was shallow but even.

"And Flight 93?"

Chin Lee wanted to be somewhere else—wished that she *could* be somewhere else. She began searching for words. She took a deep breath, held it for two seconds, and then exhaled. "I believe that I do not need to spell it out for *you*, Agent Daggard…"

"What the hell is going on?" Hanalin broke in.

"But I will." Chin began, ignoring General Hanalin's remark. "The plane was to destroy the Capitol Building, the White House, and the ground area in between. Extra explosives had been placed in baggage stowed in the belly of the plane.

"Models of plastic horses and dolls were made out of C-Four. Simulation of the flight pattern had been practiced for five years to insure the plane would come in at the precise angle and altitude to insure detonation would accomplish the desired results."

Skip Daggard flipped the table over causing General Hanalin to jump back and fall as he rolled out of the way.

Chin Lee stood her ground as Skip glared at her then took two long strides toward her. He stopped two feet in front of her and began to smile. Chin Lee did not move nor did she return his grin. She stood straight with her arms down at her sides and both fists clenched, ready to strike.

"Reminds me of the eagle and the rodent," he said.

Chin Lee took a few seconds to process his words; she returned his smile as she raised her left hand, middle finger extended. They both broke out in laughter as General Hanalin rose from the floor. "Yeah, well, I don't see the damn humor..."

They placed the table upright, arranged the map and other objects back on the tabletop then Skip responded to her last comment. "So," he glared at her, "now your people know about the Apaches?"

Chin Lee nodded her head. "Now they know. However, the Soviets do not know what happened to Flight 93. They do know it could not have been the Apaches over Washington because they did not fire their missiles."

Skip and Hanalin stared at each other. Skip looked down at the map.

"Only a select few know about those Apaches. They fly in stealth mode most of the time, and their flight patterns change daily."

Skip began to study the map again. He took a sidelong glance at her while he placed his index finger of his right hand on New York City.

Chin Lee sighed twice before she spoke. "You are well hated by many people. It was not difficult to draft the terrorists."

"When most people thought the Communist opposition had been dealt with, it simply bided its time then slipped in through our back door, huh?"

"What in the *hell* are you talking about, Skip?"

"The 9/11 attack, General."

"What about it?"

"It was an inside job, perpetrated and executed by spies and the Middle East Terrorists, with the aid of the Communists, of course. I have spent several hours studying the collapse of those buildings and reading hundreds of reports." Skip turned to Chin Lee. "Was your attack supposed to take place then?"

Chin Lee sighed. "Yes, but when the attacks on the Pentagon and Washington failed, we were not sure how to proceed. Your President Mantle presented the Soviets with a most extraordinary proposal, but your intervention destroyed that opportunity.

"The Soviet spies in your system of government proposed an alternative plan. Our attack was to take place in March of next year. But, once again, your intervention has had ramifications, so the timetable has been pushed up to October 30th...this month."

She knew that it was imperative for her to continue. "Your continued meddling has created a severe paradox for the Communists, so, by October tenth the vote will be done...your constitution rendered useless, and the attack will take place at 0530hours on October 15th or 17th."

Skip took in deep breaths of air then exhaled. He sat down in a chair, raised his left arm from his elbow, and rested his chin in the 'v' of his left thumb and index finger.

Chin Lee stood two feet to his left, while General Hanalin sat across the table from Skip.

Without lifting his head, Skip raised his eyes. "Maybe old GW should have left the capital in New York, Mac, instead of creating Washington, D.C. Perhaps the history of the world would be different."

General Hanalin studied Skip for a few minutes. He was now grasping the concept of the 9/11 attack. "I do not understand how what you just said has to do with anything, but you mean," Hanalin whispered, "that the attack was a conspiracy plot?"

Skip Daggard rose from his chair still studying the map. Without looking up, he nodded his head. "It appears so anyway."

"J-e-s-u-s Christ!"

Skip began to pace along the length of the table. Back and forth he moved with his hands clasped behind his back. The generator emitted a soft, low hum, and the wall clock's ticking was loud during the silence. Skip paced for ten minutes before he spoke.

"The Communists used the terrorists to try and take out our finances, government, and military leadership.

"Their plan was simple, Mac; if one plane failed, the commies figured that we would strike with our military might...and we did. So now our forces are divided with most of our military deployed and stretched thin in the Middle East, and one hundred seventy-seven other locations."

"Son of a bitch!"

"Now, you understand, Mac. We've been fighting the wrong war."

Chin Lee stared in sheer awe and amazement at Skip's uncanny ability to dissect and connect unrelated incidents correctly.

"So, now what do we do?"

Skip worked Hanalin's question over in his mind for four seconds. "We throw away the rule book, kick ass, and forget the name-taking." No smile followed his statement.

Hanalin and Chin stared at him. Skip took a seat at the table and looked off into space. When he looked back at them he expressed his thoughts. "No rule books in this war, Mac. We make our own rules of engagement once we meet the enemy."

NSA
Fort Meade, Maryland
General Bardolph's Office
Wednesday, October 6
0730 hours

General Bardolph sat at his desk with a fresh cup of hot coffee before him. His face was crimson. He studied the telephone on his desk as if it was the strangest creature he had ever seen. He rose to his feet, took his coffee cup in his left hand, turned around, and walked to the window. As he sipped the black brew, he studied his reflection in the windowpane.

He was completely bald, but his wife found that sexually exciting so he kept his hair cut to please her. His face was red-blotched due to his alcoholism. He was muscular; not fat, and his military bearing was prominent. Yet, in his mind, his physique and life itself was now mute because of one goddamn American.

For twenty-five years he had lived in this damn country working his way up to the position he now held for one purpose—to take down the Americans so the Soviet Communists could rule the world. "After all, that is the sole reason for the existence of the Russian Communists; to rule the world and enslave all of the races," he declared to his image looking back at him.

The whole plan seemed simple, he thought. That was, until East Germany fell and the liberal socialists took control of Russia. He knew even then, that the Soviets could still achieve world domination, but it would require the assistance of North Korea. As it turned out, the timing was perfect to acquire their assistance. They were building their nuclear capabilities and were pushing for armed conflict with the US.

Everything was looking promising for his forces to make their move except for that one *goddamned* American. One damned American soldier who refuses to die, one son of a bitch who has been his main adversary for thirty-five years. Skip Daggard, the American bulldog, who just doesn't know when to quit or let go. How many times had he himself tried, and once had the opportunity to destroy this rogue operative, this self-appointed champion of his people—this, this...this damn bastard who has charged in on too many occasions and foiled his plans. Now, with victory so close, who in the hell is it who challenges the Communist victory? "Damn you to hell, Agent Daggard," Bardolph shouted at the window.

General Bardolph turned back toward his desk. He slammed his empty coffee cup down against the edge of his desk, cursing as the handle of his cup broke off in his hand. He threw the broken handle across the room.

He removed his cell phone from his left pants pocket and pushed the speed dial button. When a voice answered, Bardolph said, "The thorn has not been plucked. We must step up our operation by two weeks, as planned earlier. The present condition must be resolved before Thanksgiving."

Bardolph put away his phone and whispered out a challenge into the atmosphere of his office, "Now, you bastard, let's see what you can do without an army."

Chapter Ten—Skip Daggard

Bunker System
Georgetown
Wednesday, October 6
1500 hours

Skip had spent the day exploring the bunker system. He wasn't interested in the structure and how the rooms were laid out. What he wanted was time to himself so he could think and plan. He wanted to be alone…to grieve. War had taught him that grieving periods are short. He had not eaten lunch with Hanalin and Chin, but took his C-Rations cold to a dark corner of the war room. It was in this lonesome darkness where Chin found him.

She walked up to him. "May I sit with you?"

Skip nodded. She sat down on the floor next to him. "My father had a saying, "'a soldier must have space to grieve, but his greatest grievance will be released on a battlefield.'"

She laid her hand upon his. He lifted her hand placing it on his knee as he laid his right arm over her shoulders. They sat close to each other for an hour not saying anything allowing the darkness to shroud them.

Skip invaded the tranquility of their space. "I've spent long, lonesome hours in the dark. It has become my friend. Sometimes I've felt like giving up, throwing in the towel, but I seem to keep going. I believe the darkness regenerates me—charges my batteries."

He drew her close, inhaling her perfume. "I've always lived at the edge surrounded by horrors and death. To most people, the Cold War is some phrase that had been concocted to indicate the sparing between the eagle and bear. In reality, the whole world was at war, and still is involved in that struggle. It was Dwight D. Eisenhower who coined the phrase."

He leaned over kissing her head while sniffing the aroma of her perfume that she had rubbed in her hair. Chin turned her head and lifted her lips to him. They kissed for three passionate minutes. When they parted from their kiss, Skip stared off into space. Chin leaned against him.

"Life moves too fast. We shouldn't be here."

She waited.

Skip sighed several times. He looked at her. "You should be in your homeland. I should be in my mountains. I'm a career soldier, Chin, but I hate war."

He paused placing his left hand to his chin and lips. She studied him, realizing that he was not a monster or a wonton killer. He was a man filled with passion and a genuine love for his people. She gently squeezed his right hand.

Skip looked at her. He studied her face committing to memory its shape, size, color of her eyes, hairstyle, and the position of her ears. He reached out letting his fingers caress her smooth face. He lost himself in the smoothness of her soft, olive skin. Their eyes locked as he continued to caress her face. "The average citizen has no concept of the violent world we live in, even though some of that violence makes headline news every day."

He stopped to breathe and feather her raven hair with his fingers. He leaned forward. She met his lips with hers. Fire from their kiss surged through their bodies. They sat gasping for air once they separated from their kiss.

Skip reached out to touch her face again, but Chin took his hand in hers. She held his hand next to her chest so he could feel the pounding of her heart.

He sighed. "The lay citizen doesn't know about or understand the violent world we intelligence people live either. We try not to think about it ourselves as each day we go to work…to war."

Skip took back his hand and stared off into the darkness. Without looking at her he said, "For people like me…those who deal with missions…we see the evil and the violence, and we're expected to… handle it…deal with it…to stomp it out."

She wanted to hold him, take him in her arms and hug him. She wanted to lie down and make love to him. She witnessed his sudden change. His face had hardened. His eyes had narrowed. Her heart froze with fear when he looked back at her.

His movement was sure and swift. He rose reaching out for her hand. "Come on, we'll go find General Hanalin."

Once they were all in the war room at the table, Skip explained his plan. "Mac, you have to identify a central Command Post. Once that is done, all of the organizations must be contacted, that includes all of the military units. We will initiate a battle cry and flyers to broadcast across the US and the world. We will have to call this operation… something—any suggestions?"

Hanalin and Chin burst out with a barrage of possibilities. Then Chin came out with one. It made Hanalin and Daggard take notice. "What did you just say?" both men asked, staring at her.

She stepped back looking at them in quiet surprise. Then she said, "Operation American Freedom—This we will defend."

Hanalin and Skip stared at each other as tears swelled up at the corners of their eyes. "Perfect!" was their response.

"Now," Hanalin said, "all we have to figure out is how we're going to incite the American population to fight."

Skip allowed a grin to spread out over his face.

Chin stared at him. Hanalin scowled, as worry lines creased his forehead.

Skip stood there with a shit-eating grin on his face not sharing the idea that apparently had come to his mind.

Skip jumped. "Ouch!"

"Kick him again, Chin…harder."

As Skip leaned down to rub the area of his calf where Chin had landed a hard kick from her right foot, they attacked him taking Skip to the floor with both of them on top.

"All right, all right already. Get the hell off of me."

Once they were on their feet, they sat down at the conference table.

"You better not make us wait much longer," Hanalin warned.

Skip let air escape from his lungs in a long sigh. "It's short and sweet; something Patrick Henry once said…"

Hanalin jumped to his feet in exasperated frustration. "HOW in the Hell do you figure that statement is going to incite the people to fight—'Give me liberty or give me death' and then the British hanged him."

General Hanalin stomped around his chair for three minutes before he sat down again.

Chin studied Skip with questioning eyes. She noticed the twinkle. She smiled. "There is more?"

"Oh! You want me to share that?"

"You son of a bitch!"

Skip took a long look around the room as if insuring himself no one else was listening. "I can't remember where he was, or to whom he was speaking; I think he was addressing the twelve delegates in Philadelphia when Patrick Henry said,

"'They tell us, Sir, that we are weak, and unable to cope with so formidable an adversary. But when shall we be stronger? Will it be next week? Will it be next year? Will it be when we are totally disarmed and a guard stationed in every house? Shall we gather strength by irresolution and inaction? Sir, we are not weak if we make proper use of those means, which God of nature has placed in our power.'"

Chin Lee felt her heart flutter and a tremor charge through her body. She stared at the two men before her and asked herself, "Who *are* these Americans."

General Mac Arthur Hanalin felt tears drip from the corners of his eyes as a surge of emotion became an electrical charge surging through his body. He let a sigh escape from his mouth, a sigh that had originated deep down in his lungs. "That will do it."

They were changed. They now were three soldiers bonded together for one cause. They could feel the change as the millions of pinpricks violated their bodies.

They sat down to a hot meal of MRE's and coffee—two old soldiers and one Communist colonel, united as the wheels of war continued to turn.

Bunker system
Georgetown
Wednesday, October 6
2400 hours

Skip sat at the conference table in the war room watching General Hanalin and Chin Lee disappear down a corridor towards their sleeping quarters. He bent over and turned on the brass table lamp. He sat frozen in time. He knew what he had to do—he had put it off long enough.

As he crossed the gray-painted cement floor and opened the flap of his backpack, he understood that he was a realist, and that what the three of them were trying to perpetrate was insane. "Well, GW," he said, "I guess no more insane than what you folks did on that July day back in 1776." Skip picked up Pearl's cell phone. He wished he had Kristine's scrambler, but all those things were gone now. He was surprised to hear a dial tone as he flipped up the lid. He pushed several buttons, and waited while the phone rang.

"Da!"

"Pop..."

"Skip, how are you?"

How was he? Good fucking question.

"Pop, Kristine and Eilis are dead."

He waited as the man on the other end broke down and cried.

"How?"

"That Communist coalition force you folks had lost, they're here in America. They have seventy million, and the bulk of their forces are in the Arctic preparing to attack Europe."

Skip paused to give Kristine's father time to process the information.

"What will you Americans do?"

Skip hesitated for two seconds. "We'll do what we've always done Pop; we'll fight. We are going to send out an official alert to the world in a few days. Look and listen for it."

"I will. I will notify my people immediately."

There was a long pause from Pollov. "Did she die well?"

Now it was Skip's turn to linger on a pause. "Those responsible paid, but the one who had ordered their deaths will die a thousand deaths before I am finished with him Pop." Skip knew this to be a lie because he did not have the luxury of time.

"Good!"

Skip hesitated six seconds, "God's speed, Pop!"

"God's speed to you, son."

They disconnected.

Skip Daggard grasped the countertop near the sink with both hands and broke down. His tears flowed free as his heart ached. There was no stopping it. He had kept it all bottled up for thirty-five years: the death, the destruction, the grief and pain. His guts retched in dry heaves as he gave himself over to all of his sorrow. He cried while trying to breathe as his grief poured out of him through his eyes.

He fell to his knees calling out into the darkness, "Bryanna, I love you. I have never stopped loving you. My heart had always belonged to you. Bryanna…Bryanna, I need you.

"Kristine, I am sorry! I loved you as best I could, and you accepted that. I think you knew that my heart belongs to my Bryanna.

"Bryanna, my Bryanna, I had to let you go to give you a chance at life. Now, it doesn't matter; the future of the world will be decided by Christmas. I wish I could turn time back so I could hold you once more."

He rose and washed his face off using water from the kitchen faucet. Using a dishtowel, he dried his face and hands. He took three deep inhales of air and walked with a purpose to his quarters. He found his old friend leaning against the wall close to his headboard. He lifted his rifle to his lips with both hands and began to kiss the receiver group and stock.

Skip sat down on the edge of his bed hugging his M-14/M25. Freeze frames of his life were nanoseconds flashing before his eyes. War! Death! Hate! Destruction, and love and sex! A realization washed over him. It was so sudden that its revelation made him sit straight up—he almost dropped his rifle. Since January 1970 he had been running towards something—Bryanna? But he knew that he'd never see her again because Death waited for him beyond these cement walls. In reality, what he had been running towards was the upcoming event. He sat alone with resignation in his heart. It was *this* war for which he had been bred, and it would be *this* fight which would release him from his grief and suffering.

Bunker system
Georgetown
Thursday, October 7
0130 hours

Skip's eyes flashed open as tears were splashing on his forehead. He found his face buried in soft breast tissue. Chin was holding him tight against her as she rocked back and forth. Her words were soft and soothing, "I have you; you are safe."

He did not move nor speak as she held him close to her body. After a few minutes he said, "I can't breathe!"

She looked down into his blue eyes. She smiled and stopped crying. She released her tight grip, but would not let him go.

He took the dark, hard nipple of her right breast into his mouth.

Neither one spoke as the ticking of the second hand of a wall clock pounded off sixty seconds. Skip released her nipple. "What happened?"

Another minute ticked away. She looked down at him. "You were screaming. I came running as did General Hanalin." She began to cry. Skip waited.

"I came to you. You were chasing around your bed on hands and knees, screaming."

She burst out into tears. Skip reached up and wiped them away. "You rose up on your knees; both arms hanging at your sides then you clutched your chest and fell over backwards." She stopped crying.

"You were asleep. General Hanalin departed as I lifted you into my arms. What was your nightmare?"

He stared at her remembering how her nipple had responded to his touch of his tongue. No! No! He shook his head.

He sighed, "Emotional momentous from Vietnam, battles, and a hundred other conflicts. Thanks! You can go now."

She studied his features. She could see many scars all over his body.

There were several places on his chest where hair did not grow. She counted twenty long scars across his abdomen and chest.

Skip took in her nakedness as he breathed shallow breaths. He laid down pulling the sheet and blanket over him. "You can stay. Just keep your hands to yourself."

The room contained a single oak-framed bed with a box spring and firm mattress. An oak student desk was three feet from the bed against the wall with a small gold-base table lamp sitting on the table's right corner. A nightlight illuminated the room with a yellow glow.

Skip stiffened as Chin pressed her warm breasts against his back. "That goes for your breasts as well."

He heard her sigh but she did not move.

Chin Lee lay on her left side with her breasts pressing into Skip's back. Her right arm was draped over his right side while her hand lost itself in his chest hairs caressing his scars. "You do not trust me?" she whispered her question.

"Hmmm! Maybe it's me I don't trust."

"Perhaps I have made a grave error!"

"Perhaps!"

She allowed his comment to filter through her brain. "I did not make an error in judgment, Agent Daggard. Lying here like this, my heart pounding between my breasts, I know I have made the right decision."

He did not respond.

"I do not understand how you plan to win, or that you will. There is much against you, but my heart has chosen for me...I will live with you no matter what the outcome or, I will die with you"

Skip's breathing was shallow as the tic, tic, tic of the second hand of a clock was the only sound in the room. Chin felt that an eternity had passed before Skip rolled over to face her. He feathered her raven hair with his fingers of his left hand. Skip felt compelled to share with her so he did. "I don't know what's going to happen, either Chin."

He sighed has he continued to feather her silken smooth hair. "I think we are going to lose. I believe it will be over by Christmas. That once the smoke clears, there will be a new 'world order'."

He shifted onto his back looking up at the ceiling, which was lighted by the dim, yellow glow from the nightlight. "I'll let you stay, but if I get an inkling…"

"I know; you will kill me."

"I'm a soldier," he said rolling back onto his side to face her. "I have made sacrifices for my people. I gave up my high school sweetheart for my country. We were to be married, but her father would not give his consent until I returned from Vietnam. But what returned was a killing machine, a covert operative for Military Intelligence.

"I never gave her a choice. I never told her…never allowed her to choose. I told my mother and I let the army bury me, and I faded into the shadowy world of espionage, lies, and deceit."

He paused to catch his breath.

"I love only one woman, Chin. Even though I had loved Kristine, my heart belongs to Bryanna, and it has ever since a warm April day in 1965. I can love you, but you will not have my heart. I believe Kristine had come to understand my feelings.

"Many people believed the Cold War had ended when the Berlin Wall came crashing down. We tried to tell them…people in the agencies tried to warn them…especially Congress and the president, but no one wanted to listen or believe.

"So, now here it is; the Communist military ready to strike, and my people, nor government are even aware that Hell is about to erupt on our soil."

Chin placed gentle fingers against his mouth. "For someone who knows many secrets, you often say too much."

He studied her eyes. He laughed.

Chin sat up and crossed her legs. She felt no shame with this man. Although the atmosphere was warm, she shivered.

"I have something very important to tell you."

Skip could hear her swallow. He waited.

"I overheard you speaking with General Hanalin about taking control of your offensive and defensive missiles in Nevada, Yakima, and New Mexico…it is too late."

Skip Daggard jumped from the bed, pulling Chin Lee erect. "What the *hell* do you mean?"

She punched him in his stomach to get free from his crushing grip. Once he had regained his composure, she said, "The Soviets have spies in place. They control mission launches; once North Korea launches their missiles those spies will launch your offensive missiles at Europe. They will either destroy your defensive missiles, or, if needed, the defensive missiles will be launched against US military targets."

Chin Lee stood frozen with fear. She had never imagined such a demon could reside in a man as she now was witnessing in Skip Daggard. She felt her breath constrict in her chest, her water ready to spill out from her body, and it seemed that her heart had stopped beating as she gasped in horror.

Now, at this moment, she finally realized and understood what her father had told her about soldiers and war—that a soldier is forever changed. She did not know when it happened; she did not know that she had moved, but her arms were wrapped around the demon, and she was burying her face in its chest as she cried, "It is all right! You are safe! I am holding you! It is all right! You can let it go! I will be here…I will stay with you."

Chin felt the creature's uncontrolled trembling as he vibrated and shook in her arms. She followed him with her eyes, as he slid down her body to his knees. She felt the fire from his face as the demon pressed his right cheek into her naked belly.

Her movement was ever gentle as she placed her hands over his head pressing him into her. Chin could not restrain her tears. They flowed from her eyes, down her cheeks, and splashed on Skip's head. She looked down as she felt him pull away from her. His blue eyes were drowning in sadness. Her breath stopped in her throat. Her heart ached to relieve his suffering.

He lowered his head so that his chin was resting on his chest. She looked up and found herself staring at the wall clock in amazed disbelief that such rage, emotional fury, and hate could explode from a human being and be brought back under control in less than two minutes.

She looked down at him as he caressed her legs with his hot hands. She stared into his blank eyes. There was nothing there; no pain…no sadness…nothing.

Chin took two steps backwards as Skip gained his feet. She was frightened by his urgency as he lifted her up heading for the bed. Yet, she was aroused as her excitement surged through her body.

An hour later they lay sweating and panting. "You all right?"

She could only muster a grunt, "Ah huh!"

Chin lay on her back next to him panting trying to catch her breath, while her body continued to tremble from their lovemaking. Her olive skin glistened in the amber glow of the nightlight, her body drenched in perspiration.

Skip lay quiet allowing his mind to soak up their experience. He blamed the upcoming dangers and his nightmare for their copulation. It was the thrill of the killing and dying, and of the unknown, which drove his lust. But it was more, which he had found hard to explain. To him, lovemaking and orgasm was his gage, his indicator that he was still alive.

He lay still listening to her labored breathing. Seven seconds passed. Skip heard her breathing begin to palpate at a normal rate as her tremors subsided.

Skip wanted to reach out to her, to pull her to him...to experience her again, but he knew that their time had passed; that this would be his last campaign and that neither he, nor she would survive. His only regret, which had continued to attack his heart, was letting go of Bryanna.

Chin sat up, crossed her legs, and saw sadness emitting from his light blue eyes. She leaned over to caress his sweaty face. "If we never have another moment like this again," she whispered, "thank you for this time."

He smiled and allowed his finger to glide across her soft skin. They were soldiers. They didn't need any words to explain what his eyes were telling her.

She laid her head down on his chest as she draped her right arm over him. "We will die together," she whispered.

Skip stroked her hair. "Come on," he said, "let's change the sheets and shower. Then we can get a good night's sleep."

While they slept safe in each other's arms, opposing forces were closing in.

NSA
General Bardolph's Office
Fort Meade, Maryland
Friday, October 8
0730 hours

The sky was a vast ocean of blue as NSA stirred with humanity. Security had been beefed up. All personnel were filtered through three entrance areas: the main lobby, the west entrance, and the east entrance near the credit union.

When the Pentagon went into a complete lockdown mode all agencies were notified. General Bardolph acted with swift and decisive action. He wasn't sure what had happened, not yet anyway, so he sent his own people to the Pentagon. His instructions were explicit and simplistic. "Find out what had happened, and report to me immediately."

General Bardolph sipped coffee while he studied his reflection in the west wall window of his office. He did not smile. He could not smile until he was spitting in the dead face of that damn patriot. He took short swallows of his hot, black coffee as he began to reminisce about lost opportunities do to MI Agent...Bardolph stopped. "Just who the hell are you anyway, Agent Daggard?" he asked his reflection.

In Vietnam, he was Code Name Snoopy. In Germany and Korea, he was SSG. Derry Batair, and then he became Military Intelligence Chief Warrant Officer Skip Daggard. "Just *who* in the *hell* are you?"

General Bardolph could feel his antagonism rising as his hate for Daggard exploded. He had thwarted Soviet opportunities in Vietnam, Germany, Paris, and Korea. He had terminated Soviet assets within the 3rd Armored Division, and other US units around the world.

Bardolph believed it had been Daggard who had destroyed the Warsaw Pact Forces assault on Europe and the Middle East in November 1974.

He had Daggard naked, chained, tortured, bleeding and half-dead, stretched out like a side of beef. He had him trussed up and suspended by chains in August 1975. He had left Brutus behind with a baseball bat to finish the job, yet somehow that goddamned son of a bitch had escaped to continue shooting holes in the Soviet's plans for world domination for another twenty-five years. Now, the bastard is on their scent again at a most crucial moment in world history, and it is a crucial time for the Soviets because victory is at hand. They were now in a position to take down the US and control the world. And, who is it that could usurp their plans? Who? That damn patriot that's who. "Who in the hell are you, and where did you come from?"

Bardolph sat back in his chair as he finished his coffee trying to smile. He knew that somewhere Colonel Lee was hunting down their quarry, and his own team was closing in on the bastard. "There is no escape this time, Daggard, or whoever you are. We have you now."

Pentagon
Arlington County, Virginia
Friday, October 8
0900 hours

Military leaders were going ballistic regarding the recent assault on their fortress, and the killing of three ranking officers. The Joint Chiefs had viewed the surveillance tapes six times still refusing to believe what they had seen. They replayed the tape over and over again still refusing to believe that some unknown general and General Hanalin simply walked into SOD Beuford's office and open fired.

Secretary of Defense Beuford spoke up. "Turn that damn thing off. They called those who had been killed spies, and the one who did the shooting pinned papers to their lapels attesting to that fact. There must be something going on that we don't know anything about, and Hanalin does."

Just then, two agents from NSA entered the conference room accompanied by twenty armed soldiers. "By the order of General Bardolph, everyone in the Pentagon is hereby placed under military arrest."

"Secretary of Defense Beuford jumped to his feet. "You can't do that…" His body was riddled with bullets.

"Any other objections?"

Once the Soviet force had secured the Pentagon, Colonel Barker notified General Bardolph. "Yes, sir one casualty; the Secretary of Defense. The way is open."

"Excellent!"

"Now," General Bardolph thought, "Now, I take the offensive."

"Find out how Hanalin and that other general had escaped and go after them."

"Sir, the mysterious general was Chief Daggard. He left notes identifying our agents as spies."

General Bardolph slumped in his chair. "How could he have known?"

"I do not know, sir, but I know how they escaped. We are preparing to go after them."

General Bardolph smiled. "Good! Be careful my friend, Daggard plays by his own rules."

"We will leave in a few hours once I receive reinforcements."

"I will send you three hundred more. Leave one hundred at the Pentagon."

Colonel Barker removed the receiver from his ear. He studied it for ten seconds."

"Sir, I do n…"

General Bardolph interrupted, "DO NOT underestimate your quarry, Barker. Take two-hundred men with you. When you find them…kill them. Also, Colonel Lee from the North Korean contingency is missing. See if you can find out what Daggard had done with her."

General Bardolph hung up his phone. He went to his coffee bar and fixed another cup of hot, black coffee. He turned and went back to his desk. "So, Colonel Lee had failed. Now, she was either dead or a prisoner."

He sipped at his coffee as his life long dream was becoming like the sands in an hourglass.

Bunker System
Georgetown
Saturday, October 9
0305 hours

Skip's eyes flashed open. He did not move. He lay on his back listening…something had surfaced from his subconscious causing his conscious to evaluate—what? He listened to the normal sounds within the confines of their sanctuary. His ears listened to Chin's even breathing, the ticking of the clock, the minute humming of the generator; everything seemed normal. Yet, his mind had alerted him. His sixth sense had awakened him to some danger that his conscious had recognized.

He rose up into a sitting position searching the room with his ears and eyes allowing his ears to absorb sounds beyond his room. He listened for ten minutes while his mind recognized and cataloged each sound. Once he was satisfied that all the sounds were normal, he rose and collected clean clothing, then headed for the shower. As he stepped into a stall, Chin stepped in close to him. "It is early."

Skip turned on the water without comment. His senses continued with their pulsating warning signals. "Something," he said to himself, "something from his past, or was it something that he had forgotten to consider—what?" Whatever it was remained elusive.

Once he was dressed, Skip went to the command room. He began to study the map. As he looked at New York and Washington, old memories began their assault on his conscious mind from hiding places within his subconscious.

"Something is on the wind, General Toomey." He was trying to plead his case, but his superior officers were not so inclined to listen, especially since he had just capped eight NSA officers during a conference at NSA.

He studied the map with close scrutiny, remembering his warning.

"I can't put my finger on it, but the Middle East is on fire and will explode. Info is coming in on a global scale, but reports are sporadic so our linguists and cryptographers are having trouble pinpointing anything definitive.

"But something terrible is about to happen."

Skip stepped back from the table as Chin handed him a cup of scalding coffee. "What is wrong, Skip?"

He turned to face her. The change in address did not go unnoticed. He measured her as he took long sips of his coffee. Sensual images of their lovemaking began to weave through his mind. He shook his head to clear out those scenes.

Skip stared off into space. His stargazing was caused by Chin's question which was compounded by that something...that something which was trying to break through from his subconscious to his conscious. Some of the warnings had something to do with the map, but there was this powerful gnawing at his brain. Something he had forgotten—something he should have done but didn't. "What the *fuck*, over!"

Chin stared at him. She wasn't sure if she should respond, so she kept quiet while she watched him begin to pace along the length of the table sipping his coffee. It took her five seconds to realize that he had stopped and was staring at her.

"Damn, you're beautiful."

She took in a slight amount of air; pleased with his praise. Then she witnessed the vacancy in his eyes. "How does he *do* that," she asked herself.

Skip Daggard began to speak, not to her, but as if he was addressing a general audience. "I tried to warn them in 1999 that we were heading for pending disaster."

He finished his coffee and placed his cup on the table. "They weren't listening to me because they were pissed. I had just killed eight spies in our organization, right in front of them. The powers-to-be were outraged with my behavior."

His sudden smile caused her to step back and study him for a few seconds.

"They argued that I should have told them; they would have handled it."

His rising rage sent her back four more steps away from him as he snatched up his coffee cup throwing it across the room. It shattered against the far wall.

"They were the same idiots who changed policy regarding the handling of spies. They'd handle it all right, well, fuck them..."

Once again she witnessed how quick he can regain control of his rage.

Skip took eleven deep breaths inhaling and exhaling getting his system back to normal. There was five feet of space between them when

Skip turned to her. "But those spies had caused severe damage, and they had caused the deaths of American service men and women, so, they had to pay—not be sent back to Russia."

Chin observed the strain on his face. "There is something else which troubles you. Is it our lovemaking?"

Skip smiled at her. "No. I think I fucked-up, and we are going to have visitors. I believe that's what fired up my senses."

General Hanalin came into the room. "Don't you know how to get a good night's sleep? And what's this about visitors?"

Chin asked, "Why do you study the map with such intense scrutiny? I do not understand your comment referring to visitors either."

His mind erupted with visions of the past. He collapsed into a chair at the table.

Chin and General Hanalin looked at each other and shrugged their shoulders.

He was driving along Route 295 North heading for a meeting at NSA. The encrypted message he had decoded provided a small hint that the US was about to be attacked. He contacted Director Rochelle to call a meeting, and have all Intelligence leaders standing by for a conference call.

Skip inhaled the beauty of the morning. The sun was shining, and the sky was a rich blue on this warm September morning as he maneuvered his government dark blue SUV through the heavy traffic. He had 'Oldies' playing on the radio.

Warrant Officer Skip Daggard was four miles from NSA when news broke in on the regular station.

The commentator shattered Skip's world with his news breaking report. "An American airliner has just crashed into one of the World Trade Center towers in New York City. Oh my God, another plane just crashed into the second tower."

Skip almost lost control of his vehicle. He had to pull over to the side of the road. He noticed that many vehicles were following suit. The commentator was screaming through the radio. Skip sat there for five minutes digesting the news. If the linguists and cryptanalysis' at NSA were right, then this might be the attack they had alluded to in the message. He could feel his heart sink as the rage began to seep into his being. "Why can't the fascist, warmongers leave us alone?"

Skip Daggard shook his head as he tried to regain control of his trembling body. He looked across his left shoulder at Chin Lee. "You killed our women and children. Not one person in those buildings was combatants."

She could see the evil rage and hatred as fire shot out of his eyes. Once again he disappeared.

He steered his vehicle back onto the highway and made his way toward NSA. As he entered the main lobby and clocked in, the security person at the desk was crying. He turned and saw the TV. On the screen was each plane crashing into the Trade Centers...one building disintegrating and crashing towards the ground, the screen flicked over to Washington. Smoke was billowing up from the Pentagon.

He stood rooted to the floor. His tears began to fall as his mind began a casualty count, and a realization that war had just been declared against the US by an unknown enemy, for what reason or purpose was yet to be determined.

A commentator announced, "A plane had just crashed in Pennsylvania. It had been rerouted from its scheduled course and redirected on a flight-pattern for Washington." Skip whispered to himself, "So, that was the mission for those two sorties from Andrews.

"Your coalition force used the terrorist militants to draw our forces across the sea while your forces sneaked in through our back door."

She stood her ground.

"The plan was conceived in 1991." She took a deep breath.

"It took eight years for the training and maneuvering to be completed. Then, all that was needed was to attack. We were concerned and had to step up the attack time-table because your intelligence people had intercepted damaging information and were plotting out our plan."

Her words sent him back.

As he stormed into the meeting on the third floor conference room, the news was playing out events that were taking place just thirty miles from their location. General Brittner, the Director of NSA was throwing documents at the west wall. "This damn information is mute now, ladies and gentlemen. "And you," the general chastised Skip. "Why didn't you figure it out?"

Skip jumped him with both feet, "Because you stupid bastard, you all tucked me away in the basement of the White House. I had tried to warn them that something was going down back in '99, but they were all pissed because I had terminated enemies in our mist."

Skip Daggard looked over the map at General Hanalin and spoke to Chin without looking at her, "So, the North Korean nuclear missile testing in 2008 and '09 were antagonistic ploys?"

Chin Lee sucked down air. She exhaled as she stared at Skip. "No, Skip. The tests were not ploys. It was a maneuver to let the Soviets and our comrades above us know that we were challenging the US. As I have stated, Skip Daggard, this war has been planned and plotted since 1991 by the Soviets who are spearheading the operation."

Chin stepped close to him. She took his left hand in her right hand with a gentle squeeze. As he looked into her deep, brown eyes she said, "When you had shot your president, the Soviets went mad with disbelief and rage. President Mantle conspired with the Soviets-in-hiding; if they would support the US in a global war, then the Soviets could take control of Russia and all that they had lost in 1989 and 1990.

"You destroyed that opportunity for them when you fired that bullet; however, the Soviets simply fell back on their original plan for war." Chin wrapped her arms around him, hugging him. She lifted her head so she could look into his bright, blue eyes. "I have been trying to tell you in words and with my body, Skip Daggard, that America is finished, as is all of the free world. You cannot win."

She pushed herself away from him staring at his face in disbelief.

Skip was smiling. "Chin, that's the same thing King George the III said to the American Colonists. But to his dismay, the "American Experiment" won out, and we've been fighting ever since to keep that which had been won and handed down to each generation since."

Chin sighed. "You do not understand the enormity of the enemy force which you face. Your navies will be attacked first. Your forces in the Middle East will be wiped out. North Korea will lay waste to your West coast, while the Soviet subs destroy Pearl Harbor and the East coat. The ground forces, with the aid of air and missile support, will destroy your military bases.

"It was not the murder of my father that had been the deciding factor in my decision to defect, Skip Daggard. His death was crucial in my decision, but it was my heart that gave me the strength to defect and make this stand with you. I know what is going to happen. We are going to die."

Skip moved toward her taking Chin into his arms. He kissed her soft-skinned forehead. "I can't predict the future, Chin, but out of three hundred million Americans, I can guarantee that at least eighty million will fight. And should the Communist coalition forces win the field, then they will be faced with a problematic deficit—they will have to hold it." He bent down and kissed her red lips. "And that, darlin' will be their downfall. We will be like the ankle-biters, little Chihuahuas, snapping at our enemies' heels, implementing guerrilla tactics. However, the enemy will never take the field."

She smiled at him, which took him by surprise. "Well," she said in a trembling voice, "we shall soon see."

"Reckon so!"

While Skip and General Hanalin studied the legend on the map, Chin stood close to Skip. He inhaled the aroma of her cleanliness without the cover up of perfume. Skip began to shake his head. Both General Hanalin and Chin looked at him. Skip turned to General Hanalin. "I hate commies, General."

Chin frowned and took a step back away from him.

"Tell me Mac, what is it that makes the Communist females fall in love with me?"

Chin stepped closer while General Hanalin mustered up his response. "Maybe it's your charming personality?" They broke out into hysterical laughter.

Chin Lee scolded, "Perhaps...it is love."

"Yeah, right, bitch!"

It came from nowhere, but Skip knew that he had been struck as he lifted himself up from the table rubbing the left side of his jaw, which was already turning black and blue.

"Damn, Skip! She put all of her ninety-nine pounds into that one." Hanalin couldn't hold back as he bellowed forth in righteous laughter.

Once Skip regained his feet, he glared at Chin. "I don't..."

She was up in his face. "Do not use that word ever again referring to my person, Skip Daggard. I am a woman—not a bitch."

As he rubbed his jaw, Skip mumbled, "Yes, ma'am; I apologies."

"Now, back to the legend," General Hanalin broke the tension.

As the two Americans leaned over the map, studying the legend, Chin rose up on her toes and kissed Skip on the spot of his chin where she had smashed him with the heel of her right hand. "Apology accepted!"

Skip laid his left arm across her shoulders drawing her close to his side.

The legend of the North Korean map of the US provided much information. Skip began to read, and then caught himself. He turned to Chin, "All right, sweetheart, you'll have to decipher for us."

Chin stared at him as suspicion began to leak out from her eyes. She studied Skip's facial expression for a few minutes trying to detect deceit, but his eyes were blank.

"The Korean letters next to the small, red dots, NK, meaning those targets will be destroyed by North Korean missiles. The larger dots with a sickle next to them indicate that these are Soviet missile targets."

Chin Lee stopped to breathe. She was stalling.

Skip glared at her. "Any time tomorrow would be fine, Love."

She swallowed. "The Korean writing in the Legend refers to information on another map."

Skip bent forward studying the writing. "Where's the other map?"

His question evoked a memory.

The Huey was flying at six hundred feet. "Ask them where the other map is," he said to the South Vietnamese interpreter. He did! None of the three prisoners responded. "Ask them again." The question had been asked again without any response. "Order them to strip."

The oldest girl blinked as she stared at the interpreter.

"Ah! So you speak English." Skip directed his question towards the interpreter. "You two know each other?"

"She my sister," he replied thirty seconds later.

"I do not know where the other map is, Skip," Chin said.

"So, what's all the scribbling in the Legend?"

Chin Lee was not sure how to answer. One thing was obvious: Skip Daggard could read her language. "IR stands for Iran and ME for the Middle East." She waited for a reaction but none came. "Iran will take out all United States military units in the Middle East."

Skip crossed his right arm over his chest. He rested his left elbow in his right hand as he stroked his chin with his left hand. After three minutes had passed, he looked over at General Hanalin. "I had informed the president that he didn't need Congress' approval to invade Iran back in '06. I explained it to our new president last year that he had sixty-three days to send in the troops, get to Congress, and accept Iran's Declaration of War, and declare ours against them. Then he could wipe out all of their military installations and their nuclear capabilities. Neither one took any action"

General Hanalin nodded his head, but Chin stared at him, puzzled.

Skip recognized her confusion. He gently took her small, olive brown hands in his. "When a country's embassy is attacked, Chin, that's a declaration of war. When the Iranian militants stormed the US Embassy in Teheran in 1979, under the order of Ayatollah Khomeini, killing Marines and assaulting US citizens, they declared war against the United States.

"We waited for President Carter to accept their declaration and go to Congress to declare war and take back our embassy. Instead, he tried a feeble attempt, making us look foolish. Meanwhile those militants were torturing and raping our people."

Chin waited for more, but she saw, in Skip's vacant eyes, that he had gone to some other place.

"I don't fuckin' believe it. Those bastards declared war against us and nobody is doing anything about it."

"Look, Skip I have already talked to many of our people. If the president doesn't come up with something better than that fucked up aborted attempt to rescue our people and take appropriate action, there's about three hundred of us going to resign our commissions and go get our people."

Skip glared at General Hanalin. "Hmmm! Somehow word got out and the CIA put us under house arrest."

General Hanalin sighed, but Chin Lee could not refrain herself. "*W-h-a-t?*"

"What?"

"That was my question, Skip."

Skip looked at General Hanalin. "You got diarrhea of the mouth, Skip. You expressed your thoughts."

Skip stood against the table ringing out his hands. He stared at his feet. He lowered his head, looking into Chin's eyes. "I was in Augsburg in '79 to roust out a few spies assigned to our field station. Two days after President Carter's aborted attempt to rescue our people, three hundred MI types decided we'd resign our commissions, go on a killing spree and rescue our people.

"Guess it leaked out, because when we went to the arms rooms to gather munitions for our mission, the CIA counterintelligence people were there waiting and placed us under house arrest until we had been convinced to scrub our idea. But the fact remains, Chin, a declaration of war still exists between Iran and the US—a war they had declared. Therefore, the president doesn't need any approval to attack; the reason he can attack is already on the books."

Skip stepped back from the table as a lifetime of images flash-framed in his mind. So many, that he finally shook his head. "I've got to whiz!"

Once he had left the room, Chin looked at General Hanalin. "I do not understand; this true?"

"Yes, militarily speaking. But diplomatically, this issue had been swept under the carpet—forgotten."

"Not by him."

"No. He was there. Americans suffered, and our flag was burned."

General Hanalin studied the map. He looked up at Chin as she asked her question. "Who is he, General?"

General Hanalin stared off into space focusing on the far wall. He locked his hands behind his back as he began to pace along the length of the table trying to formulate an answer.

In the silence, they could hear the ticking of the second hand of the brown wall clock, and the low hum of the generator. The aroma of brewed coffee was strong.

Hanalin stopped when he was positioned at the center of the table. He looked across the Formica-covered table at her. "There isn't one word I can use, or even a phrase to describe Skip Daggard. I've been with him since 1968, forty-two or forty-three years, and I still don't know him.

"I'll share with you what I know. You can draw your own conclusions. I remember when he first came to me. My unit was located at a small fire base ten miles northwest of Saigon. We were a special military intelligence covert operations unit. He reported with his duffel, an M-14, his orders, and a set of dead eyes."

General Hanalin looked off into space as he continued to recall those early years.

"He came from STRATCOM, a strategic communications unit that was located in a rice-paddy somewhere in Thailand; a top-secret site. I ordered him to secure his weapon in our arms room."

General Hanalin trembled remembering. He looked across the table at Chin Lee. "I looked into his eyes. There was a vacancy in his eyes. A void I had never seen before in a soldier's eyes, but there was something hiding in the shadows of his eyes, something deep down inside of him… waiting." General Hanalin sucked down a lung full of air and let it escape on a slow exhale.

"It was like staring into two deep blue wells; wells without end. When I ordered him to secure his weapon, again, his eyes changed. They turned into two glowing horizontal slits of fire. He took a step forward. I took an involuntary step backwards."

General Hanalin paused to wipe sweat from his brow and inhale a deep gulp of air. "In that instant, Chin, I learned what death looks like, and death, Chin, is Skip Daggard.

"He doesn't hate as in the meaning of the word. He dislikes. How he rationalizes the differences is beyond me. I suppose that you could say that Skip Daggard is a heroic villain. He is the only person in US History who has terminated a president, and has had no charges brought against him. Yet, his action cost him his career, but he was allowed to retire. I had a hand in that resolution." What helped was that the shooting could not actually be blamed on him. Yeah, he and

Kristine were in the vicinity, but CIA people swore that they had him trapped under ground."

They were silent for several seconds staring at each other, while mulling over the general's words. She knew the face Hanalin had spoken of, she had seen it herself.

Skip came back into the room and marched over to the table to gather up the map. "I've decided..." He studied their faces. After twenty-five seconds had elapsed, Skip sat on the edge of the table near the center. "Okay, what's up, you been talkin' about me again, Mac?"

They both stared at him.

"Don't believe anything he says," Skip said as he sauntered toward Chin. He gently reached for her drawing her into him. His lips were aflame as his burning tongue darted into her moist mouth. His hot hand caused her to tingle and tremble with excitement as he moved his right hand under her blouse, along her warm, brown skin and over her breasts. She felt the heat from his sweaty palm, as he squeezed her right breast through her shear, silk bra. Her nipples exploded to erect hardness as his hand slipped under her bra and caressed both of her breasts. Then, without warning, he withdrew his hand and his lips with a quick, sudden action. She was left breathless, hot, and confused.

Skip stepped back away from Chin. "She's going with you; she's okay." He reached for the map and handed it to General Hanalin. "I don't know how much time we have, Mac; two weeks...three...maybe. But, as Chin had said, they will step up their timetable now that they know we are on to them, and that we've captured one of their officers. For now, I want them to believe that. I don't want them to know that she has defected.

"So, figure on two weeks to put an army together and recapture our silos. That gives me the same timeframe to take out 170 spies and rejoin you."

Skip looked at Chin. Her olive cheeks were still rosy from the treatment he had just given her. "This is your last opportunity!"

"I have made my decision," she replied while gulping down small amounts of air.

So had the three Fates, who control the humans' life span.

As Skip rolled up the map handing it to General Hanalin he said,

"By Christmas, we will be dead, free, or learning how to be Communists. Now, you two scoot. I have a welcome mat to set out for our guests."

Skip's body went erect and stiff. Both Chin and Hanalin studied him for five seconds. Skip finally spoke. "They're coming! It's time to pack and get out of Dodge," he said as he turned away from them. As he marched back into the interior of the bunker, he said over his right shoulder, "God's speed...until we meet again."

Chin looked over a Hanalin, "What is Dodge?"

General Hanalin smiled. "This place is Dodge. It's a metaphor meaning we have to get out of here."

"Why did he not say that? Who is coming?"

Hanalin shrugged.

Chapter Eleven—Death to a Nemesis

Bunker system
Georgetown
Saturday, October 9
0810 hours

As Chin and Hanalin prepared to leave, they watched Skip begin to place explosive charges. As he planted his booby traps, Hanalin said, "Welcome mat for those visitors you think we're going to have?"

Skip took out a small packet of C-4. He looked over his shoulder at Hanalin, "Yeah! Plus, they won't be able to use this bunker once the war begins."

When Skip placed his last charge, he stood up and sighed. Hanalin came over to him followed by Chin. Skip looked at him for a long minute. "I've always wanted to be a soldier, Mac. But I never dreamed that my wish would lead me to this. This situation gives me a feeling for what those delegates must have felt when Thomas Jefferson read the minutes of the first three days of their gathering. It turned out to be a declaration of war and the Preamble to our Constitution. I can imagine hearing a church mouse scurry across the wooden floor as their silence gripped the atmosphere.

"You know what the damnedest thing is about this atrocious garbage? I'm not even getting paid!"

Skip and Hanalin broke out into laughter. "But you are getting paid, Skip, Hanalin corrected him, "you're drawing a monthly retirement check."

They both chuckled again while Chin Lee stood there shaking her head wondering if she would ever understand these Americans.

General Hanalin and Skip gripped each other's right hand. Neither one wanted to let go as they stared into each other's eyes. It was Skip who disrupted the moment. "It's time to go, old soldier."

"I know."

Five minutes passed before they let go of their grips and patted each other on the back. Skip went to Chin; he gave her a long French kiss. "If this all goes to shit, remember, you were a prisoner because you tried to kill me." He drank deep of her beauty. "This is what was bothering me; that the general and I would be followed."

She forced a smile. She stood on her tiptoes to kiss him again. She squeezed him against her.

He took her arms; pushing her away. "Go!"

Chin Lee studied General Hanalin as he looked through a periscope type device in the left corner where two tunnels formed a right angle. She stared at him as he turned the periscope with slow movements. The tube actually looked like an air pipe for the tunnel system so it seemed to be in an appropriate place.

When Hanalin was finished surveying whatever he was studying, he pushed the pipe back into the corner and refastened the hold-down brackets. "Skip's little invention. It's all clear on top. We can go."

When they had reached the top of the ladder, Hanalin pushed aside a manhole cover, climbed out, and then he helped Chin Lee out. He closed the cover and turned toward the interior of the parking plaza. "We will have to go to the second level for our vehicle."

Chin Lee followed without speaking.

Once on the second level of the parking plaza, Hanalin scrutinized the fifteen vehicles, which were parked there. "Come on! It's over there." Hanalin marched over to a metallic blue Tahoe with Chin Lee in tow. He lay down on his back, slid under the vehicle, and retrieved his prize that was secure to the chassis near the catalytic converter. As he slid open the top of a small, flat tin box and took out a key, he said, "There are vehicles like this one all across the country."

Chin Lee stared.

General Hanalin smiled at her bewilderment. "Skip being Skip, he purchased a handful of vehicles from the MP impound lot on Fort Meade when he did a two year stint with the 519th Military Police Battalion. Then he placed them in strategic locations. Only two people know about them, Skip and I.

"That's one thing you will have to accept Chin, Skip does not trust anyone. It took him a long time to trust me. And he never trusted Kristine, and they had been together for five years."

"Hmmm, will he ever accept me?"

"Haven't you two made love already?"

"Yes!"

"Then he's accepted you, yet, he does not trust you."

Chin stared at him with her head cocked over her right shoulder.

General Hanalin looked at her as he opened the door for her. "Skip trusts one person, Chin, himself. Last night you witnessed the thing which lurks in the shadows behind his eyes. So, I believe you understand."

Hanalin closed her door, then went around and slipped into the driver's seat of the Tahoe. General Hanalin put the silver key into the ignition and started the engine.

"I do not understand why you are doing this, General Hanalin. You are the Army Joint Chief of Staff an officer in high standing."

He sat with his hands wrapped tightly around the steering wheel. After several seconds had passed, he looked at her. "I am convinced that our ideologies are the cement which has bonded Skip and I. We don't fight for governments or politicians. We fight for our people.

"That is why I am here, I've earned his trust. I am a leader he can depend on. A person gets but one chance with Skip Daggard. You prove your loyalty to the American people or…he shoots you."

They drove out of Georgetown under a dark sky threatening to storm. General Hanalin drove north toward Frederick and I-70 west.

Hanalin wasn't sure why he had chosen this roundabout route to Harlan, Kentucky because it would have been a more direct route if he had simply selected route 64. He had decided to go north, then west on I-70, pick up I-68 west, then go into Ohio, then south to Harlan. Maybe it was something Skip had said, 'Be devious.' Perhaps his route was pre-selected.

Chin Lee sat quiet, lost in her thoughts, her heart pounding against her chest. She still felt Skip's blazing hand toying with her nipples. She smiled as she unconsciously rubbed her breasts.

She knew in her heart that she had made the right choice. She came to a sudden realization as the rain began to splatter against the windshield, that her decision to defect would render her future null and void. She was traveling with a man who had been her enemy all of her life, yet, she was going to help him try to put an army together to fight against her countrymen and the Soviet Communists.

Neither had spoken during the hour or so it took to get to I-70. Once General Mac Arthur Hanalin made the loop at Frederick, and began the western trek on I-70, Chin Lee smiled as she reached up and touched her right breast again.

Hanalin observed her movement out of his peripheral vision and took a quick look at her then back at the road. The fierce, heavy rain, which poured out of slow-moving clouds, slowed to a steady downpour.

General Hanalin argued with himself for a few minutes before he took the plunge. "I don't know if any of us are going to survive this, Chin…oh, hell, maybe I should shut up!"

Chin Lee looked over at his taut face. "What is it you have to say, General Hanalin?"

"Nothing, forget it!"

"Is it about Skip Daggard?"

Now he was angry with himself for opening his mouth. "I had rehearsed three smart aleck ways of saying this, but I will just say it. That kiss Skip gave you and groping your breasts wasn't out of passion, Chin…"

She swiftly raised her left hand to stop him. "I know."

Hanalin stared at her then focused back on the road. "*You know?*"

"Of course, General Hanalin; it took me a few seconds to realize what he was doing, but even so, it felt good, so I let him continue."

They both chuckled. "You knew he was feeling you up for wires or bugs?"

"Yes! Where are we going?"

He thought about what Skip had often said, 'Commies, they're always asking questions.'

The rain turned into a light, but continuous drizzle as they drove up the mountain above Frederick, Maryland. Fort Ritchie was about thirty-five miles to the north, and Fort Detrick was about fifteen miles northeast.

General Hanalin answered her question. "To put an army together…I hope."

Bunker system
Georgetown
Saturday, October 9
0840 hours

Skip stood in the dimly-lit corridor near the steel door to the tunnel, surveying his handy work. He used his mental process, checking the placements of the C-4 charges. Once he was satisfied that the trip wire he had laced around the handle of the steel door would ignite all of the C-4 packages he had placed in the tunnel and the door area, he turned towards his escape route and moved out smartly.

He knew that they were coming. When he was showering he remembered what it was that he had forgotten. He had focused his attention on the fact that there wasn't a security camera in that section of the hall in the Pentagon, but that the secret door had been armed with an alarm. "Dumb shit," he chastised himself. "It's that kind of forgetfulness which gets people killed." He started laughing. "Yeah, and a bunch of dumb shits are about to get theirs."

Skip Daggard lingered at the base of the ladder, inhaling the remnants of Chin's perfume. The aroma evoked images of other women who had been important at crucial moments in his life. Dtoy, who was a Thai operative, saved him from drugs and being knifed by a female North Vietnamese spy, who had tried to fillet his back. Corporal Sarah Knott, a spy in US Military Intelligence, who had saved him from having his head bashed in by her people, actually she was a double agent, and a few others whose names he could not remember.

Skip shook his head. He leaned against the wall and smiled. "Well, Kristine, the enemy is about to take more casualties." His position was good. Skip was one hundred yards down range from the bunker; the explosives were on the east of the bunker, and in that tunnel leading to the Pentagon, so he waited for the explosion. While he waited images of tunnels in a foreign land snaked out of his subconscious mind dragging him back in time to hell.

Sergeant Daggard was squatting on his heels ten yards from the tunnel opening. He did not look at the team leader. "How long has he been down there?"

Staff Sergeant Opel responded in a long sigh, "Toooo long!"

They heard the tunnel rat screaming, but the American soldier was two hundred yards east of their position. By the time they reached him, the corporal was already dead…twenty green pit vipers were slithering away into the tall grass. The net, which held the poisonous snakes, was still wrapped around the tunnel rat's head and face.

Skip shook his head forcing old horrors back into their hiding places as a slight tremor from the explosion shook the ground he stood on. He allowed himself a short, satisfying smile; he ascended the ladder to hunt down, and kill enemy spies.

Pentagon
Arlington County, Virginia
Saturday, October 9
0905 hours

Major Timmins was sitting at General Hanalin's desk. He was in constant radio contact with Colonel Barker.

"Major, we are closing in on the bunker. My advance patrol is at the door" Then the explosion; communications was severed. Many people in the Pentagon felt the tremor. Major Timmins jumped to his feet shouting, "My God, it was a trap." He tried for fifteen minutes to reestablish contact to no avail while waiting to hear from the team he had sent in to find out what had happened.

His men returned at 0930 hours. Captain Hedge reported. "The tunnel is sealed off 300 yards into the system. We have to presume that they are all dead."

Major Timmins fell into General Hanalin's chair, his face a mask of horror. His breathing was labored, and he had to contact his leader.

It was a call he dreaded to make. He looked at his captain, "Thank you! Take up your position, Captain. I have to contact the general."

"Two hundred men...gone, and we haven't attacked yet...damn!" He dialed the general's number.

"This is General Bardolph! Tell me you have good news, Colonel Barker."

"Sir, this is Major Timmins, Colonel Barker and his men are dead."

General Bardolph jumped to his feet sending his chair across the floor. "*WHAT?*"

Major Timmins wished he was home in Moscow with his wife... anywhere but here. "It was a trap, sir. The tunnel is now sealed off."

Heavy breathing came over the phone. General Bardolph spoke in a distant voice, "Thank you, Major, you are in charge at your location now."

"Yes sir!"

General Bardolph stood behind his desk fuming with rage. He did not move. He stood still. He had resources to find Daggard, but if he used them, then American loyalists will be alerted. His breathing was shallow as he tried to figure out a plan. He had given up on Colonel Lee; her people had not heard from her—she was considered dead or a prisoner. "Well," he said as he retrieved his chair, "I have issued orders to my field officers, so Daggard will have to wait." General Bardolph shuffled to the west window. Once again he looked west aggravated and disgusted. "I hope you survive so I can torture you, you bastard," he said to the windowpane.

World War Two Memorial
Washington, D.C
Saturday, October 9
1045 hours

Washington lay under a dark cloud as a cold, penetrating rain fell upon America's capital and its inhabitants.

Skip left the bunker using a maze of tunnel systems. He stood near a blue 2000 Chevy Impala in the parking lot near the WWII Memorial.

The Washington Monument was about three hundred yards off. Skip stared at the white, obelisk finger of stone pointing Heavenward.

The monument was closed now. It had been closed ever since that fatal day three years ago. He smiled as memories flooded out from his subconscious. How she had told him she was pregnant as she relieved herself in a drainage area of a tunnel. How she had goosed him when he started his ascent up the ladder into the monument. He had looked down at her.

"How did *you* like it, sweetheart?" Kristine had said sarcastically.

He smiled over his response. "I liked it. Can you do it again?"

She retorted, "*Figures!*"

At once he went somber remembering other things that he had shared with her that day. He remembered something he had told her. That something was a nagging persistence thumping against his brain wall. "My memory didn't serve me well that day, Kristine. I have no clue to what I was thinking when I told you there were 255 steps up the monument when there are 897, and there are 455 rungs on the iron latter we had climbed. You see, that kind of forgetfulness is what gets folks in our business killed."

Skip Daggard moved in behind the steering wheel. He put the key in the ignition and started the engine. He stared out of the windshield at the World War II Memorial, the Washington Monument, and Washington. "It seems that we've only postponed the inevitable, Kristine. The enemy is here, as is the war. Why can't *they* just leave us the fuck alone?"

He drove out of DC heading towards CIA Headquarters at Langley thinking about the future and how he was going to inform CIA Director Leo Pike about the spies in his organization. That those spies must be terminated immediately—not interrogated—nor spanked, but shot dead...now. It was the only solution.

His ultimate destination was Drainsville Park. As he drove, Skip began formulating plans for his attacks. It would have been simpler for him to go to his secret room in the Lincoln Tunnel, but he never did the simple or expected. "I wonder where the general and Chin are right now?" he asked himself in a quiet voice.

1-68
Friendsville, Maryland
Saturday, October 9
1115 hours

As they left Frostburg and Allegany Country, crossing into Garrett Country, Chin Lee shifted in her seat. "Why are we *here?*"

General Hanalin turned off the wiper blades. "This is where it started for us just a few days ago, Chin. Skip figured to give you your last chance to bail."

"By bail do you mean to go back to the North Korean side?"

Hanalin nodded his head.

They drove in silence for several miles, until they saw the sign, Friendsville 19 miles.

Chin sighed. General Hanalin stole a glance at her. Chin swiveled in her seat toward Hanalin. She studied the wrinkles of his face and his scars. She looked at him. "I had been ordered to kill him."

General Hanalin almost lost control of his vehicle. He stole a glance at her. "*What?*"

"I tried twice, but I could not squeeze the trigger."

He took two minutes to process her words as he glanced at her three times. He smiled at her as they came up to exit 4, the Friendsville exit. He continued past the exit. "I guess you're staying!"

"What?"

"Your face and eyes! You love him."

She exhaled a deep sigh. "Yes, he is the first man to ever touch me—to kiss me, to fondle me. I have always been a soldier. My life was devoted to the Communist party."

They rode in silence. The sky cleared but clouds lingered in the west.

"Did he love her?"

Hanalin maneuvered their vehicle around a fuel tanker as they started up the hill past Friendsville. "You mean, Kristine?"

She looked at him.

"I heard him crying once…a long time ago. He was calling out to someone named Bryanna." Hanalin became emotional. Tears began to gather at the corners of his eyes.

Chin studied him, waiting.

"I didn't intrude. I never asked who she was."

He wiped the tears from his eyes. "I waited for him. He was thirty-six hours overdue from a mission. I took a Vietnamese interpreter and three Special Forces MI soldiers with me."

Hanalin went somber as he remembered. It was difficult for him to talk. Chin waited, staring at the pain on his face.

"We found him five hours from home."

Hanalin wiped more tears from his eyes. "It was a small cleaning near the Mekong River. I knelt down by his right side. I threw the bodies of two Vietcong off of him."

Hanalin hesitated as he wiped more tears away. "There was no hope for him. He had been sliced and diced. We all believed that he was dead. As I reached down for his dog tags, I told two soldiers to use a poncho and make a stretcher. Then a voice said, 'What took you so long, Cap?'"

Chin watched a smile spread out from his lips and engulf his face.

"We stared at him in total disbelief. That's when he told me, Chin, who she was. While lying there in a pool of his blood mingled with the enemies, he told me that he had heard his fiancée, Bryanna calling him from ten thousand miles away. 'She said to me as I was going under, Skip, Skipper I can't take medals to bed. Don't you die on me! Wake up! Skipper wake up! Come home to me Skipper.'"

They entered West Virginia.

"Now, do you understand what I meant when I said that he can love other women, but only on woman has his heart?"

Chin nodded her head.

"He loved Kristine, yet, he almost killed her when he found out she was a Communist spy. Her father had been in the KGB. Now, he serves in Russia's new Secret Service."

"I cannot fathom the idea that she was a Communist spy."

General Hanalin nodded his head.

Chin stared at her reflection in the window as she thought about her opportunities to terminate Daggard, but she could not fire her weapon.

"I had my opportunities to kill him," she said.

He looked at her while turning on the wiper blades as a gentle rain began to fall.

"The heart can play many instruments."

General Hanalin smiled. "Yes, it can."

"It was the passion in his voice and the fire in his eyes when he talked about your people and this country. He turned his back on me and walked away tall and straight. There was passion and a hunger in that kiss he gave me."

"It's the battle."

Chin stared at him, "*The battle?*"

General Mac Arthur Hanalin let out a deep sigh. "As I was trying to explain before; Skip came to me with his demons. He had been killed once, stabbed, beaten, and electrocuted. He's had all of his fingers broken, been filleted, and it took twenty-five stitches to sow up the second crease in his ass from machine gun bullets."

They both laughed.

"He was, and is suicidal."

She stared at him.

"It took him years to open up and let me in. He would share only small bits and pieces. It was the night he "died" which changed him."

The rain continued to fall.

"He put in a ten forty-nine, request for transfer for door-gunner on a Huey gun ship. Back in '68 the life expectancy for a door-gunner, who manned the .50 cal machineguns in the open doorway of a helicopter, was twenty-four hours in-country."

The rain stopped as they drove past Hazelton, West Virginia.

"His request was denied because he was privileged to too much top-secret information. When he let his demon loose; all the command wanted to do was get rid of him. I ended up with him."

General Hanalin stopped at Little Sandy's in Bruceton Mills for gas and a meal. As they sat at a table in the truck-stop restaurant, they looked around listening to laughter and westward road conditions that truck drivers were sharing. Chin studied the sadness in Hanalin's eyes as he said, "They have no concept that their world is about to come crashing down."

Dranesville Park, Virginia
Saturday, October 9
1220 hours

He stood in the southwest corner of the park near the ruins of the cabin. It had been a sanctuary he had shared with Kristine until they had been found. He sucked down huge amounts of the wet, fresh air. He didn't try holding back his tears. He let them spill out from his eyes, run down his cheeks, and splatter on the ground as he fell to his knees. When three minutes had passed, he rose to his feet and wiped his tears from his face. Skip could see her in the kitchen twenty minutes before he destroyed the cabin, sexy and hot; they had made love on the kitchen table.

Skip took a deep breath and sighed. He took out Pearl's cell phone. It would be his first contact with Leo Pike. "The Dog is ready to howl. It's Party Time! Let's Rock and Roll! Maintain!" He closed the cover on the phone.

Director Pike stared at his phone. He did not have to retrieve a code-decipher book in order to decipher Daggard's message. Dog meant Daggard, and "Party Time" meant the US. Rock and Roll meant war. Maintain meant wait, keep a low profile, and don't share with anyone. Pike knew that Daggard would call again. He rose as a solemn frown marched across his face.

Director Leo Pike walked to the east window of his office. He studied the Apache helicopters as they landed on the tarmac. He stared at his reflection in the windowpane. He was fifty-nine, of Italian ancestry, and gray had not yet advanced against his wavy brown hair, which he had styled in honor of Elvis Presley.

He reached up with his left hand touching the three pox marks, and tracing the four scars along his cheeks. Without warning, the memories invaded his conscious.

Explosions shattered the silence. Darkness became flash-frames of light.
"You Lt. Pike?"
"Yeah, who are you?"
"I'm the Dog…Code Name Snoopy. What're you doing tied up to these posts?"

"We were to be executed in the morning."

Director Pike turned around when he heard his door open. "What's wrong Agent Norton?"

"Sir, we've intercepted encrypted messages from NSA."

Silence became sand in an hourglass.

"And?"

"It's Cold War stuff, sir; Soviet."

Director Pike took printouts from his agent. He rifled through the documents. Pike looked up at Agent Norton, "This it?"

"Some of it, sir."

Daggard's warning was a bell clanging in his head. "When the transmission is complete, Agent Norton, bring me the rest of the documents."

"Yes sir!"

Director Pike spoke up as Agent Norton wrapped his fingers around the doorknob, "Recall all of our personnel, Agent Norton."

Norton stared as his leader. *"All personnel, sir?"*

"To include the pilots."

Agent Norton studied his leader as confusion spread across Norton's face. "Yes sir; everyone."

Director Leo Pike fell into his maroon chair behind his desk. Memories came back to haunt him.

"Compton?"

"Snoopy?"

"Yeah, stay hidden, Compton; tell us when they're coming."

"Okay, Snoops!

"All right! This is our first defensive position—get ready."

"Can we help?"

Sergeant Daggard spun around, *"NO! Just sit there."*

"Can we have weapons?"

"No, Lt. you can't," Daggard did not face Pike.

Once his men were situated, Daggard went to Lieutenant Pike. *"What did you tell them?"*

Pike stared into the eyes of death. *"Nothing!"*

Daggard rose from his squatting position. He walked over to Sergeant Davies. "Something's fucked up here, Davies."

"I don't know about that Snoopy; orders are orders."

Director Pike shook his head vigorously. He could still see the threatening posture of his rescuers. A vision he tried in vain to clear from his head for years.

"Sergeant Daggard! Snoopy, I didn't tell them anything…nothing."

"Davies, take everyone and get to the LZ. If I'm a no-show, take off and I'll find another road home. I'm goin' back for Compton. He should have been here by now."

"Everyone, Snoop?"

"Everyone!"

"Well, you better beat feet back to base before we land because I'm not taken' the heat."

"Get going."

"Come in!"

Agent Norton marched across the carpeted floor. "These are all the transmissions, sir."

Director Pike took them from his subordinate. He rose to his five feet nine inches and sighed.

"The recall has been initiated, sir. Agents are beginning to report."

"Thank you, Agent Norton; report to your station."

"Yes sir!" As he began to turn around, Norton turned back to his superior. "Sir, what's going on?"

Director Pike studied Agent Norton. Should he trust him? Should he tell him? Hell, what did he know himself? "Agent Norton!"

"Sir?"

"I want four Apache's up immediately, following the Alpha-Baker coordinates."

"*SIR!*"

"Carry out your orders, Agent Norton."

"Yes sir!"

Twenty minutes had elapsed. Director Pike observed the helicopters take flight from his window observation point. He leaned his forehead against the windowpane. His breath clouded up the pane. "I *hope the hell* you know what's going on, Skip. Due to your conversation, I just put in motion the destruction of NSA." He let a heavy, saddened sigh escape from his mouth. "I pray the order isn't given." He stayed his position as memories returned.

Huey's began to lift-off. Sergeant Davies shouted to the pilot, and the chopper landed as Daggard came running across the field carrying Compton.

Once the two soldiers were inside, Davies shouted, "Go!"

"Take care of him, Doc," he said to the medic, "Reckon you'll live, Compton."

The choppers landed at an MI site ten miles west of Saigon.

Director Pike observed the Apaches disappear into the afternoon airspace.

Once the Apaches had disappeared, Director Pike turned from his window. "What in the hell is going on, Skip? W-h-a-t in the h-e-l-l is going on?" As he returned to his seat behind his desk, Director Pike allowed another memory to move into his conscious mind.

Pike helped Daggard with Compton as an ambulance approached. He had noticed Daggard's somber attitude during the flight. A Lieutenant and a colonel approached. "YOU FAILED TO CARRY OUT YOUR ORDERS. SERGEANT," screamed the colonel.

And then the most unbelievable thing happened. Daggard drew his .45 and shot the colonel in the head. As the colonel fell to the ground, Daggard said, "I hate spies," and walked away. Then Daggard stopped, turned around and said to Pike, "I was supposed to kill you, but there lies the traitor."

Director Pike shook his head as he began reviewing the documents Agent Norton had given him.

Daggard stood over the steel grate, remembering that Kristine didn't want to go down, so he went first and copped a feel as she descended. She had pretended to get mad.

He took out a key and unlocked the rusty, silver, Masters Lock, put the key in the right front pocket of his Levis, and lifted the grate. Skip climbed down the iron ladder, closed the grate and locked it again. He heard the helicopters as they made their circle from Langley to begin their flight pattern. "I was on my way to see, Pike; I have something to finish first,' he said as he descended the latter.

It took him four hours to reach his destination in D.C. He stood before the stone-walled door feeling for the trip wire. It took him four minutes to find it. He held it in his left hand as he pushed on a cut stone in the wall. The stone door slid open. Skip stepped in and defused the block of C-4. He closed the door by pulling on a brick, and saluted the grave. He went about defusing the rest of the twenty booby traps that he and Kristine had set three years ago.

He sighed several times trying not to remember while he rummaged threw his gun cabinet for his Ruger 7mm sniper's rifle and a box of shells. Once he had what he'd come for and put away his M-14, Skip stood over the grave. "It seems that the Fates have found it necessary for us to be intertwined." He saluted and left the sanctuary.

Once again he stood near the Washington Monument. This time he selected a Ford Expedition SUV.

Goddard Space Center
Route 32 and 295
Near NSA, Fort Meade
Saturday, October 9
1500 hours

The position he was in was not new to him. Skip had lain in a prone position in mild and extreme weather conditions before…blizzards, monsoons, sweltering heat, pleasant mornings and frigid evenings.

He had chosen the roof of the Goddard Space Building, one mile west of NSA so he could snipe his quarry, General Bardolph the Deputy Director of NSA. He didn't know his target, but knew the official vehicle for the Deputy Director, and the underground parking area he'd depart from.

To Skip's surprise, the vehicle pulled up close to the topside west entrance doors at 1505 hours. As he fine-tuned his scope, Skip froze. "No fuckin' way," he hissed removing his eye from his scope and looking over his rifle. Then he quickly stared through his scope again as the general opened the left side back door and slipped into the vehicle.

Skip placed the crosshairs of his scope one inch down from the top of the right rear passenger window and began to apply pressure to the trigger. His hand trembled and his rage charged forward from its hidden depths within Skip's soul as the demon began to stir.

After all of these years, the son of a bitch who had ordered his execution was here in America, the Deputy Director at NSA, and the leader of the Communist coalition force.

He stayed his finger on the trigger because of his initial shock. It had been his demon that had whispered, "No! A bullet is too quick. This man must pay."

The demon knew exactly how to make Bardolph pay.

Fort Meade, Maryland
Saturday, October 9
1735 hours

Skip Daggard sat in his vehicle. He was parked at the end of Officer Road near Burba Lake on Fort Meade. He had acquired Bardolph's address through the Post Locator. The rain had stopped, making it easy for Skip to use his handheld listening device. At 1740 hours, Skip overheard the phone conversation that would give him his entry into the general's quarters.

By 1800, a Domino's driver signed in at an MP gate. The MP on duty called the household where the pizza was to be delivered. Once the MP was satisfied, the driver was allowed on post with a time limit to deliver the goods and be back at the gate to sign off post.

Skip waited fifteen minutes after the call to Domino's had been made. While waiting, he looked around the SUV. Skip had taken this one from the parking lot near the World War Two Memorial.

At 1810 hours, he left his vehicle, and arrived at the front stoop of Bardolph's quarters just as the pizza driver came to a screeching halt.

"Great," Skip said to the redheaded teenage driver as he stepped onto the sidewalk holding two large boxes of pizza. "I need your help."

Skip looked around. "I haven't seen my uncle in fifteen years, so when he opens the door, I'll grab the pizza from you and barge on in, okay?"

"Wow! Sure, but how do I get paid?"

"How much?"

"Thirty-two fifty."

Skip handed him a fifty, "This all right?"

"Hell yeah, mister!"

The delivery guy rang the bell. As the door opened, Skip grabbed the boxes, pushed his way in slamming the door shut with his right foot. He drove the pizza boxes into Bardolph's face forcing him back against a wall near the stairwell. Skip produced his knife, slicing the arteries on both inside thighs. Bardolph screamed out in pain while trying to disarm the mad man who had invaded his house.

Skip plunged the eight-inch blade into the fleshy part of Bardolph's right shoulder. He twisted the knife as he withdrew the bloody blade.

He shouted in Russian to Bardolph's wife and two daughters, who had come running from the kitchen into the dining room. "Shut up and lie face down on the dining room floor."

They obeyed as tears cascaded from their eyes. Mrs. Bardolph began to plead for her husband's life.

"You want him alive, huh?"

Mrs. Bardolph pleaded, "Please!"

Skip stared into Bardolph's eyes. "Yeah, I wanted my wife and daughter alive too."

Skip placed the sharp tip of his knife under Bardolph's chin. He turned his attention back to the women. "Nice family," Skip said, "which one dies first?"

Bardolph's eyes went wide with fear. "Please, not my family."

"I had you in my sights today until I recognized you. Thought I was dead, didn't you?"

The whimpering by the three women made Skip turn his head again. "SHUT UP!" Once they quieted down, he turned back to Bardolph. "So, you don't want me to harm your family, huh?"

"PLEASE! I beg you…"

Skip smashed him in his mouth splitting his lips and damaging teeth.

"But it was all right for you to order the rape and murder of my family, huh? My daughter was only three."

His wife looked up at him.

"Your daughters are lookin' good. Maybe I'll violate them," he said punching Bardolph with an uppercut, which caused Bardolph to crumble on the floor.

Skip squatted. He retrieved a slice of Supreme Pizza and began to eat it. Once he finished that slice, he took out handcuffs. He locked Bardolph's left wrist in one cuff, snaked the other cuff and chain around the post of the banister, and locked Bardolph's right hand in that cuff.

Skip took another slice of pizza and rose in one swift movement. Stepping over the women, he went into the kitchen and took a beer from the refrigerator. He twisted off the cap, taking three long gulps from the bottle. "I was supposed to die in that fire too, wasn't I?"

General Bardolph gulped air. His face was covered in sweat and etched in pain as his blood formed a large pool on the hardwood floor under him.

"That's twice now, you bungled the kill. Guess what," Skip put down the bottle of beer on the dining room table and finished the slice of pizza. He sat down on the small of Bardoph's wife's back. "That's two too many." He wrapped her long, brown hair around his left hand yanking her head up exposing her throat. In an even cross motion, Skip slit her throat almost severing her head.

Bardolph was too weak to cry out, but his daughters weren't. Their screams were short-lived…they died in the same manner as their mother.

Skip grabbed the beer bottle from the table. He squatted on his haunches in front of Bardolph as he reached for a third piece of pizza. "No senses in letting all of it go to waste. Three slices is usually my limit."

He finished the slice, and then downed the beer in one long gulp. "I know who your associates are. Your man talked. I want you to take this thought with you to Hell…your people aren't going to win."

Skip leaned forward ripping off Bardolph's Polo shirt, exposing his chest. He cut away a circle of flesh over Bardolph's heart. He yanked a huge chunk away. Bardolph screamed in pain. The flap of flesh dangled against Bardolph's exposed belly. With a few quick flicks of his blade, Skip held his enemy's heart in his hand.

Bardolph's lifeless body slumped against the stairwell wall.

Skip let the heart slip over his fingers and splatter onto the floor next to Bardolph's left leg. He stepped over the dead women, and took out another cold beer. He opened it taking several long pulls on the beverage. He cleaned his knife on a kitchen towel, and then washed the blood off of his hands and face. Next, he got a piece of paper and a pen from the center of the kitchen table and wrote a note.

These spies are leaders of a Communist coalition force that is going to try and take over the United States—there are over one hundred fifty more to be dealt with before I rest.

Skip Daggard
Military Intelligence Chief Warrant Officer, Retired

When he left Bardolph's quarters, Skip contacted NSA. "You need to send agents to General Bardolph's quarters immediately. I heard screaming coming from inside." He hung up, threw Bardolph's cell phone onto the front lawn smashing it into pieces with the heel of his boot. He marched to his vehicle, slid in behind the steering wheel and drove away toward Washington and another rendezvous with spies.

Chapter Twelve—Chin Makes a Decision

Secret room
Lincoln Tunnel
Washington, D.C.
Saturday, October 9
2300 hours

Earlier in the day the House had passed a bill to delete the Second Amendment. The bill was now before the Senate. At 2300 hours, the senators were deadlocked. They had just heard from the president that if the bill passes the Senate, he would veto it. The senators voted to retire until tomorrow.

Skip sat on an army cot in his secret room off of the Lincoln Tunnel. His room in the tunnel was three hundred yards from the Ford Theater and two miles from the Capitol Building.

It had been in this room where Kristine had revealed her true identity. She also informed him of his true target. And, it was in this room that he began to share his nightmares with her.

He moved his left hand over the spot where Kristine had peed. He could hear her voice as his tears swelled up at the corners of his eyes.

"What had they done to you over there, Skip?"

"They killed us, Kristine. We all died."

He had told her about the Battle for Hue, and other horrors, and then she peed. He rubbed the spot again. "It's hard to believe," he spoke to her memory, "that it was only three years ago when we terminated a traitor in the White House. Now, when I need you most..." He bowed his head. "But, it has always been that way, honey, and this is one mission when I'm definitely better off by myself because what I'm going to do tomorrow will make our excursion three years ago…well, you'll see."

Skip undressed, lay on his cot and pulled the sheets up and over his war-scarred body. As he slept, he dreamed of a world at peace. It had been this utopia that had been the driving force for his continued service. He woke up at 0215 hours and sat up on his cot. He reached under the sheet retrieving his rifle. Skip wrapped his arms around the stock drawing the rifle close to his body. He lay back down with the rifle cradled in is arms.

Ohio
A Holiday Inn
Saturday, October 9
2305 hours

General Hanalin and Chin had taken adjoining rooms in a Holiday Inn just inside Ohio after they turned south towards Kentucky. Chin lay under the warm blankets staring up at the ceiling in the darkness of her room. She had her hands clasped together resting on her stomach just below her breasts.

Many events of the past three days were like movie frames in her mind. Her memory of Skip's flaming kiss, his hot lips, and his burning hand caressing her breasts kept exploding in her brain causing sensations to erupt in her body.

She lay analyzing the new direction she had chosen in her life. It was still leading her toward conflict and battle, but this time her future was shrouded in uncertainty. Her mind could not comprehend how these Americans were going to win.

Chin sat up drawing her knees to her chest, wrapping her arms around them, then resting her chin on her knees. "They are not organized," she said to the darkness of her room, "and they have no army. I should correct that statement; they *will* not have an army. How can they win?"

Chin rose from her bed in a slow, graceful movement, and walked to the bathroom for a drink of water. She studied her figure in the mirror. "I do not understand the Americans," she said to the face in the mirror looking back at her. "They are doomed, yet they prepare to fight. What was it that Skip had said? Oh, yes! 'If it were not for the militia, the meager Continental Army could not have won the Revolutionary War.'"

She took another swallow of water, placed the glass on the counter near the sink, and turned off the light. She walked back to her bed, slid under the blankets shaking her head. "What militia? Where will they come from? Who will arm them? Freedom! What is this? And why do these Americans cherish it more than life itself?"

Agent Daggard had told her that she had had a taste of it, and she chose to fight for it or die fighting for it. Had she? Perhaps! She had devoted her whole life to communism and had come here to America to tame the dragon, only to learn that the dragon was not the American government but the Americans...all of them. "How many are there?"

Chin stretched out lying back down, placing her hands behind her head on the pillow. She felt a stirring inside of her. A sensation she had never felt before. Agent Skip Daggard was the first man who had ever touched her...ever kissed her and her body responded with passion and a burning desire. She needed him, right now. "Where are you my darling," she whispered into the dark, confine of her room. "I am staying...I will fight...and I hope I am worthy."

Secret room off the Lincoln Tunnel
Washington, D.C.
Sunday, October 10
0430 hours

Skip Daggard awakened at 0430 hours in the manner he was accustomed, no aid from an alarm clock. He listened for several seconds, taking in the noises of his surroundings: The quiet humming of the Honda generator, the subtle tic, tic, tic of the second hand on the wall clock, and the slight humming sound of the electric oil heater going on and off automatically.

Once he was satisfied, he slipped out from under his sheets, placing his warm feet on the cold stone floor. He rose from the cot and dressed, using swift and deft movements. First, he put on his jeans, then his undershirt, then his socks and finally his hunting boots. Skip put on coffee, and went over to the grave at the far corner of the secret room. He saluted the Civil War soldiers he had buried in the mass grave about five years ago when he had first discovered this room. "I had no idea then, men, how important this room was to become."

Another salute and then he poured a cup of coffee. He put in some sugar and evaporated milk he had taken from his cache of supplies, and sat down at the field table in the center of the room. He slipped on a dark, blue wool pullover shirt.

Skip ran his fingers over the names of the soldiers that had been carved in one corner of the table. He sipped his coffee as he stared at the Corporal of the Guard's diary sitting on a wall-mounted set of shelves. "We are going to die, and we do not know why," Skip said out loud, which was the corporal's last entry in his diary.

They had been President Lincoln's military guard, placed here in this tomb by Secretary of War, Stanton. The beginning of the plot to murder Lincoln and the debauchery of the South had been put into motion.

The official record stated that Simon Cameron, the Secretary of War, was ineffective, therefore, Edwin McMasters Stanton, a prominent lawyer, was selected for the position.

"Here's a reality check for you, corporal. Ann Carol of Kent County, Maryland, conceived the North's route of attack into the south, which was named the Tennessee Plan because the plan called for a Union armada using the Tennessee River to invade the south."

Skip took four sips of his coffee while studying the mound of dirt. "So, corporal, do you see the paradox? Cameron would never take such a plan written by a woman to Congress. There had been much debate between Lincoln and his cabinet about Stanton because Stanton was an avid Lincoln hater. He never hid his feeling for the president."

Skip rose to his feet and paced near the grave. "When Stanton was invited to the White House in December 1861, offered the job and explained why, he accepted in quick order. He presented the plan to Congress on the pretense that Generals Grant, Rosecrans, and McClellan had been the authors. Congress was so pleased with the Tennessee Plan that they awarded medals to the three generals. The stage was set, and on April 14th 1865, Stanton executed his revenge against Lincoln."

He turned back to the grave. "I believe, corporal, the reason why your captain hadn't been here with you is the fact that he was Lincoln's executioner." He stood facing the grave as he finished his coffee. "The evidence is there, cleverly hidden, but there. Your captain would have been armed with a holstered side arm.

"He sat behind and left oblique to Mr. Lincoln. One well-placed bullet, and it was well-placed, and the conspiracy was complete."

Skip fixed his second cup of coffee. He went over to the table and sat down. He spoke out to an imaginary face. "I should have listened to you, Kristine. If I had, you and Elise would be alive. I agonize over your words, 'Our bags are packed, take us with you.'"

He sat in silence for five minutes sipping his coffee. "There's another girl, Kristine, an olive-brown smooth-skinned North Korean Communist. What is it about you Communist females anyway? Why do you all pick on me? She says that she's goin' to stay...we'll see."

His tears would not come...he understood why; they had been exhausted. He sucked down his grief.

"I have to pack now. Today I'm going to commit an atrocious act of treason. I'm going to take out Congress...spies. You know about those kinds of things...spies."

Holiday Inn
Ohio
Sunday, October 10
0715 hours

General Hanalin and Chin Lee met in the corridor and took the elevator from the third floor down to the dining room. They sat down to a continental breakfast when the vague news came from the huge plasma TV. "General Bardolph, the Deputy Director of NSA, and his family have been murdered in their quarters on Fort Meade." Pictures of Bardoph and his family were shown.

"*Bardolphphphph!*" The word escaped his mouth on a long hiss.

Chin stared across the table at him.

"B-a-r-d-o-l-p-h! Of course!" He exchanged a stare with Chin. "It was in 1975 while Skip was spy-hunting in Germany. Suddenly, he disappeared. Corporal Knott was instrumental in locating him. When

171

we broke in and found him in a dungeon in a section of the ancient wall around Frankfurt, a giant of a Russian soldier was using Skip's body for baseball practice.

"The colonel who had ordered Skip's execution was Bardolph. Skip has been hunting for him for thirty-five years."

General Hanalin was lost in his thoughts. Three minutes had passed when he sighed. "Bardolph hid himself well. He had always sent an aid to meetings at the Pentagon."

Chin looked at him. "So, now it begins?"

Hanalin could see the worry in her eyes. He reached over with his right hand laying it on her left hand. "Yes, now it begins. Your people and the Soviets declared this war, Chin. There won't be any rules or Geneva Convention. Skip never followed those rules anyway." His words evoked a memory.

He sat frozen in his seat with his back rigid against the wall of the Huey as the screams of the second prisoner dissipated in the air. He wanted to challenge his operative, but he had seen that Daggard's demon had taken control. Only a fool would challenge the demon.

Daggard reached for the third prisoner. The man cried, and gave up all of the info Daggard had required and much more. Yet, Daggard grabbed the VC, yanking him from his knees and threw him out of the chopper.

"What the hell did you do that for? He gave you the information."

"General, are you all right?"

He focused back on Chin Lee, "Yeah! Just a bad memory." He could still see the amber glow of light shooting out from the slits of Daggard's eyes.

"There won't be any rules, Chin. We'll be fighting for our right to exist. We'll be fighting on *our* soil."

They listened to the news reports while they ate their meal.

"What will Agent Daggard do now, General?"

He didn't have to think long before answering. "He will do what Skip does best. He will hunt down the spies and kill them."

They finished their meal in silence, then left to continue their journey. Yet, a persistent issue kept resurrecting itself. As they drove out of the hotel parking lot, she finally asked, "What is Skip going to do about the spies in Congress?"

Kentucky
Sunday, October 10
1105 hours

They had entered Kentucky about 0930 hours. At 1105 hours, General Hanalin pulled into a Bob Evans for lunch. They ate in silence, each lost in his and her thoughts. When they finished and were sipping coffee, General Hanalin broke the silence. "We've been so wrapped up in preparing for war, Chin that we haven't given much thought to your feelings. I'm sorry for our seeming uncaring."

She looked at him as she took two sips of coffee while processing his words. Chin placed her cup down on the saucer looking into his eyes. "I have cried for the loss of my father, General Hanalin. I feel that my government has betrayed me. That they have swept my loyalty out with the dust."

She picked up her cup with a trembling hand. "I have deserted my people," she said in a hushed voice. "I have no country. I cannot comprehend General, that is, I have no basis to understand how you Americans plan to win."

She took three sips of her coffee before looking up into Hanalin's eyes, "Two men challenging seventy million?" She shook her head.

General Hanalin smiled. He finished his coffee in three swallows. When he put his cup down he studied her as she finished her coffee. "In ancient times," he began, "a formidable force marched across the known world enslaving those they had concord. On a mountain pass, three hundred Spartan warriors met this force in order to defend their people. They fought that enemy for several days inflicting severe losses.

"By the time the enemy was able to crush this small force, ten thousand more Spartan warriors were there. Sparta didn't fall."

She studied Hanalin, while he spoke trying to isolate meaning in his words because she knew there was a meaning to his story. She had learned that there is always meaning in his words. She stared into his eyes. "There are too many front lines, General. Opposing forces will come from many locations using a vast array of weapons. She lowered her head squeezing her coffee cup between her hands.

"I realize that we are only three, but the enemy has already taken casualties. I'm sure Bardolph had some key role to play. Now that he's dead, they will have to plug in a replacement for him."

She raised her head staring at him. "You said three?"

General Hanalin smiled, "Skip, you, and I."

Chin smiled. Then a sad and sober look took its place. "General, you do not have any time."

General Hanalin's eyes widened as he glared at her.

"Because of Agent Daggard…" She stared into the old eyes of General Hanalin. "They will attack in seven days."

She watched General Hanalin digest her information. She was not prepared for his response.

"Well then, I guess we better get going."

Her mouth fell open as Hanalin rose to his feet. She sat there with her eyes wide open staring at this huge man. Chin gained her feet; her movements seemed animated as they left the restaurant.

He stole glances at her while they crossed the parking lot to their vehicle. He wanted to say something to her, but he could see that she was lost in her own thoughts. He unlocked the doors by pressing a button on the key pad. Hanalin opened the passenger side door for her. Then he went around the front of the vehicle and slid into the driver's seat. He inserted the key into the ignition while he looked over at Chin Lee. She returned his stare.

"I can't predict the future, Chin. I can only use the past as a gage to make approximate assumptions. Many of my people won't fight. They will become prisoners of war. Some will hide, but the majority will fight.

"I believe that Skip has a death wish, that he's crazy, and that he's completely unpredictable. He has always taken the missions where survivability was questionable, and, somehow he has always survived." He paused for a deep breath.

Chin studied the wrinkle lines along General Hanalin's forehead. She noticed his worry lines stretching out from his eyes, his dimples, and his hard-skinned face and his soft friendly eyes.

He didn't know whether he wanted to proceed. He shrugged his shoulders and took the plunge. "There was an incident one month after the moon-walk. US forces' morale was at an all-time low." He paused again as memories began to seep into his conscious. "Skip had completed his mission. He was on his way back to our base. Voices flooded the airways over our radios. A large enemy force had a unit from the 1st Calvary Division pinned down. They were in communications with their rescue choppers. They were calling off their rescue."

He paused, wiping perspiration from his forehead. "We were on the same radio frequency as the two units so we could hear everything regarding the rescue mission. Everything that was being said could be heard by thousands of US forces that were listening in on that frequency. The voices went silent, but we could hear the intensity of the battle increase because the operator continued to key the mike." He took a deep breath. "What came over the radio next, made me and the members of my unit stand up.

"'Rescue Leader this is Alpha Leader. The DOG has arrived, do you copy?'"

"'Alpha Leader this is Rescue Leader. Am I to understand that SNOOPY is at your location?'"

"'Affirmative, Rescue Leader. He had charged the enemy position from the rear entering my location.'"

"We could hear the battle raging. Ten minutes passed, and then there was silence. Then we heard, "'Rescue Leader, this is Alpha Leader abort! I repeat…abort. Our resources have been depleted. We are fixing bayonets…we are not surrendering. Do you copy?'"

"There was silence for about a minute before the Warrant Officer responded. We could hear that he was crying. "'Make them pay for your lives. We'll come back for your bodies.'"

Hanalin had to stop so he could wipe away the tears from his eyes. "What happened next was unbelievable. "'Rescue Leader, this is Alpha Leader do you copy?'"

"'Alpha Leader, this is Rescue Leader, affirmative.'"

"'The LZ for extraction is about one hundred meters, 270 degrees from our position. We're coming out.'"

"There was complete silence. I can tell you, Chin, that the twenty-five soldiers hovering around my radio held their breath, staring at each other and at me."

Hanalin looked at her, remembering. "It was one of the craziest acts of heroism. We could barely hear the singing in the distance of the *Battle Hymn of the Republic*, When *Johnny Comes Marching Home*, and the US Army song."

Again, Hanalin had to stop so he could wipe his eyes. "The singing was getting louder. "'Good God almighty! Hack, Get your camera and get pictures of this because no one will believe us.'"

"We could hear cheering and screaming."

General Hanalin stopped his narration to catch his breath and drive his vehicle out onto the interstate. "Skip didn't share what had happened, but I was privileged to a copy of the "Official Report" three days later. Their ammunition was expended. The DOG had them fix bayonets and issue out the 31 hand grenades they had left. He then ordered them to hunker down in the depression where they had been fighting. They would wait for the enemy to jump in, bayonet the enemy then detonate the grenades.

"A few minutes had passed and nothing happened, so Skip stood up ordering the men into columns of twos. When the men were formed, Skip gave the order, 'Forward, March!' And up out of the depression they marched. They were carrying their wounded and dead. By the time they had marched ten yards, the enemy began forming on both sides of the trail. Skip ordered, "Present, arms." The Americans saluted. A command was shouted down the line, and the Vietcong and North Vietnamese soldiers snapped to attention and presented arms."

General Hanalin drank down three gulps of air before he smiled. "I'm not sure why I shared that with you, Chin. Perhaps it was to show you how crazy and unpredictable Skip can be, or to reiterate that Skip writes his own rules of engagement. Or, perhaps to give you an idea how the American military responds in an unconventional manner… they don't follow the rules."

They drove five miles before Hanalin said, "So, we have one week! Guess we better get our 'Welcome' mat ready."

Chin Lee sat frozen in her seat. She had just listened to one of the most profound stories of bravery she had ever heard. She looked out at the countryside, letting her imagination recreate the scenes of battle. Her body trembled.

She did not look at General Hanalin when she said, "You are correct in your estimation of Agent Daggard, General, he *is* crazy—crazy like a fanatic."

He shook his head in acknowledgement.

"Where are we going, General Hanalin?"

"Home!"

Chin stared at him.

"Harlan, Kentucky. I chose Harlan as our CP for a few reasons, Chin. One, it's my home, and two because the enemy can be lured into the mountains and trapped.

"Our second Command Post will be in Bailey, Colorado. It is situated about a mile and a half above sea level. Vehicles have to be modified for the change in altitude or they will overheat and break down. If the enemy gets that far, they will be afoot. We will have a Command Post somewhere on the East Coast; more than likely at Fort Ritchie, and one on the West Coast at Fort Lewis."

He looked over at her. "I think your leaders thought this would be a cake-walk, easy, but we'll make it so hot for them they will rue the day that they made the stupid decision to attack us."

They drove in silence for several miles. Chin sat in awe of the countryside thinking how colorful and beautiful and peaceful it is. As they drove around towering spiral pillars of stone formations 200 feet tall, and up and down mountains about 3, 000 feet above sea level along route 119, Chin's mouth fell open in awed admiration for the country's beauty. "It is beautiful country, General Hanalin. I fear that soon, it will all be destroyed," she said around a forced sigh.

General Hanalin stole a careful glance at her. When he focused his attention back to the road, he said, "You love him...don't you?"

She shifted in her seat so she was facing him. "Is that a statement or a question, General Hanalin?"

"Ha, ha, ha...I súpose it is both. You're wearing your heart on your face."

Chin toughed her face involuntarily, *"Really?"*

"Your cheeks are rosy, and your eyes have that sensual, subtle, bright twinkle shining from them."

"Yes, I love him."

Their breathing and the road-sounds of the tires filled the silence.

After a few minutes had passed, Hanalin cleared his throat. "I do not know when this war will end. Conflicts that people thought would only take weeks lasted years, like the Crusades. According to Skip, they lasted 800 years."

She sat up straight-backed at the mention of his name.

"This war could last a week, a year, or it could be the end of America as we know it, leaving the three of us dead." He paused. "Give him time, Chin. Kristine and Eilis were his world…and there's always Bryanna"

Chin sat in silence, processing the words of wisdom from this father-like man. She came to a sad recognition in that instant that she was passionately in love with a man who may never return that love. *"Who is Bryanna?"*

Hanalin took a deep breath wishing he had kept his mouth shut. He stole a glance at Chin, who was staring at him. He shifted his gaze back to the road. "She's the woman who has captured Skip's heart, as I have stated earlier. I've never met her."

Chin puzzled over this information. "Why is he not with her now?"

Hanalin wanted to sew his mouth shut, but her name was out. "Ask Skip."

She stared at Hanalin. She knew that he would not tell her any more.

"And what about you, General Hanalin, have you never been in love?"

Her question caused memories to explode in his mind. "Oh yes! She was German, and her hair was the color of an autumn morning. Her skin was a rich, dark tan. She loved the semi-nude beaches because of the freedom to choose to wear a bathing suit or go naked.

"I would have to apply the tanning lotion on her body before she could go out into the sun."

Chin studied his facial expressions as he spoke. She smiled. He had loved this woman.

"Her name was Heidi. I met her in Frankfurt, Germany in 1975. The fireworks were instantaneous for the both of us. Skip was best man."

She shuddered at the sudden change in Hanalin's mood, which had gone from happy to somber. She sat placid, waiting for him to continue.

"It was September, 1985. A knock came at our door at 2130 hours. When I opened it, Skip was standing there. His face was cold and hard. His blue eyes were blank and ice-coated. His arms hung at his sides, and he held a handgun in his right hand.

"I knew! I knew immediately why he had come as he stormed passed me, shoving me to the floor, he whispered, 'She's a spy.'"

He choked on the words. "Heidi came into our living room from the kitchen. She appraised the situation quickly.

"Skip told her to get on her knees. She did so. He placed the muzzle of his .45 against her forehead and cocked the hammer."

Chin jumped up in her seat. "*You did nothing?*"

"What could I do? The woman I loved—my wife had betrayed me. Besides, her executioner was Skip Daggard, the terminator of enemy spies."

The vision he had tried to elude for years had burst forth on its own accord.

"Heidi looked at me. 'I love you Mac Arthur Hanalin. I love with all my heart.'"

He shifted in his seat remembering, as he explained to Chin, while his tears began to fall.

"Skip stared at her for a few seconds. Then he turned his head to the left studying her eyes and facial expression. I still cannot believe what happened next."

He took a deep breath reliving those precious moments between life and death.

"Skip released the hammer with his thumb allowing his arm to fall at his side. He reached down for her and helped her to her feet. 'Who,' he asked Heidi. Her response was, 'KGB!'"

Hanalin paused to catch his breath.

"He told her that they would never bother her again. He had been true to his word. On a hot August afternoon, twelve years later, she lay dying in a hospital bed at North Charles in Baltimore. I was holding her left hand. Skip held her right hand. At 1400 hours, she sat up, looked at Skip and said, 'You're going to fall in love with a spy.' She looked at me, kissed me and said, 'I love you Mac Arthur Hanalin with all my heart.'"

Hanalin began to choke on his words. He didn't try to hold back his tears as he burst out crying. "Those were her last words." He had to pull off the road. Mac Arthur Hanalin wiped the water from his face. He looked at Chin Lee. "Two years later, Skip fell in love with Kristine Anderson. She was an MI sergeant at NSA. When Skip was ordered to the White House Communications position, she went with him; she was a Soviet agent. Only he didn't find out until they were on their way to kill a traitor in the White House."

He smiled an honest, friendly smile at her, "And now, you!"

She smiled at him. "Do you think that he will fall in love with me, do you really think so?"

As he drove the vehicle back onto the highway he said, "Just give him time, Chin; just a little time. But remember, his love will be real but not complete.

Chin let out a deep, foreboding sigh. "Time, General Hanalin is something we do not have."

Chin stared at him as hope opened the door to her heart. Then, she made a grave mistake. "Why fight? If we surrender, we can live."

General Hanalin steered the vehicle to the roadside once again stomping the brake pedal down hard. If they had not been wearing seatbelts they would have been thrown through the windshield. "SURRENDER, who the fuck do you think you are talking to?"

His anger filled the compartment with a frosty chill.

She believed the air was crystallizing.

He sat trembling. He gripped the steering wheel, his knuckles turning white. It took him five minutes to collect himself. He shifted to his right, glaring at her. "Why did you say something like that?"

"Because that way we could survive…live"

He stared at her for a few minutes in cold silence.

"Maybe you better get out."

"*What?*"

"Get out of the car."

Fear began to squeeze her…choke her. She could hardly breathe. She started to tremble in its effect on her psyche.

"I do not understand."

"That's apparent! Chin, this isn't about us, you and me and Skip. It's not about the men and women who are going to die. It's about passing down the baton; giving the next generation of Americans freedom. And, DO NOT ever say that word to Skip. He will shoot you immediately."

She trembled. "Do you still want me to get out?"

"That's your choice. But if you choose to continue the journey, then it's to the end, no matter what happens. Understood?" "Yes! I will stay."

General Mac Arthur Hanalin exhaled a deep breath of air as he smiled at Chin Lee, "Figured you would."

Chin looked at her reflection in the passenger window wondering who this Bryanna is, and how important she is to Skip. She spoke the question without thought. "I wonder where he is and what he is doing."

Chapter Thirteen—Out of Options

Secret Room Lincoln Tunnel
Washington, D.C.
Sunday, October 10
1150 hours

Skip sat at the table studying a schematic of the structure and layout of the Capitol Building. He did not make any marks on the blueprints, but logged the places in his mind where he would place the C-4 charges so that the building would implode. "Fewer innocent by-standers will be injured by implosion," he said out loud.

Skip had a hard time keeping his thoughts on his mission. Kristine was everywhere in the confines of the room. He could hear her voice echoing back at him from the walls.

"Your target isn't the Secretary of State, Skip, but the President of the United States."

He could see her defiant face looking at him as he had pressed the muzzle of his weapon against her forehead.

He rose and went to the army cot and ran his hand over her pee stain. He had shared so much with her in this room about 'Nam and himself. He closed his eyes as his tears collected at the corners.

"What did they do to you over there, darling?"

"They killed us. We all died." His eyes flashed open as he realized he had spoken. But to his dismay and complete sadness, Kristine was not there. He meandered over to the grave. He cried because the grave had more of a meaning now. It wasn't just the grave of the ten Civil War soldiers; it was Kristine and Eilis' as well.

"They're going to pay, honey. They're going to pay dearly for what they did to you and our baby. When this is over they're going to wish to God that they had stayed home and had left us alone.

"I promise you, Kristine every one of those spies is going to die, and we're going to crush their military force. We will put all of them to the bayonet."

When he turned to walk back to the table, Skip allowed a long buried memory to come forward. He could see her sitting next to his mother at his gravesite at Arlington, the sounds of the 21-gun salute and *Taps*, and Bryanna taking the triangular flag from the Military Intelligence Sergeant.

Skip stifled his tears sucking down his grief and pain as he picked up his rucksack shifting it over his shoulders. He retrieved his .45 side arm from the table and stuffed it into his shoulder holster, and then walked to the door looking back at the grave. He stood at the door and saluted the grave. "Today another war begins."

"I cannot be with you on this mission, darling, for that, I am truly sorry. We both know that you operate best when you are alone. It appears that your destiny has been set before your birth. Remember, darling that other men and women have stood at the same threshold you now find your self, and most have persevered."

Those were the words his imagination thought Kristine would say… or…had there been a whisper from…?

He stood facing the stone door thinking about truths that were locked away, and when revealed, how many people were privileged to those documents as portions of those truths were allowed to become public knowledge because of the 1997 Freedom of Information Act. However, certain intelligence organizations refused to adhere to such a policy, so some secrets remain beyond the eyes of the public or the government.

Skip pushed on the stone lever with his right hand. The stone wall made a loud grinding sound in the silence as it moved open. He stepped out into the dim lighting of the Lincoln Tunnel. As he pushed on the stone lever to close the door, another memory exploded into his ever-active mind but he fought for control. He managed to suppress that night when Mrs. Daggard's only son died in a rice-paddy during the Southeast Asian War Games. Some Vietnam Veteran had coined the phrase probably a communications operator, but the phrase had caught on; "Southeast Asian war games."

Capitol Building
Washington, D.C.
Sunday, October 10
1400 hours

Congress was in an emergency session. The senators had returned to deliberate on the bill the House had unanimously passed yesterday to delete the Second Amendment from the US Constitution. The democratic controlled Senate was in an uproar. Senators had formed into pro and con groups and the heated debates erupted as each group hurled accusations at the other.

A steady, light rain splattered against the ground.

Skip Daggard stood at the bottom of the white marbled steps leading up to the building. The security in and around the Capitol Building had been beefed up, so there was no way that he could simply walk in carrying a rucksack over his shoulders containing one hundred eighty pounds of C-4, and a concealed weapon.

While he stood there staring at the building, a thought infiltrated his conscious. He spoke in silence to himself. "There're many good folks in there, and we're going to need some of them to rebuild." This was not a new notion; he had given considerable thought to this idea while he had stood over the grave of the Civil War soldiers in his hideout.

When the crowd dissipated, he took out his cell phone. He dialed in a code-specific number and waited.

"Capitol Building, Security Sergeant Johnson speaking, how may I help you, Mr. Vice President?"

"Sergeant Johnson, the president wants to meet with Senator's Henderson, Brock, Gari, Zane, Murphry, and Tully; you have that?"

"Yes, sir," he repeated the names.

"They are not to divulge their leaving to anyone and neither are you...understood?"

"Yes, sir, understood."

Skip closed his cell phone and put it away.

Federal Police Officer Johnson stood just inside the doorway to the Senate gasping in shocked horror to the mayhem before him. "Jesus," he said out loud, "if someone doesn't come in and break this up it will turn into fisticuffs."

He boldly stepped away from the door into the interior of the Senate looking for his quarry. To his joy, he found them together. "Ladies and gentlemen, the six of you must come with me right now."

Once out in the lobby, Officer Johnson explained, "I just received a call from the Vice President. The president wants you six at the White House immediately. You are not to tell anyone you are leaving. Let's go!"

Fifteen minutes after Skip had spoken to Johnson, he saw the six senators walk down the steps of the Capitol Building and get into a black, oversized Cadillac and drive in the direction of the White House. Skip had ordered the vehicle prior to contacting the FPO Officer.

Skip left the Capitol Building complex. He walked the few miles to the subway station near the old Redskins' ball park. He went down a set of stairs to the subway platform and waited. Once the train had pulled away, and all of the people had gone, he jumped down to the tracks and began to walk into the tunnel. He route stepped for fifty yards before he came to the small blinking red light that indicated he had reached his destination.

He blended against the cold, damp, gray wall for several seconds as he studied his back trail and the tunnel in the direction the train had disappeared. Once he was satisfied that no one else was there, he turned to the wall and placed his hand against a metal plate directly under the blinking red light. A four feet wide by six feet high section of the wall slid open. Skip stepped in, moving with rapid steps into the corrugated-pipe system. He stopped three feet into the system, turned, counted to four, then turned and moved towards his ultimate destination once the wall had closed.

Capitol Building
Sunday, October 10
1435 hours

Just as Skip reached the subterranean level of the Capitol Building, the six senators were being ushered into the Oval Office and General Hanalin was seventy miles from Harlan, Kentucky.

Skip climbed up an iron ladder fastened to a wall of a ventilation chute. He came out of a steel door into the control room of the building where all of the machinery for the heating and AC units was located. He moved deftly and swiftly, placing the C-4 charges around the entire basement at exact infrastructure locations—locations he had memorized from the blueprints he had studied in his secret room.

He knelt down on the gray-painted cement floor. Skip connected several wires to the plus and negative terminals on the detonation device. As he turned the silver wing nuts tightly, an eerie sensation swirled around him like a dark shroud. "War. Why couldn't they have just left us alone?"

He raised his head staring as if he could see through the ceiling looking upon the faces of the members of Congress. His breathing became labored. Skip Daggard sighed. His vision was flooded with the sites of three twin tower complex buildings crumbling. According to reports of the structural design, the buildings were constructed to implode instead of explode. But there had been one slight problem with that theory and explanation, so he and three of his colleagues had spent fifty hours studying films and footage of the collapse of those buildings and blueprints of the structure. They had come to a singular conclusion: Explosives had been strategically deployed at ground level in order for the buildings to collapse in the manner in which they had. After all, isn't that precisely what he was doing? Yet, two questions he had were never answered: Who was taking the videos of the planes, and how did they know to be there? And two, what was wrong with the structural look of those planes? As he tightened the last wing nut, he sat straight up. "Goddamn," it came to him, "of course, those planes were drones…son of a bitch!"

Then, a nagging persistence seeped out of his brain, which made Skip sit up and take notice. "Suppose," he whispered to his detonation device, "suppose those who had placed the charges were US operatives. It wouldn't be the first time the American people had been duped into a war by their sworn, elected officials. "Wasn't it President Franklin Roosevelt and his three top Naval Intelligence Officers who conceived "the splendid arrangement," an eight point plan to antagonize Japan into attacking Pearl Harbor in order to bring America into World War Two?"

Skip knelt on his knees sucking down several breaths of stale air, thinking, "If Roosevelt hadn't had the balls to do what was needed, Europe and Asia might have fallen. Canada, the US, and all of the South American countries would have found themselves surrounded by two huge opposing forces and ordered to surrender or be destroyed.

He thought about the Oklahoma bombing. It was that one frontal view which had brought him to his feet, "What the *fuck*, over!"

He had gone to three EOD (explosive ordinance division) experts assigned to the White House. They confirmed his belief that bombs had been placed on several floors. It had been the concave shape of the building after the explosions, and the fact that every floor had been destroyed, which convinced them. When evidence came up missing, it was apparent to Skip that the FBI had been the agency specifically targeted.

"And there was the American Revolution! All the colonial leaders wanted was the King to ratify the Articles of Confederation and stop seizing colonial ships and its men and cargo on the open seas. In other words, stop stealing from the purses of the wealthy leaders of the American colonies.

"Then one day Thomas Jefferson reads his summary after three days of heated discussion to the colonial representatives in Philadelphia, and, the 'American Experiment' is given its breath of life, and that summary would eventually become the Preamble to the American Declaration of Independence. Thirteen colonies became thirteen United States without an army or navy, and were about to duke it out with the most powerful military force at the time."

Skip reviewed several scenarios in his mind for the thousandth time. He could walk into the Senate and shoot the spies, but he would be shot down before he could kill all 107. Another option was to snipe them as they left the Capitol Building, but, again, he would not be able to take them all out.

He checked the tightness of the wing nuts. He tugged on the wires insuring that they were secured while arguing with himself about his course of action. One other option persisted: He could take out the spies at their quarters. Again, he dismissed this option because it would allow for the majority to seek refuge with their comrades.

Skip shook his head. "Well," he said out loud, "millions of Americans have been debating the idea of a revolution for years, which meant starting all over with a new Congress." His smart-ass comment did not produce a smug smile.

Skip Daggard rested his chin on his chest with his eyes closed. What he was about to do went against his grain and attacked his principles. He tried again to search for an alternative; there was none. "After all," he stated to the machinery, "didn't I take an oath to defend my people against all foreign and domestic enemies."

Slowly, he gained his feet. A deep, heavy sigh escaped from his lungs as he took one more look around. "Well, this is war," he mumbled, "and in war there is always collateral damage...non-combatant casualties... except for those spies who are about to get theirs."

As Skip Daggard retraced his steps, he whispered out a promise to those who were about to die, "The enemy will pay dearly for your sacrifices."

Skip left the subterranean basement of the Capitol Building through the same tunnel system he had used to gain access to the building. He leaned against a square, white tiled pillar on the underground platform waiting for the train to depart and the people to leave. Once he was alone, Skip removed the remote firing mechanism from his right coat pocket as he walked toward the stairs. When his left foot touched down on the third cement step, he flipped open the black cover and tripped the silver toggle switch with his right thumb.

The ground shook topside with earthquake force as smoke and soot swirled down the steps coating him with gray soot.

He never looked back at the destruction as he marched down the street full of people rushing past him shouting and crying. The wail of sirens from emergency vehicles sounded like Banshees moaning for lost souls as they raced to the scene of the destruction.

One mile from the Washington Monument, Skip stopped. He placed the palm of his left hand against the bark of a tree and lowered his head. He wanted to vomit, but all he could do was cry. His sorrow lasted thirty seconds. Skip drank deep of the cool, fresh air, then stood straight on his feet.

As he walked toward the Washington Monument, he began to say to himself, "I am a soldier of my land, willing to give my all for the oath I took. I am a soldier of my land, sworn to defend my people against all foreign and domestic enemies. I am a soldier of my land..."

White House
Washington, D.C.
Oval Office
Sunday, October 10
1455 hours

While Skip was stepping out on the platform, President Short and Vice President Aims stood up looking puzzled at the senators as they entered the Oval Office. "I take it by your presence, that the Senate has cast their vote."

Senator Adal Gari, a Teutonic name meaning noble spear-maid, looked at her colleagues, then back at the president. "Sir," she said, "we are here at the request of the Vice President. We were informed that you wished to discuss this issue with us."

President Short glared at Vice President Aims.

"What the *hell* are you talking about? Sir, I have no idea..."

An explosion shook the windows at the White House with such violent force that the outer panes of several windows actually shattered. Everyone in the Oval Office crumbled to the floor. Several Secret Service agents flooded the Oval Office falling across its occupants, protecting them.

Secret Service Director Kimble rushed into the Oval Office. "Mr. President, we have to go...NOW!"

Secret Service officers began yanking the president and vice president and the senators to their feet. The White House was a blur of activity as Secret Service and Marine guards ran through the building gathering up its occupants, and forcing their charges to the basement, through a tunnel, and into a waiting train. The evacuation took less than ten minutes.

Kentucky, Route 119
Sunday, October 10
1515 hours

General Hanalin was thinking of Carol. She had been waiting patiently for six years. Now, on the "Eve of Destruction," he would propose to her. He was focusing on her image, her golden hair streaked with silver, the freckle-lines under her hazel eyes, and her straight-backed plump figure.

The news boomed out from the speakers of his vehicle's radio. "My God! My God, the US Capitol Building has just been destroyed."

General Hanalin had to pull over to the side of the road because his tears made it impossible for him to see the road.

The commentator was crying as he announced; "Emergency vehicles are rushing to the scene. My God, the whole building is destroyed. It's feared there are no survivors. The full Congress was in session."

General Hanalin rested his forehead against the steering wheel. Chin Lee sat against the backrest of her seat in complete shock. "*He killed all of those people!*"

Hanalin turned his head so he could look at her. "Now, Chin, do you understand why there is no simple explanation to your question?"

She stared at him.

He wanted to smile, but could not muster the will. He sat somber wiping his tears from his face. "There is no accounting for Skip Daggard. He plays by his own set of rules; rules he often makes up in accordance to situations.

"That's why North Vietnam had put a fifty thousand dollar price on his head. That's why he was so effective during the Cold War. There's just no accounting for Skip Daggard."

They sat in silence listening to the news. "Washington, D.C. has been shut down. National Guard units are rushing to seal off all roads.

They have surrounded the White House. We are going to Beth Decker at the scene; Beth?"

"Yes, John it's been confirmed that the Capitol Building has been imploded," she said through her tears, "and…and…my God, John… my God, there are no survivors—our Congress has been wiped out. I'll get back to you."

He looked over at Chin Lee. She returned his stare. He exhaled four long breaths "So, it begins. Skip has accomplished two things: One, he's just given the world a wake up call; and two, he's stopped the enemy from disarming the American people. "How long do you think it will take the Communist Coalition leaders to respond?"

There was no hesitation with Chin Lee's response, "Immediately! There is too much at stake."

"Yeah, like world domination, huh?"

Chin Lee stared out of her passenger window studying her reflection in the window. Her words came out as a whisper, "He destroyed the entire building…killing all of those people!"

General Hanalin drove their vehicle back onto the roadway. "Skip must have rationalized that it was his only option. There's something you should know about Skip; he's a patriot. When it comes to the American people, he'll fight. Skip has a simple philosophy, war is man's insanity against himself and the only rule is…to win.

"It's the American soldier's attitude. An enemy can slap us around a little, but when they attack our people, then we're goin' to kick ass. Skip is the epitome of that attitude."

They listened to the news in silence for several miles. Most of the story was a repeat because firefighters were still fighting the blaze and no rescue attempts could be made. However, according to news reports, there would be no survivors.

Chin Lee sat lost in her thoughts. She began to recall stories that she had heard about Agent Skip Daggard while she was growing up. That he was a vicious protagonist, and a killer of women and children. He had no morals or scruples. Now, she realized that everything she had been told was a lie. Agent Daggard does have morals and values, and he is the epitome of a true soldier. She exhaled a deep, long sigh. It all seemed so easy the way the Soviets had presented their quick and decisive war against the Americans. When her father had voiced his question regarding Agent Daggard, General Ashfort Bardolph waved his hand. "He is retired," General Bardolph had said, "and if he meddles, then Daggard will be killed swiftly and efficiently."

Chin Lee exhaled another sigh. She knew in her heart that her countrymen had trusted the Soviets—and now? The Soviets were going to be hard-pressed to win, and might get her people killed. She watched the countryside of Kentucky pass her window. Still staring out of her window, Chin asked, "*Who is he*, General Hanalin?"

General Hanalin took deep breaths as he pondered her question. "Hmmm, that question again, huh? As I said, Chin there is no easy way to explain Skip, and what he has just done is a prime example of what I mean."

He sighed then began. "I guess circumstances shaped him just as much as his loyalty. When he first came to me in Vietnam, he was fuming with anger and hatred. All he wanted to do was to get out into the jungle and kill...and...die."

Chin Lee stared at him.

"Years later he shared with me what it was like to face the enemy and die. To have his soul taken from his body, and get so close to Heaven only to be returned to earth.

"I had looked into his sad eyes, Chin, eyes that were dead. Then he said, 'That's when the demon came...the rage, the hate, the need—his need to kill...and...his need to die.' He never shared with me after that, and he never went anywhere without his weapon. I mean, you would have thought that M-14 had grown out of his hand."

A light snow began to fall. General Hanalin was arguing with himself, wondering how much he should share with her. After all, she had come here with an army to take over his country.

He stole a glance at her while she was staring out her window. She saw his reflection in the glass and turned to face him. "You do not trust me?"

"No, I do not."

"That is accepted behavior, General Hanalin. I would expect nothing less."

"Why did you defect?"

Chin Lee stared out of her window again examining those reasons which made her a traitor. It was five full minutes before she answered.

General Hanalin had to turn on the wiper blades because the snow was steady yet still light.

"There are three reasons why I have defected, General Hanalin. I suppose you have concluded that Agent Daggard is reason number one. The second reason is what he explained to me about freedom and how the American people will fight to their deaths to pass on that freedom to their children. It was the excitement in his voice which made me take notice and question the plausibility of our victory. And, of course, you know the third reason...President Huong had my father killed.

"But who can account for the heart, General Hanalin, when it begins to pound against the chest, pulsating erratically, pushing blood through the veins causing lightheadedness? Who, General Hanalin, can account for the heart?"

He smiled a fatherly, understanding smile.

They listened to more news reports in silence as they drove toward an unknown future.

Chapter Fourteen—Spies' In-Charge

Lincoln Tunnel
Washington, D.C.
Sunday, October 10
1600 hours

Skip Daggard stood a quarter mile from the Washington Monument near the bushes close to the parking area and the World War Two Memorial. He studied the area in deep concentration, but no one was around because they had rushed up streets towards the destruction.

Once he was satisfied the coast clear, Skip swiftly removed the man cover lid, dropped down into the opening, found his footing on the ladder, and then slipped the cover back into place.

He made his way to the Lincoln Tunnel through this old section of the Washington Tunnel. It was the exact tunnel that he and Kristine had used three years ago to evade capture by the CIA.

Skip knew that he wasn't being followed, yet, old habits die hard. He used his escape and evasive maneuvers for forty minutes switch-backing through tunnel systems; he was a soldier again. He finally arrived at his secret hiding place.

As the stone wall was opening, Director Kimble of the Secret Service was contacting Director Pike of the CIA. "Lima Papa this is Kilo, my package is Sierra-Alpha-Foxtrot-Echo, Kilo clear."

"Leo Pike this is Kimble, the president is safe, Kimble clear."

Skip pulled on a stone and a section of the wall slid open. He stepped inside after a long look up and down the tunnel. He entered the room and pushed on the stone to close the wall. He fell back against the cold, damp earth stone. He could feel the damp seep into his back through his clothing. Skip Daggard crumpled inside. His tears fell as he let out his pain and grief. He raised his head from his chest. He stared over at the grave. "Today, sergeant I've killed Americans. It isn't the first time. But this time...this time..." The memory exploded from his eyes.

The jungle twenty miles south of Phnompenh reeked of foliage, decay, and roasted flesh. Skip tried to outdistance the odor but he could not. He fell to the jungle floor and broke out in a gut wrenching, fit of tears. He poked into his eyes, trying to rip the images of their twisted, pain-etched faces from his eyes. He cried out, "I had to, you know that I had to...you guys were being overrun."

"That wasn't the worst," he said to the grave as he crossed the room and started the generator. "No, sir, that wasn't the worst!" Tears began to form at the corners of his eyes. "The Ashau Valley...that was the worst...we dropped bombs on ten thousand of our own on that fucked up day." Skip grabbed the corner of the table, which stood in the center of the room, and let loose his pain and grief. Thirty seconds later, Skip sucked it up and whispered, "It was a ploy, a sucker play to draw the enemy into the valley, then fly-boys were to annihilate them from the air. One top-secret flash message...the last message in a series of four that were transmitted to set up the whole operation...the last funkin' message to have our guys withdraw was never sent, and those ground-pounders paid for the mistake."

Skip wiped away more tears from his eyes and spoke out loud, "I hope you're recruiting our army, Mac. I pray that you are because those bastards are goin' to pay."

Skip Daggard crumbled into a chair at the army green field table. It took him five minutes to collect himself. He began to write out his message to the president.

Harlan, Kentucky
Carol Blanche's house
Sunday, October 10
1700 hours

They drove along Route 119 towards Harlan. A creek about eight feet wide ran parallel with the highway into Harlan. Mountains surrounded the small town.

General Hanalin drove down the main street through the town, and then he maneuvered his Tahoe left onto an asphalt driveway a quarter mile from town. "Well, we're here," he said.

The snow and rain had stopped. The gray sky threatened more. He stood holding onto the door of his vehicle while his aching legs gained their strength. He said, looking up at the sky, "We'll either get more snow, rain, or both; it feels like it could snow."

He walked stiff-legged around the SUV and opened the door for Chin Lee. When they started up the cement walk towards the front door, Carol came rushing out of the door. She skidded to a stop when she saw Chin.

The question in her eyes held daggers. *"Mac?"*

As they approached, Hanalin spoke with authority, "Chin Lee this is my fiancée, Carol Blanche. Carol this is Chin Lee formally of the North Korean Army. She's with Skipper."

Carol glared at them. "Is that so," she said in a belligerent tone, "and how does Kristine feel about that?"

Hanalin strolled over to her and took Carol in his arms. She made an attempt to fight him but lost her will as soon as he kissed her. He held her close feeling the tears building up at the corners of his eyes. "She and Eilis are dead." He waited ten seconds for his words to seep into her brain.

"What!"

"They were killed by Soviet spies. Skip killed the spies, and then he rescued me from spies that were keeping me under house arrest at the Pentagon."

Carol stared at him in shocked disbelieve. "Mac, the Capitol Building had been destroyed. And there had been an explosion near the White House."

Hanalin looked off toward the west at a threatening sky. He looked down at Carol through sad eyes. "I will explain it all, Carol, right now we need to get inside. Please contact your brother and the rest of your clan. They need to be here… now. Do you have some clothes that will fit Chin?"

She glared at Chin for a few seconds before her eyes softened. "I don't understand, Mac. Kristine and Eilis are dead?"

General Hanalin nodded his head. Once inside he explained, then he asked, "What explosion near the White House?"

"It's being kept hush-hush, as if being quiet about it will pacify the people." Carol turned to Chin, "You can find something in that closet." Carol showed her.

"Some news reports say that there has been only one explosion—the Capitol Building, but that the White House has also been affected."

Chin stood by the closet door, afraid to open it. She made a quick surveillance of the foyer. The solid wooden front door was behind her. The closet door was five feet in front of her. The small living room was sparse of furniture, and the dining room was just off of the kitchen. There was a hallway leading to a bathroom and a bedroom and a set of stairs that rose to the second floor landing. The living room and dining room walls were painted off-white.

Carol came to her. She opened the closet door. "Rummage through these clothes hanging on the wooden hangers, and select something that fits you. Carol looked again at the brown uniform Chin was wearing. "We're gonna have to bury that; my brother fought in the Korean conflict."

Hanalin came up to them. "Skip wanted her to wear it incase we were captured. That way, she could say she had been held as a prisoner."

She showed Chin to the bathroom and made the calls which Hanalin had directed her to make.

By the time he came down stairs dressed in ACU's (Army Combat Uniform) and entered the kitchen, several men stared at him. Mac Arthur Hanalin stepped over to Carol's kitchen table and laid out the map Skip had given him. As he studied the faces of the men in the room, he made a command decision; these would be his officers, some of his generals in the field.

Twelve men gathered around the table staring at the map. General Hanalin thought, "How ironic! Jesus had twelve disciples at his Last Supper; one would betray Him."

Carol was fixing coffee at a counter. Chin Lee came into the kitchen dressed in faded Levis and a white chiffon blouse. The men looked up at her. General Hanalin gave her a serious and stern review.

"Gentlemen," Hanalin said, "this is Chin Lee. She is the one who provided us with this map."

Greetings were dispensed. Chin accepted a cup of coffee from Carol.

Ted, Carol's brother asked the question, "Who the *hell* is she?"

General Hanalin ignored Ted's question. "Gentlemen, the United States have been invaded. The enemy is here entrenched across America. They are waiting for their orders to attack. If you look at the red line which begins in Maine and runs down the eastern seaboard, swings inland over to California, then up to Washington, that gentlemen is where the Communist Coalition forces are entrenched.

"They have spies in our government and many within our intelligence communities as well. Skip Daggard is taking out the spies. What we have to do is put an army together. We have to align our forces along this blue line, which parallels the enemy's line."

General Hanalin took a deep breath and exhaled, "and that, gentlemen, is where you come in."

The men who were gathered around the table in the quiet kitchen sipping coffee stared at him. The two women were leaning against the countertop near the stove sipping their coffee and listening to what General Mac Arthur Hanalin was saying.

"You must have heard by now what has happened in Washington." Everyone nodded. "That was Skip opening the ball. There were one hundred and seven spies in the House and Senate."

The men gathered in the small kitchen with its blue walls with white flowers, stared at him. Hanalin waved Chin over to the table. The men looked at her. "Chin is going to explain everything. Pay attention."

She did not know how to start. She had not been expecting to explain anything. Chin felt trapped by the presence of these Americans. She swallowed then she recovered her military bearing. After all, she was a soldier, and these men were to be part of an army that did not exist.

"Where you see red dots, those are targets for North Korean nuclear missiles. The sickles indicate Soviet nuclear missile targets..."

Ted interrupted, "Wait a minute! How do you know this?"

Chin Lee looked over at General Hanalin. When he did not speak, she looked into each man's face gathered around the table. "General Hanalin did not give a good introduction. I am Colonel Chin Lee formally of the North Korean Communist Army."

It took a few seconds for her words to seep into logic circuits of their brains. Ted jumped back from the table glaring at Hanalin, "Mac, what the fuck!"

Ted wasn't just Carol's brother; he was a Korean and Vietnam War veteran. He had been a Special Forces Intel operative, and retired in 1980 as a colonel. He knew Skip Daggard. They had met three different times in the jungles of sunny Southeast Asia. One time, they had to fight their way out of Cambodia just as President Nixon was telling the American people that US forces were not engaged in any military action in that region.

"She has defected to our side," Hanalin piped in.

"Yeah, what does Skip have to say about this?" asked Ted.

General Hanalin sighed. He had anticipated some flack.

"'Keep an eye on her, Mac. If she gives you any indication that she's snowing us, shoot her.'"

Chin Lee glared at General Hanalin. So, she though, that is what those two had been whispering about before they all departed from the bunker.

Carol went around filling their cups. She stopped in front of Chin Lee. She looked into Chin Lee's eyes for several seconds then she smiled. Still looking at Chin Lee, Carol said, "She's on our side all right; she's in love with Skipper."

NSA
Fort Meade, Maryland
Colonel Deniska's Office
Sunday, October 10
1750 hours

Colonel Alek Deniska, General Bardolph's second-in-command

had taken the helm as Deputy Director of NSA after Bardolphs' demise. Colonel Deniska, in actuality, was a general and second-in-command of the Soviet forces of the Communist coalition forces. He had graduated from West Point in 1985, and advanced through the ranks in intelligence to be assigned under his leader at NSA.

He wore his blond-grayish hair in a nineteen fifties style flat-top. His face was dotted with pox marks. He walked straight-backed, and studied the world and its occupants through gunmetal blue eyes, and he hated everything that was not Soviet.

Colonel Deniska sat in his captain's chair in his office at NSA. Sweat beads forced themselves from his pores on his face. He sat, crushed, as if he was Atlas, but all at once the world became too heavy for him to support. "U-n-b-e-l-i-e-v-a-b-l-e," he blurted out to Major Pete Rouke who was a Colonel in the Soviet forces.

"He killed all of those people including one hundred and seven of our people. I like this man. He thinks like me."

Major Rouke rose in an easy movement from his chair. He leaned on his commander's desk glaring at his leader. "I thought he was supposed to be dead!"

Colonel Deniska rubbed his chin with his left hand. "Yes! I wonder what happened to Colonel Lee." He waved his hand through the air and jumped to his feet. "We have to attack now. Make it happen."

Major Rouke stared at him. "We did not disarm the Americans!"

"No, and we will not be able to do so. We will attack simultaneously— the Americas and Europe. We will engage our entire force."

"But we will have no reserves!"

Colonel Deniska sighed, lowering his head. "I know." Breathing heavily, he stared at his desktop. Then in a fit of rage, he grabbed his desk under the center drawer and flipped it over, screaming. "One man, how? How can this be? General Bardolph ordered his execution in 1975, and yet the bastard escaped. And now we are so close to achieving our destiny and one son of a bitch…"

Colonel Deniska fell back into his chair. "How can this be?" Colonel Deniska shook his head. "Genocide will be the Americans' price."

"*Sir!*"

"We will kill them until they submit."

"Yes, sir" Major Rouke smiled.

When Major Rouke left to carry out his orders, Colonel Deniska lit a cigar. He spoke around the tip of his cigar, "The whole damn building! He destroyed the w-h-o-l-e building. That damn patriot should be on our side," he said, admiring Daggard's deed. "I will have to recall the rest of our agents before Daggard can kill them," he explained to his cigar.

He looked out of his west window toward Route 295. He could see the gray smoke rising from Washington. "The w-h-o-l-e d-a-m-n b-u-i-l-d-i-n-g—marvelous, but try as you may, Agent Skip Daggard, your people's reign is about to end."

Colonel Deniska turned from his window. He spoke as if he was facing Skip Daggard. "It will be over by Christmas. We Soviets will have achieved our destiny. Then we will put you Americans in your place; those who have survived, that remain." He began to laugh a sadistic, hysterical laugh.

However, Colonel Deniska was unaware of one factor, the Fates. Those mystical creatures who have guided Skip Daggard through his entire life, and as Colonel Deniska sat down at his desk enjoying his cigar, the Fates were mobile, guiding Skip Daggard down his life's road in accordance to *his* destiny.

Chapter Fifteen—Little Pentagon

Fort Ritchie, Maryland
Sunday, October 10
1812 hours

The underground rail project had begun in 1985 and was completed in August 2003. After September 11, 2001, the project became priority number one. The train utilized most existing rail lines, both underground and over land. At Frederick, Maryland, the rails went underground through the Catoctin Mountains and ended at an underground platform under the communications center where the underground "Little Pentagon" is located at Fort Ritchie.

By now, most Americans and the rest of the world had heard of the destruction of the US Capitol Building and the deaths of the senators and representatives.

Once the train had passed the Langley area, President Short looked across at Senator Gari. "You stated that an FPO had instructed you to go to the White House according to the Vice President's orders?"

Senator Adal Gari smoothed out her gray skirt and white silk blouse. "Yes, Mr. President that is what we had been instructed to do. We weren't allowed to announce our departure either."

Silence filled the car while President Short paced the length of the plush carpeted compartment. He was a tall, thin man with military bearing, he walked straight-backed. He studied everyone present in the train car, then he turned back to the senators, "Six senators, three Republicans and three Democrats," he said out loud, "but no representatives; is there a significance here?"

President Short turned to Secret Service Director Kimble. "Kim, what in the hell is going on?"

"We do not have a report yet, but we do know that the building had been imploded."

President Short fell into a chair. He stared at Director Kimble for a few seconds. "Terrorists wouldn't have done *that*!"

"No sir! We also know that no one survived."

The president rose in a slow, unhurried motion. Once he gained his feet, President Short turned to look at Vice President Jack Aims, "Are we under attack; if so, from whom?"

The Presidential families sat subdued and silent, as did the Secret Service Agents.

Director Kimble was called to the communications car.

He returned to the president seven minutes later. His face was pale and grave. Kimble handed the president a communiqué.

President Short began to read the message in silence then stopped. "What in the *hell* is this, Kimble? We've lost the Pentagon?"

Director Kimble choked on his worlds, "Yes, sir! We are definitely under attack."

"Who the hell is in charge?"

No one moved or answered due to the immediate shock.

Director Kimble stepped forward. "Sir, I believe we can surmise that the enemy, whoever he is, is in charge."

At 1815 hours the Presidential train stopped at the platform of the Little Pentagon. It was a subdued president and his entourage who entered the building and found chaos.

Sunday, October 10
1830 hours

At 1830 hours, Major Rouke was moving troops through the Lincoln Tunnel, under Washington, D.C. while Colonel Deniska was crushing out his cigar in his office at NSA. General Hanalin and Chin Lee were discussing the map with Ted and other, soon-to-be field officers, while Skip Daggard was about to open the wall to his secret room and step out into the Lincoln Tunnel. All hell was about to break loose.

Major Rouke walked tall, which gave an exaggerated height to his five feet, eleven inches. He looked down his nose at everyone through steel, cold, gray eyes, and accepted a fact that General Bardolph had been an incompetent, bungling fool. The first and only time he had encountered Agent Daggard was thirty-four years ago in Frankfurt, Germany. Bardolph had Daggard in chains, yet somehow Daggard had escaped.

Major Rouke ran his index finger of his left hand along the bullet scar on the left side of his face. He had been on patrol with an NVA unit in Cambodia in December 1969. If he had not stumbled over some overgrowth, the bullet would have blown his head off. The NVA officer had stared at him. "Daggard," is all he had said.

Major Rouke had his men move quietly through the tunnel; as quiet as two thousand soldiers could maneuver through the poorly lit subterranean passageways. They were to position themselves near the exit at the White House. When the order was given, they were to storm the White House, kill everyone inside and take control of the government.

Skip Daggard was about to open the wall to his hideout when he detected noises coming from the tunnel. He listened for a few seconds, then he went to a locker and took out a hand held, micro dish listening device. He put on the earphones, and then placed the cone against the wall. He heard the sounds of shuffling feet—many feet.

Colonel Deniska marched across his office floor to the inside east wall. He ran his finger of his right hand along the backside of the right frame of George Washington's picture. He activated the dime-sized button imbedded in the frame. The picture frame swung open revealing a wall mounted, gray-faced safe. Colonel Deniska turned the tumblers with deft fingers. He placed the top-secret documents into a brown, leather briefcase, closed the door, and secured the gold frame.

Colonel Deniska was preparing to leave NSA. He sat at his desk writing down his plans. He had to modify Bardolph's original plans because everything had changed with Daggard's interference.

He rose and went for a cup of coffee, and then he sat down at his desk. As he sipped his coffee, he reviewed his plans. "SHIT! I hate to engage the entire force, but I have no choice. *Damn* you, Daggard."

Colonel Deniska finished his coffee. "It is time to leave." He would drive home, eat supper then have his wife and son pack a few essentials, then they would join the forces in the underground bunker system in Tyson's Corner, Virginia, where he would conduct "Operation Takeover." However, Colonel Deniska had committed the same huge mistake that his predecessor had, by underestimating Agent Skip Daggard and the American People. He also failed to comprehend past events in order to understand just how far, and to what extent Skip Daggard would go in order to protect his people.

Major Rouke placed his troops in the tunnel near the entrance into the White House. "This is going to be our difficult hour," he said in their native tongue. "We MUST be still until our orders come."

Skip Daggard waited one half hour after the noise in the tunnel subsided. He put away his listening device, retrieved another weapon and ammo bag, and then he opened the section of wall. His M-16 A4 was locked and loaded with a thirty round clip. He stepped out into the tunnel with his weapon aimed from his hip ready to mow down any antagonists. No one challenged him. He closed the wall by pushing on a stone. Once the wall was secured, he waited, listening for another fifteen minutes. He detected a faint sound. Now he knew where the enemy had gone. He argued with himself whether to engage or proceed to Langley.

His adrenaline washed over him. His heart began to pound in his chest as his blood rushed to his head. He stood at the line of demarcation, or, the battle line. Once troops moved up to this point, there was no turning back. A smile cracked his somber face. Skip Daggard knew the history of Washington, D.C. A history that would set in motion the War of 1812 and as the blueprint for the city was being drafted, so too was the ground being broken for the American Civil War.

In 1792, many of the southern representatives had approached President Washington about moving the government and capital closer to the center of the country, and out of New York. Washington agreed, and helped establish the area along the Potomac as the new capital.

Skip allowed a sardonic smile to crack his face as John Travolta's words, from the movie, *Michael*, came to him. Travolta, playing the Angel, Michael, faced a bull. He declared "BATTLE," then engaged the huge, black beast. He did it again in a bar against several human antagonists.

"Okay, Skipper," he said silently to himself, "the enemy is here. It's time for... battle." He turned back to the wall and moved the stone. The wall opened, and he went inside to his arsenal locker. Skip retrieved a small black explosives trigger device, and once again stepped out into the tunnel, closing that section of wall.

Major Rouke and some of his men turned their heads looking back down the tunnel. The grating sound the wall had made, while opening and closing, had reached their ears. He gave an order for the last unit to defend their rear. However, he would soon learn that he had given a futile order; his last order.

Skip Daggard was a man of puzzles. He gathered information, and then used that information to create a puzzle to solve a problem. Once the problem was solved, he would act accordingly. He had studied the formation of D.C., and why the capital had to be moved from New York. Skip was also a strategist. During his studies of ancient and modern warfare, he tried several strategies in the taking of the US. He knew that the Cold War had not ended with the downfall of the Soviet Union and the Berlin Wall in 1989. The Communist doctrine was quite specific, and it did not lend to any conclusion except world domination, no matter how long it took.

In theory, he could only make assumptions until 9/11 but then it became clear that Washington had once again become a target for destruction or takeover. So Skip followed his instincts. It took him a year to place the charges. He knew that he was loyal, honest, and practical, and, sometimes, cunning as an animal. Therefore, like an animal caught in a trap, he had to sever a limb so that the body could survive. That limb, of course, in this case, being the White House and president.

Skip walked a mile through the Lincoln Tunnel. He came to another movable wall and opened it by pushing on the same sand colored stone as his hideout's wall. A small section of the wall opened. Skip stood on the threshold for a minute. He reached out as if stroking Kristine's face. "Do you remember the question you asked me three years ago when we stood here, Kristine? 'Do you think they will find us, Skip?'"

He allowed himself a moment of grief. "I told you, no honey, they won't because I know something they don't." He inhaled trying to smell her perfume.

"Well darlin', another enemy is here, and guess what? Yeah! I know something they don't, but they're soon gonna find out."

Skip Daggard stepped across the threshold. He turned to face the opening, and then he pushed on a stone. The wall closed. He exited the tunnel system through the precise manhole near Constitution Avenue where CIA Director Rickard had waited for him and Kristine to emerge three years ago, with several of his agents…waiting to kill him and Kristine.

His movements had gone unnoticed due to Washington's ghost town like appearance. The normal crowds that would have been visiting the memorials were staying home. He strolled to the parking lot close to the World War Two Memorial. He spotted a dark colored SUV, and, with purpose of movement, walked up to the vehicle, reached under the rear right wheel-well, and removed a black metal key container.

He removed the key, placed the container in his right jeans pocked, unlocked the driver's door, slipped in behind the steering wheel, and then started the vehicle. He removed the small black trigger device from his camouflaged fatigue jacket, and flipped up a protective cover.

He looked towards the White House, hoping that Secret Service Order #129 had been implemented after the Capitol Building had blown up. Without any expression on his face whatsoever, Skip spoke out into the interior of the vehicle, "What was that phrase that Bruce Willis used to say at the end of his *Die Hard* movies? Oh yeah! Hideous mother fucker," he flipped a toggle switch. The earth near the White House rumbled and shook as smoke escaped into the atmosphere. "Well," Skip said, "that takes care of whoever was down in that tunnel."

He drove towards the Pentagon to quiet a suspicion. He turned around at once. He had seen the military forces surrounding the building. "Fuckin' idiots; we don't need those leaders anyhow."

Skip Daggard drove out of Washington heading for Langley. He could feel depression beginning to set in as it always had during this time of year. Bryanna will have another birthday in twenty-one days; she'll be sixty. He shook his head violently to clear his brain. He didn't have time for depression; his country was at stake.

CIA Headquarters
Langley, Virginia
Sunday, October 10
1915 hours

Leo Pike stood at his window staring out at the two gray and black funnels of smoke rising into the late afternoon sky. His operations officer had been keeping him abreast of the situation in Washington. He knew that the Capitol Building had been imploded, killing the entire Congress. He also knew that Secret Service Order #129 had been implemented, and that the president and vice president were at Fort Ritchie with their families and six senators.

What no one seemed to know, however, what was the cause and effect of the second explosion near the White House? Director Pike turned from his window and shuffled back to his desk with his hands cupped behind his back and his head tilted down. He collapsed into his chair, leaned back, and clasped his hands behind his head staring at the picture of his wife, Julie. He let out a long quiet sigh. "I wish you were still here, Julie I surely do!"

He let a deep sigh escape from his lungs.

"What was it that Skip Daggard had told me once? 'In our business, wives are a liability.'"

He clutched the picture frame in his trembling hands. Leo Pike could see it all as if the events were happening right now. But it wasn't happening now. The events unfolded in the fall of nineteen ninety-eight.

Skip stormed into the command center in the basement of NSA. He walked up to Leo, "What's the situation?"

"They took her, Skip," Leo said as he handed Skip a note. They want me to turn over top-secret information about our stealth bomber or they'll kill her."

Skip stood in front of Leo reading the note. "This is from the Russian Secret Service, therefore, this is bullshit—they already have the information they're asking you to provide."

He stared into Skip's eyes as a realization flooded him with dread. "I know. I also recall you warned not to get married while in this business. I'm not like you, Skip. I couldn't walk away from the girl I love."

"Good! You can be the one to kill her. They already know that you're not giving them the information. How long have they had Julie?"

"Twenty-four hours!"

"She's already dead!"

"Skip was right," he said to her picture, "you were already dead."

The ringing of his red phone interrupted his thoughts. It was hidden in his left bottom desk drawer. "SHARK," he used his code name.

"Sniff, Sniff...SNOOPY," another encrypted message. "Prepare to move at a minute's notice." Director Pike stared at the receiver as the dial tone hummed. "Now what in the hell; prepare to move at a minute's notice meant only one thing—attack was imminent."

A knock at his door interrupted his thoughts as his operations officer came in.

"Sir, we have received confirmation from our people at the Federal Building that the Capitol Building has been destroyed by implosion. There are no survivors. All of the senators and representatives and their cabinet have been killed."

Director Pike jumped to his feet. *"Imploded?* So, it's confirmed; no guessing?"

"Yes, sir; there hasn't been any destruction to other structures, but several passersby have been injured. Our agents, FBI, and Homeland Security are at the site right now."

Director Pike rushed across the room and switched on his television. CNN was at the scene reporting as was several other news media. Director Pike studied the destruction with intent interest.

Sam Norton, the operations agent, stared, shocked. "We're not sure how the terrorists managed it yet, sir."

Director Pike stood straight up and glanced over at his operations officer. "Terrorists, Sam? No, they would want mass destruction. Terrorists would have exploded the building causing more destruction and death."

As a helicopter flew around ground zero providing further viewpoints of the disaster, Director Pike began to recognize a specific signature.

"Daggard," he whispered to himself. "Sam, I want updates as they come in from our agents at the disaster site."

"Yes sir. One other thing, sir, the other funnel of smoke near the White House is from the Lincoln Tunnel. Here is one more piece of information." He handed Director Pike a message.

"Sir, the Pentagon has been taken over by a military force. We were fired upon as we tried to gain access to the complex. National Guard units are engaging this huge force right now. Reinforcements have been called up. "

Signed,

Agent Brent

"What the hell is going on, sir?"

Pike went to his desk. "Sit down, Sam. The president is at the "Little Pentagon," and I just received an encrypted message from Chief Daggard."

Leo Pike fumbled with some papers on his desk. He looked into the eyes of his friend. "Sam, what I gather from Daggard's message is that attack is imminent."

Sam leaned forward, "Sir, you mean the United States is under attack?"

Leo Pike rose to his six-foot height. "Yes! I don't know who our enemies are. He didn't elaborate."

He turned and went to his window looking off towards D.C.

"Sam, the destruction in Washington has Skip Daggard written all over it."

"*Sir!*"

Director Leo Pike felt old as he turned to face his subordinate. "Sam, Daggard has been in contact with me; that's why I had you conduct a recall."

When Sam left his office, Director Pike gave more consideration to Skip's coded message, 'Prepare to move at a minute's notice.'

He knew Skip Daggard; he knew him as well as anyone could know him. He and Skip had served together in the 29th MI Group at Fort Meade and NSA, and had worked together on several covert operations. It had been Skip who had tried to save Julie, but failed.

CIA Director Leo Pike knew Skip all right; knew that Skip was not a showboat, nor did he go around killing for…well, almost never. He knew Skip for what he was, not just a MI subversive operative, but specifically, a spy killer. He answered to no one, and he took orders from no one except General Mac Arthur Hanalin.

He stepped back to his window. As he studied the spiral smoke swirling into the eastern sky, his mind went back to Skip's message, 'attack imminent.' His jaw dropped. His mouth became a human flytrap as realization squeezed the air from his lungs. If Skip had done this, as he believed…then…then, "My God," Director Pike blurted out, "then there were spies in the House and Senate. Skip had no alternative. Yet, why didn't he turn it over to NSA?" Skip's earlier order about the helicopters and NSA flooded back into his conscious thoughts. He shivered with realization.

Director Pike turned from his window as an icy chill rippled up his spine causing the director to visit the rest room. "He couldn't go to NSA."

CIA Headquarters
Langley, Tyson's Corner, VA
Sunday, October 10
2130 hours

Skip Daggard drove to the gate at Langley and showed his identification credentials. He entered the building and signed in at the desk. Skip entered Director Pike's office. "Hey, Leo!"

Director Pike jumped to his feet behind his desk. "Skip, you want to tell me what in the *hell's* going on? Washington is burning. The president has gone underground, and Congress has been wiped out. And I just received word that the Pentagon has been breached. Not to mention that I'd appreciate a clarification on your last transmission."

Skip waved his hand. "I have other business first," he said and handed Pike a slip of paper with six names written on it: Scott, Brant, Alex, Bunting, Franks, Bender, and Traffard. "Are they all present?"

Pike studied the names. "Yeah, what the hell's this?"

Skip fixed a cup of coffee then collapsed on a soft cushion on the left side of a brown leather couch close to Director Pike's desk. "Are they all located within the area?"

Director Pike nodded his head. "Jesus, Skip, you look all done in."

Skip took three sips of his coffee. "I'll tell you Leo, I'm tired. I should be relaxing at home enjoying my family and fishing. However, the Communists banded together and decided to put the Americans in their place, Where?"

"Where, what?"

"Where are those agents?"

"Are you going to tell me what's going on?"

Skip took three more sips of his coffee, put down his empty cup and rose to his feet. "They're spies; you coming?"

Director Pike stared at Daggard as he walked toward the door. Daggard turned looking back.

"I'm coming!"

"Stay behind me and don't interfere."

The men walked down a well-lighted corridor to a large room. They entered through a double set of wooden doors. The room was divided into cubicles by six-foot high cushioned partition sections.

They strolled down the main isle looking for their quarry. At the seventh cubicle, Skip could not believe his good fortune. He stepped in and spoke a greeting in Russian. Before the men could collect themselves, they all responded in Russian. Skip took out two weapons and shot them dead. "Now, Leo you want to know what this is all about?"

Leo Pike shook his head.

Skip looked at several agents who had come running with drawn weapons after the shooting. "All right, I will tell all of you. Those asswipes were Soviet spies. They had been sent here for the sole purpose of gathering information and confusing issues to keep our people in the dark. Right now, their forces are preparing to attack."

Skip and Leo sat at the computer the spies had been working on. The spies had managed to shut down the computer when Skip and Leo had approached. Leo booted up the system but could not access any files.

"Wait a minute," Skip said, "that was two tries; one more and we may lose everything. I have the code name for their war, type in *Operation Takeover* using Italics."

Leo typed in the requested words; the computer opened the last file the spies had been working on. "It's encrypted," Leo hissed."

"It's a message to a Lieutenant in Tango-Echo Group at NSA telling him to shut down Star-Wars, and override the capabilities of I-Spy."

Leo stared at Skip. You find this funny?"

Skip looked down at Leo. "Yeah, for as long as these pukes have been operating within our infrastructure they're still a bunch of dumb-shits. I can counter everything they try to do with our system, except for the missiles at White Sands, New Mexico."

Skip stood looking at the agents who had gathered around him and Leo. It was time to bring them into the loop.

"Within a few days, their comrades are going to attack the US and Europe. Those of you who are in guard or reserve units are to report to those units immediately. Now you know."

Skip followed Leo back to his office. Leo held the door open until Skip was inside, then he closed the door behind them. "What do you want me to do with their bodies, Skip?"

Skip walked over and sat down at Leo's desk. He looked up at Leo. "You have an incinerator furnace don't you?"

Leo stared at Skip. "Yes."

Skip reached over Leo's desk. He picked up Julie's picture with gentle fingers. He looked back at Leo. "Burn them!"

Leo glared at Skip. He wanted to shout, "Put her picture down you rotten son of a bitch," but instead he went to his desk and called over the intercom giving orders for the bodies to be burned. Skip became somber as he studied all of the lines on Julie's face, her smile and rosy cheeks. Then, without warning, a memory flashed across his consciousness. Skip Daggard shivered.

Leo stood in front of his desk, studying Skip's facial expressions, or, lack of any facial expressions.

"How much time do we have?"

Skip replaced Julie's picture frame back in its place. He looked up at Leo. "*What?*"

"How much time do we have...before they attack?"

Skip rose to his feet. "I figure three to five days. I've caused a ripple in their plans. I don't think that they want to be fighting in Alaska during the winter..." Skip let his words trail off as he thought of Julie.

"I believe they were going to attack next spring once the weather broke in Alaska. I surmise that their whole plan revolved around disarming the American people, depleting our military forces, taking out the Americas—Canada included, then feign a major assault on Europe, and demand the surrender of all the free countries, since this continent would be in their hands."

Skip began to smile. Leo stood staring at him in utter amazement.

"They overlooked one variable in their calculations."

Skip walked to the window and looked out toward D.C.

Leo couldn't stand the suspense any longer. "What variable?"

Skip turned around to face Leo. "Why, us damn Americans," he said and began to laugh.

Leo couldn't contain himself, "You're crazy!" But he had to laugh as well.

He looked at Leo, and then walked over to a small bar that was situated against the east wall and fixed two cups of coffee. He remembered that Leo liked his coffee black, no sugar. He carried the cups over to a round oak table in the center of the 12x12 square room; both men sat down sipping at their steaming beverage.

"Did I ever share with you how I got hooked on coffee, Leo?"

"No."

Skip took two sips. "My Aunt Mary turned me onto the brew. When I was a kid I'd visit with her and my Uncle Clarence at the violet farm he maintained—they lived there. It was located in Floram Park, New Jersey. She'd fix coffee in the morning with evaporated milk and sugar...Man I tell you nothing smells better than walking into a warm kitchen with fresh brewed coffee perculatin'."

Leo was astonished. "What in the *hell* does that have to do with anything?"

Skip studied his friend as he sipped the last of his coffee. "Not a goddamned thing!" He rose to his feet and went to the bar to fix another cup of hot coffee. When he turned around and faced Leo, he said, "Sometimes, Leo...sometimes it's a good thing to reflect on where you came from in order to understand why you're fighting. I expect D.C. to fall along with Florida, Texas, California, and if they manage to get subs into the Puget Sound, Washington State."

Skip's sadistic smile caused Leo to respond with a question, "*What?*"

Still smiling his sadistic smile, Skip answered, "Then they have to move inland, and that Leo, is when we'll crush them."

Both men took long sips of their coffee before Leo broke the silence. He looked across the room at the picture frame on his desk then he looked at Skip. "You never told me what happened."

Skip took two small sips of his coffee. He looked at Leo. "No, I did not...and I won't. Remember her the way she looks in that picture, Leo."

Skip finished his coffee. "Leo, I can't tell you what to do, but you've been a colonel in the army, so you know the drill. Seventy percent of the Intel people are vets. Collect your agents, Leo, get all of the Intel folks out of D.C. and prepare for war. I'll be back in the morning; have a chopper waiting for me."

Skip placed his empty cup on the counter of the bar and turned to leave. When he reached the door, he turned back to Leo. "We've lost the Pentagon and our government is gone. They may have nuclear subs in the Baltimore Harbor as we speak. If I were you, I'd get my forces together and marry-up with the troops at Fort Detrick, and head northwest into the mountains and establish communications with the president at the "Little Pentagon." It will be the East Coast command center. See you at 0700."

As he opened the door, he looked back at Leo again. "You look at her picture often?"

Leo glared at Skip with hate in his eyes. "Yes, every day."

Skip accepted the hate emitting from Leo's green eyes. He remembered the first time they had met.

Skip Daggard spun around in his prone position rolling on his back, pointing his M-14, "Who the fuck are you?"

"Snoopy?"

"Wrong answer ass-wipe, I'm Snoopy." He began to squeeze the trigger.

"I'm Lieutenant Leo Pike, US Army Counterintelligence. We have to haul-ass out of here."

Daggard smiled. Ever since that first meeting, they had saved each other's lives on numerous occasions in the jungles of sunny Southeast Asia, Europe, and the Middle East.

Skip marched to his vehicle. He fell against the driver's door with his arms across the roof, resting his forehead against the edge of the roof just above the door. He had buried her image long ago, but seeing her picture brought it all forward.

"I warned you about having a wife. Now, we're at this damn junction. So what are we going to do?"

"I know you warned me, Skip, I'm not like you. I can't walk away from the girl I love."

"No. So here we are, Leo, you and me, and Julie is a prisoner in the hands of our enemy. And who is it that has to go in and rescue her? Me."

I'm going with you."

"Like hell! I don't need some emotional shit-for-brains covering my back."

Skip stood up. He hadn't cried as he remembered, but his heart felt crushing pain. "Remember what she looked like, Leo. Because what I had found was a shell of a woman who had been raped repeatedly, broken, bleeding and tortured," he whispered.

"Julie, it's me. Skip."

"Sk...i...p?"

"Yeah, I'm sorry, Julie that it has taken so long for me to find you."

"Sk...i...p! L...eo?"

"He's not here, Julie. Julie, they're all dead. I killed them."

"They hurt me, Skip. Th...e...y hurt me."

He wiped the blood from her face and eyes. "I know, Julie. They paid."

She reached up for him taking his hand in her broken fingers. "Kill me...kill me, Skip. Please...kill me."

He took her head in his hands hugging her against his chest. In one swift motion, he snapped her neck.

He sucked down his grief and slid in behind the steering wheel. Julie had been taken for one purpose: to coarse Leo into turning over top secret military troop strengths preparing to move into the Middle East.

Skip drove out of the parking lot heading for Dranesville Park. He gave thought to contacting Kimble and the president, and his friend in the MP's at White Sands.

Chapter Sixteen—Mobilization

Dranesville Park
Sunday, October 10
2330 hours

Skip Daggard stood in the clearing studying the ruins of his cabin. Images of a rifle muzzle came to him, and then her image as Kristine burst out of the door skipping steps as she came running into his arms, their lovemaking, and their hasty retreat from the CIA.

He had to have time to think, analyze, plot and plan, and make a few phone calls. He had chosen his favorite, quiet place to be alone, but discovered that too many memories exploded from his subconscious. He moved away from the burned cabin.

"All right, Skip," he said to himself, "many of the enemy spies had been dealt with, some still remained, so Kimble has to be notified as does Butts at White Sands. I hope that Hanalin is gathering his leaders."

Skip lay down in the back of his SUV and went to sleep with visions of battles, mutilated bodies, and white doves riding a wind current over the White Cliffs of Dover.

While Skip slept, opposing forces were beginning to lift and shift into position.

NSA
Colonel Deniska's Office
Monday, October 11
0630 hours

General Deniska sat behind his desk studying a map of the United States, Canada, and South America. He rose from his seat and walked to the window as a crimson dawn began to break in the eastern sky. He clasped his hands behind his back. "Damn! Who could have done such a thing?"

His mind was already providing him with an answer. "It had to have been Daggard, but how? How could he have known Rouke was advancing underground toward the White House? And twenty-five hundred of my soldiers wiped out...just like that; boom."

He turned away from the window and walked over to the coffee bar. He poured a cup of coffee and placed three jelly donuts on a small paper plate and went back to his desk. As Deniska studied the map again, he began to write down his marching orders as he drank his coffee and ate his donuts.

Dranesville Park
Monday, October 11
0635 hours

Skip Daggard sat up after he had rested quietly for several minutes, allowing his ears to sift out all of the noises while his brain identified those noises. Once he was satisfied that the sounds were natural, he sat up, dressed in his ACU and desert-sand brown boots. He slipped out of his SUV, surveying the area.

The cool air and position of the morning sun provided him with information that it would be a cold winter with substantial snowfall. He smiled. As he studied the ruins of his cabin again he said out loud, "So, what has changed in three years? China hosted the Olympics, go figure on that one. Russia attacked Georgia sending a ripple 'round the world. Oil prices went through the roof, and now another global war. Nothing has changed. The fuckin' world is at status quo, all fucked up.

"Well, Skip Daggard you piece of shit, it's time for mobilization."

He allowed for a smile to spread out from his lips. A crazy idea had seeped into his brain; an idea that was beginning to germinate and take root. But first, he took out his cell phone and dialed in a code specific number.

Little Pentagon
Fort Ritchie, Maryland
Monday, October 11
0700 hours

Everyone had awakened and arose early for breakfast. The president, vice president, Director Kimble, and the senators were sitting at a table in the center of the war room when the presidential bat line began to ring. They stared at the red phone in amazed wonder. President Short lifted the handset to his ear.

"Good morning, Mr. President."

"Who is this?"

Skip chuckled. "Chief Daggard, sir. I'd like to speak to Kimble."

President Short handed the handset to Kimble. "It's for *you!*"

Director Kimble took the handset staring at the president with questioning eyes.

"It's Chief Daggard."

"Authenticate!"

"Sierra—November—Oscar—Oscar—Papa—Kilo—Niner. Now that's out of the way, listen. We are about to be attacked by a Communist coalition force. Your Lima Charlie will be the East Coast Charlie-Papa.

"Now, you have three spies with you. I believe they are to take out the president and vice president. They are Burk, Parks, and Huttsen. Go shoot them—I'll hold."

Director Kimble could not fathom the information he had just received. He knew Daggard's reputation. He placed the handset down on the table as his right hand trembled. "Just leave that where it is, Mr. President! I will be right back."

As he turned drawing his weapon, the three men came into the room. Kimble lifted his weapon in one easy motion and shot the three men in the head. As they fell to the floor, handguns made a thumping sound as each man dropped his weapon as he fell.

President Short jumped from the explosions in such close proximity. He shouted, "KIMBLE! What the *hell?*"

Kimble did not answer. He retrieved the handset. "Damn, Daggard talk about timing; a few seconds later and we would have been dead."

"Okay! So that's done. Kimble put me on loud speaker."

Director Kimble did as he had been instructed. "All right, Skip, you're on."

"We are about to be attacked by a Soviet-led Communist force. The three men Kimble just shot were moles. The enemy has placed over one hundred thirty throughout our intelligence community and government.

"General Hanalin is taking charge of the military because the Pentagon has been taken over. We will not adhere to any orders coming from that quarter. I expect that the spies at NSA, who seem to be the leaders of the Soviet forces, will be dealt with before I join forces in the field—if I can.

"Kimble, contact Director Thomas at the Federal Building. He has five spies in his organization. Have him take them out. They are Talbert, Hansen, Bleeks, Perkins, and Kirby; any questions?"

President Short stared at Kimble as he pressed the mute button on the phone. "Can we trust this man?"

A silence prevailed. No one moved, but all eyes were focused on Director Kimble.

Kimble smiled, "Yes, sir...with our lives!"

The dead men were removed. No one agreed or disagreed with Kimble's remark. As he took three cartridges from his right suite jacket pocket, pressed the slide button on his 9mm weapon, caught the clip and removed it from the butt-end of his hand gun and began pushed each cartridge into the clip; then he slid the clip into the butt-end and slammed it home. He replaced his weapon back into his shoulder holster, and then turned back to the president.

"You have doubts about Daggard, Mr. President?

President Short looked at his wife then back to Director Kimble. Yes, Kimble I do. President Mantle's assassination has not been resolved, and Chief Daggard was the primary suspect; however, NSA stepped in and…Well, we all know what happened. Nothing! Daggard was exonerated."

"All the evidence against him, Mr. President was circumstantial. And NSA had proof that Daggard had actually gone to Camp David and warned the president about the plot."

Director Kimble pointed as the last body was being removed. "As I said, Mr. President, we can trust him with our lives."

President Short pressed the mute button on the handset. "Chief," the president said, "who destroyed the Capitol Building?"

They could hear heavy breathing coming from the speaker. Time ticked off of the walk clock. "I did. There were one hundred and seven spies between the House and Senate. Their only mission was to disarm the Americans so their forces could walk in on us. I had no other alternative, Mr. President."

Senator Gari studied the faces in the room. "Chief Daggard, are you the one responsible for sending my colleagues and me to the president?"

"Yes, ma'am, we will have to rebuild once this is over, providing we win. You six seem to be more stable for such a task."

Gari stood straighter, and smiled. "Thank you for your confidence."

"Don't thank me senator, it was the way the six of you have conducted yourselves. Well, we have a war to win; God speed; until we meet again."

The phone went dead.

Skip made two more phone calls: "Hey Butts how's it hangin'?"

"Skip, you old dog-breath, what the hell's goin' on in Washington?"

"B, its war; we are going to be attacked, and our silos at White Sands are to be used against us. I need you to take out the three spies there and insure that our missiles remain in our hands. We'll need them for defense."

Henry Butts began to laugh. He had served with Daggard for two years at NSA before taking charge of the MI Military Police garrison at White Sands, New Mexico.

"Listen shit-for-brains, haven't you been following the news? Here are the names of the spies Blake, Olson, Maverick.

Terminate their asses and take control of those missiles. When North Korea fires theirs, you answer with ours. GOT IT?" Butts stopped laughing. "Skip, are you serious?"

"Yeah, Henry...dead serious!"

Henry Butts began to sweat. "Maverick is mine. The other two are air force."

Skip could feel for his friend, but only in a small way. He did not possess the kind of heart it takes to reach out to people in times like this. "Butts, I'm taking to the field to help put a defense together, good bye."

At 0730 hours Skip boarded the chopper at Langley heading for Harlan, Kentucky and a rendezvous with destiny. The three Fates played hopscotch with the whirling blades.

Harlan, Kentucky
Monday, October 11
1115 hours

General Hanalin, Chin, Carol, Ted and the other eleven officers sat down to lunch. They had been following the news as it was presented over the TV and radio stations. Hanalin had established Command Posts at his location, Fort Carson, Colorado, Fort Lewis, Washington, and Fort Greely, Alaska. Fort Greely was important because of its strategic proximity to the lower forty-eight states, especially Fort Lewis with the I Corps; 1st Brigade, 25th Infantry Division; 3rd Brigade, 2nd Infantry, and 1st Special Forces Group (Airborne); Signal Support, and McChord AFB. The Special Forces Group possessed bazooka style nuclear weapons, and the Brigades rocket-launch nuclear weapons. It was these types of weapons and field nuclear missiles that were going to be used against the Soviet's 8th Guard in the European Theater in November 1974. It was a few weeks before Thanksgiving when the NATO and Warsaw Pact forces faced off with each other from the Middle East to Denmark and the free world was threatened.

"It seems Skip has been quite busy in the east," Hanalin said.

Many agreed with nods of their heads as Carol and Chin put two platters of pancakes, fried eggs and bacon and biscuits on the table with a fresh pot of coffee.

When the ladies sat down, Chin expressed her concern, "What do you think Skip's next move will be, General Hanalin?"

Hanalin pondered her question while he chewed on a piece of crisp bacon. "I think," he began as he took a sip of black coffee, "he will go to White Sands to ensure we have control of those missiles."

The operations sergeant came in for a plate of food and took it back to the radio/communications room, which had been Hanalin's study. As Sergeant Hawk sat down and began to fill his mouth with pancakes, his radio came alive with traffic. "This is Delta Oscar Gulf; do you have a copy Gulf Hotel Oscar Bravo?"

"This is Gulf Hotel Oscar Bravo, that's a good copy Delta Oscar Gulf."

"Affirmative, we are ten mikes from your LC."

Sergeant Hawk put down his plate. "Delta Oscar Gulf, this is Gulf Hotel Oscar Bravo. Am I to understand that you have the DOG aboard?"

"Affirmative, Gulf Hotel Oscar Bravo."

"Ten-four, Tango Mike."

Sergeant Hawk beat feet into the kitchen. "Sir,' he directed his address to General Hanalin, "I just received a radio transmission; Chief Daggard is approaching our location, and will land in a few minutes."

They jumped to their feet. "Are you sure, Sergeant Hawk?"

"Yes, sir, I confirmed it."

"How far out?"

Hawk checked his watch. "About five mikes, sir."

"Well, he's just in time for breakfast, go figure. Shall we go greet the DOG?"

They approached the landing zone, which had been established six hours after Hanalin and Chin's arrival. It was located fifty yards behind Carol's house in a cornfield. They stayed back because a dusting of snow lay upon the ground, and the whirling motion of the blades was causing the snow to blow around in a circle.

Once the blades stopped, Skip and the pilot emerged. Chin raced past Hanalin into Skip's arms, planting kisses all over his face.

Carol looked at Hanalin, "Guess I was right."

"What?"

"That woman is most definitely in love."

Hanalin and Carol laughed as they approached Skip and Chin.

"Thought you'd be on your way to White Sands," Hanalin said extending his right arm and hand. The two men clasped in a hardy handshake.

"I puzzled over the crisis; figured I didn't have the time, so I contacted a friend of mine to take control of the situation." They walked to the house discussing the events in Washington. "We don't have much time, Mac. I killed a large force that was preparing to assault the White House."

"That was *you?*"

Once they were all out of their coats and back at the breakfast table, Skip started, "Wow! Guess we timed our visit just right, Toby," he said to the pilot.

Skip filled them in on the events that he had been involved with. "There are at least three more moles in NSA. I think one of them has taken charge of their forces since I terminated Bardolph."

He demolished a stack of pancakes, three eggs, and twelve pieces of bacon, which had been placed before him by Chin. Once he flushed down the remnants with two gulps of coffee, he continued. "Tobias is a colonel on Director Hedges' staff, and Master Sergeant Milan is now a civilian in Tango-Echo Group. We will contact them so they can act in unison to terminate the remaining moles."

Skip took three sips of his coffee and winked at Chin. She responded with a whisper, "Tonight."

"Mac, who would take charge now that Bardolph is dead?"

General Hanalin gave the question some thought as he finished the remaining pancake on his plate. "I believe it would be Deniska."

"I will contact Tobias and have him show Deniska the error of his ways. I will have Milan take control of the military personnel operating Star Wars."

Skip rose to his feet. Chin came to him for a hug. Skip accommodated her request.

As the small company moved into the command room, Skip queried Hanalin. "How's the army coming?"

This question stopped everyone. Hanalin turned to Skip. "I've established Command Posts, but we haven't really gone out to the units or the people yet."

Skip went off. 'WHAT THE FUCK! WE DON'T HAVE OUR FORCES IN PLACE?"

"Skip…"

"What the hell have you been doing? The damn enemy is preparing to attack within a few fucking days and our forces aren't… POSITIONED?"

Chin went to him. She wrapped her arms around him trying to calm him down. She didn't say anything as she hugged him tight. When she felt his breathing slow down to a semblance of normal intakes and exhales, she looked up into his blue eyes. She caressed his face with her fingers of her left hand. She had single-handedly neutralized the demon.

NSA
Colonel Deniska's Office
Monday, October 11
1247 hours

Colonel Deniska sat at his desk studying his map. He leaned back in his chair as a nagging, persistent feeling began invading his thoughts, providing him with a warning, a warning that it was time for him to join his forces at their bunker in Virginia twenty miles south of Langley and Washington. "Why did I come here this morning? My wife and son were ready to leave, yet, I came here, why?"

He felt confident in a swift victory. The Chinese had decided to join forces with North Korea, and Russia was standing on the sidelines waiting. He rose and went for his fourth cup of coffee.

Once he had added evaporated milk and three heaping spoons of sugar, he went to the window looking over the west parking lot. "So much has happened since Daggard's involvement on September 30th," he mumbled to his reflection in the window.

He studied the change in weather patterns, and knew that time was running out. His forces must take Alaska within the week, or reinforcements from Asia would not be able to make the crossing and advance. He studied the clouds as they moved across a gray sky. "How could one man cause that much destruction?" His quiet time was interrupted by a knock on his door.

"Come in." He turned to see who his visitor was.

Colonel Tobias marched in and closed the door behind him. He had been part of the support to Chief Daggard three years ago when Chief Daggard and Sergeant First Class Anderson's mission involved terminating traitors in the White House.

"I have a message for you from Chief Daggard."

It took ten seconds of the tic of the little hand on his wall clock before recognition set in. He backed up against the outer wall of his office when he saw the weapon in Tobias' extended hand. Colonel Tobias fired his 9mm handgun six times; three rounds into Deniska's head, and three rounds into his chest. Deniska slid down the wall leaving a trail of blood as his body crumbled into a heap on the floor as blood oozed out of his head and body.

Colonel Tobias opened the door, stepped out into the outer office glaring at the frightened civilian secretary. He took out the empty clip and replaced it with a fully charge one. "I'm sorry," he said raising his hand extending his arm, "but I can't take any chances." He fired his weapon four times, killing the woman.

Tango-Echo Group is a communications facility located in the basement at NSA where Milan now worked as a civilian. He had walked up to the Star Wars systems communications pod, and discovered that the operator was in the process of destroying the Star Wars systems. Milan took out his .45 and shot the mole in the back of his head.

Milan had been a Master Sergeant in the Air Force and was the person who had informed his superiors at Cheyenne Mountain Facility of the coded encrypted message decoded at NSA, which led to the termination of the traitors in the White House.

He sat down at the communications console, typed in several commands and took charge of the Star Wars satellite system.

Colonel Tobias entered the room after he had reported to Director Major General Hedge to bring the general up to speed on current events.

"I have to take the system off line, sir. The bastard fried three of the weapons firing boards."

Colonel Tobias turned when he heard General Hedge's voice. "What is the status, Colonel?"

"How long Milan?"

Milan looked at Colonel Tobias. Milan opened the system console to check the damage. "To replace the three boards and the mother board will take about thirty minutes, sir, but to replace the melted control wiring harness will take at least two days."

"You do what it takes and use whatever resources needed."

"Yes, sir, General," Milan said.

General Hedge took Colonel Tobias aside. "I have contacted General Joel at Fort Devens. He will deal with the mole situation himself on his end. He will take his forces into the mountain area around Boston. I had advised him that the East Coast Command Center is at the Little Pentagon as you had instructed."

Colonel Tobias shook the general's hand.

Tuesday, October 12

At 0530 hours a mysterious message began to be broadcast over all North American television and radio stations, military and civilian, as well as the free world.

"They tell us, Sir that we are weak, unable to cope with so formidable an adversary. But when shall we be stronger? Will it be next week? Will it be next year? Will it be when we are totally disarmed and a guard stationed in every house? Shall we gather strength by irresolution and inaction? Sir, we are not weak if we make proper use of those means, which the God of nature has placed in our power."

Patrick Henry

"Today we face a formidable foe. A Communist force of seventy million is poised to strike and enslave the free world. Twelve million soldiers of that force are hiding throughout the United States waiting for their orders to attack. American Legions, VFW Posts, Survival Organizations, Nation Guard Units, and active duty military units must unite. The time has come once again for patriots to defend our homeland. All US Forces throughout the world prepare for attack. Your orders are being transmitted."

US Military Intelligence Officer, Skip Daggard, Retired

As they sat down to breakfast at 0545 hours, Skip turned to Hanalin, "Now general, you'll have your army."

The call to arms went out over every means of communications. Planes took to airways dropping leaflets proclaiming the above messages.

As in the past, so it was on this day, they came down from the Rocky Mountains, from the Cascade Mountains, from the Appalachians. They came from the cities and farms, and up from the flatlands. They came from the valleys and from the plains—arriving by the carloads, busloads, truck loads, on horseback and foot.

They came from the lower 48 states, Alaska, the Yukon Territory, Ontario, Quebec, and Montreal. They came for one purpose: To fight for the right to be free.

They were French and English, yellow and red, white and black; of Asian and Old World ancestry with one common trait—they were Americans.

Harlan, Kentucky
War Room, Carol's home
Friday, October 15
1500 hours

General Hanalin's Radio Operator, Sergeant First Class Hawk stood before General Hanalin with tears running down his face. He handed Hanalin a piece of paper. General Hanalin read the message to himself then exploded into a torrent of tears. He turned to his OPS leaders in his War Room in Carol's living room. He reached into his left back pocket of his ACU pants and produced a white handkerchief. Once he had wiped his face and blown his nose, he read the message out loud.

"To: General Hanalin, Kentucky Operations from General Mobo, Special OPS, Fort Carson, Colorado---General Hanalin, the United American Patriot Forces now number One Hundred thirty million. What are your orders, Sir?"

Carol burst into tears and stormed out of the room. She stumbled into her kitchen, grabbed hold of the countertop as her tears splattered on her stainless steel sink.

The twelve officers in the room were shaking hands as their tears dripped from their cheeks. General Hanalin looked over at Chin Lee. She returned Hanalin's stare yet she looked mortified. All she could manage was a whisper, "How?"

Skip stood off to the side near the entrance into the kitchen. He assessed the reaction with grave satisfaction. "We are going to pay a high price for the sales tag."

Everyone turned and stared at him.

His eyes were devoid of any emotion as he said, "Freedom!"

He looked at Chin. "You see, Chin, that's what our enemies have failed to understand about us; we *will not* go gentle into that good night."

They nodded their heads in agreement as General Hanalin issued last minute orders and assignments to his twelve field commanders, shaking their hands and bidding them good luck. The men left Carol's home to join their units throughout Kentucky.

Across America, Canada, and South America, civilian and military personnel linked up, taking up their assigned positions along the perimeters directed by Skip Daggard. The wait for battle…would not be long.

Chapter Seventeen—War

Carol's house
Harlan, Kentucky
Sunday, October 17
0330 hours

Skip Daggard leaned forward allowing the scalding hot water to beat against his head and shoulders. His body went stiff as the curtain was drawn back. "You are up early," Chin said as she stepped into the tub closing the shower curtain.

They stood a few inches apart. She studied his face. Chin reached up with her left hand caressing the scars on his right cheek. She stared into his sky-blue eyes. "It is time?"

Skip let go of a long deep sigh. "I believe so." He used his right hand to stroke her left cheek while he studied the richness of her raven hair. He moved to the inside of the tub so Chin could access the water spewing out from the silver showerhead.

"Forever the warrior," she whispered. She placed her left hand against his chest. His tension pulsated through her palm. This time she knew this was a different kind of tension. She studied his eyes. They were calm. She canted her head toward her left shoulder as her facial expression created the question.

He smiled. "The soldier attitude, Chin; I am now on the line of debarkation. I'm simply waiting for orders to move out, tense, yet calm."

She used the index finger of her left hand to trail along a seven-inch bayonet scar on his right arm from his shoulder down his biceps. She followed her finger with her eyes then she looked up into his. "You are sad."

Skip rested his chin on his chest as the water splashed over their bodies. He looked deep into her penetrating brown eyes, eyes that were almost black. "I hate war." He closed the shutters of his eyes. He didn't see the puzzled look in hers. He didn't open his as he began to caress her silken face. After three caresses, he opened his eyes looking into hers. "It's the women and children who suffer. They're the ones who pay the ultimate price."

She had no words. She stood next to him awash in pride while he allowed his human side to be exposed. She declared, "He is not a monster." Chin moved the soaped up washcloth toward the silver forest on his chest. Skip defended himself against her action by raising his right arm to block her advance. She looked at him with injury in her eyes.

"Not now!"

She released a meek smile. "So, the warrior stands before me."

"It is what I am, Chin."

Skip lowered his head. "The enemy has no idea what is in store for them." He looked deep inter her dark, brown eyes. He asked the question to himself, "Should I tell her?"

As the hot water beat against their bodies, Skip decided to violate his number one rule; divulging information.

He studied the petite shape of her physique, and then smiled.

"What?"

"You may be small, but you're a lethal weapon."

She took the soap from his hands and began to lather up her body. She looked up at him, "Do not forget that point."

They laughed. Chin noticed the change in his eyes. "What troubles you, Skip?"

He exhaled a short, shallow breath. "I was working up something to tell you when I realized that it's only been eighteen days since all of this atrocious bullshit started."

She placed her left hand on his hairy chest. He was ice cold.

Skip stared into her eyes. "Remember when I told you about...oh, hell!"

She stared up at him, waiting.

He placed his hands on her shoulders. "Remember when I told you that neither my president nor Congress was an issue?"

Chin nodded her head, "I remember. I do not understand it."

Skip allowed a short breath of air to escape from his mouth. "That's because you're not an American soldier. Our president is the Commander-in-Chief, but he's not in charge. Our military leaders are in charge."

Chin's face took on a puzzled frown. "I cannot comprehend this concept."

Skip smiled at her. "I know. Even our allies have a problem understanding our military philosophy. That's why our military leaders will not allow foreign leaders to take charge of US forces in the field."

He squatted down pulling her in against his body. "The Soviets tried this twice before, war."

Skip Daggard's body began to tremble as he rested his chin over her right shoulder. She held him as she squeezed him against her body.

"We have nuclear weapons in our arsenal that no one knows about except our military." He stood up placing his hands on her shoulders again, pushing her away. He looked upon her quizzical face. "Some of those weapons were going to be used on the Soviet 8th Guard in 1974, Chin, but they had been informed by their spies, so they withdrew from the battlefield, and went home. It happened again in '86 when General Powell was a colonel in the 3rd Armored Division. Communist and Allied forces faced each other along the East/West borders near Fulda, Germany." Skip drew in a large amount of steamed air. He exhaled a slow and deliberate breath. "President Ford had no idea. It was the same in '61 at checkpoint Charley in Berlin; the military leaders had given the orders, and were going to blow the Soviets shit away. President Kennedy had no idea, but when he had found out, he went ballistic. That's what I mean, Chin. We have protocol, but when it comes to war, our military takes charge.

"Win, lose, or draw, Chin, when this is over, the world will be changed."

They stepped from the shower. As they toweled each other, Skip continued while wiping water from her back. "Your soldiers will be allowed to advance across the DMZ and through the tunnel systems..."

Chin spun around almost falling over due to her sudden move. "Yeah, we know."

She stared into his eyes. There was no doubt of his sincerity.

"Your forces will be allowed to advance to pre-designated points from the DMZ and tunnels. Your forces will be nuked and the tunnels sealed. Chin, our military has a top-secret plan. Its code name is…"No Mercy."

Chin trembled. In a steam-filled bathroom in a home that had become a military command post nestled in the mountains in America, she was learning to what extent the Americans would fight in order to defend their country.

Skip and Chin dressed in silence. Both wore the military snow-patterned Army Combat Uniform. Skip retrieved his war bag and rifle from the corner of their bedroom. When they stood on the landing at the top of the stairs, Skip stopped. His eyes absorbed familiar sights; the old cherry banister that looked new; the light colored oak paneling on the wall along the steps; the maroon indoor-outdoor carpet runner nailed to the steps and risers.

Chin clung to his left arm observing his changing facial expressions then he looked at her.

Skip let a long sigh escape from between his lips. "Maybe," he smiled, "just maybe, if we stay here and never descend the stairs, just maybe there won't be a war."

Chin smiled back at him. She stood straighter, moving her shoulders back while lifting her face, then she whispered to herself, "I have chosen well, father. My heart has chosen well."

As they walked down the stairs together, they had no clue about the world of tears and mayhem they were entering as they stepped across the threshold into the war room.

War Room
Carol's house
Harlan, Kentucky
Sunday, October 17
0415 hours

General Hanalin was using the table containing the war map, to support himself as Skip and Chin entered. Other members of Hanalin's staff had fallen into chairs, or were leaning against each other, crying.

Skip and Chin stood inside the room close to the doorway. General Hanalin looked up. "NSA is gone."

Skip released a burst of air. "Tit for Tat, huh?"

Everyone stared at him. Chin stepped away looking up at him. She could not believe her ears or her eyes. There was...nothing. No emotion.

General Hanalin was the first to recover. "*What!*"

Skip walked toward the table. "They lost three thousand, now we've lost three thousand. Get over it."

They stared at him in shocked disbelief. "You're a cold hearted bastard, Skip Daggard," Carol screamed out. "Didn't you have friends there?"

"*Friends*! *FRIENDS*!" Skip slipped his M-14 from his shoulder. He raised his rifle in the air. "*This is my friend*!"

Chin had learned to read his face. She read his facial expressions now, and went to him. She took him in her arms as a protective mother would her child. She hugged him, cradled him, and whispered, "I have you, darling."

Skip Daggard buried his face in her right shoulder. He allowed for his thirty seconds of grief to spill out as his tears wetted her uniform. When he stood up, the hard-core soldier stood before them; the soldier enemies had come to fear. "I hope Milan freed Star Wars before he went under." Skip knew the truth. He was not going to share with them, that he had issued the order...Pike's helicopters completed their mission.

Messages began to come in, and the soldiers jumped and went about their business, their faces telling the tale; once again, war had come to America.

Sunday, October 17
0445 hours Eastern Standard Time

During the late fifties and early sixties US military leaders constructed one of the most elaborate defensive systems known to modern warfare. Neither Congress nor presidents had any idea of this defensive/offensive horseshoe that protected the North American Continent. Many outraged inquiries were launched against the military for their needless spending, but those inquiries were met with a barrage of paperwork and a military force highly trained in manipulation and deception. While expenditure was showing cause for a four dollar hammer at the cost fifteen hundred, and a toilet seat costing twelve dollars and ninety-five cents costing two thousand dollars, Congress and Funds Appropriations Committees were demanding answers.

This type of funding system had been created to fund the top-secret defense of America. The only president to be privileged to a segment of the defense had been Ronald Reagan simply because the need for a Star Wars type weapon was necessary. The only personnel who had knowledge of the system were key, career military and intelligence leaders who had signed up for the duration.

Skip studied the map. When he spoke, he was speaking to a general audience. "I guess the world is going to learn." He raised his head in a slow upward turn. Skip's face looked like that of a lost basset hound. He looked across the table at General Hanalin. "Who's going to give the order?"

General Hanalin stared into the sad, blank eyes of his friend and best soldier. "I am."

The operations personnel and Chin stared at Hanalin and Daggard. Skip allowed a heavy sigh to escape from his lungs. Skip looked down at the map. "I remember complaining about the price of a hammer when I was on that mission for you in Germany." Skip looked up at Hanalin. "It was a year later when I learned the truth." Skip looked back at the map, studying specific locations around the US. Without looking, Skip said, "So, Carol doesn't know?"

General Hanalin looked at Carol as she entered the room with a tray, carrying a carafe of coffee, cups, and biscuits. "What don't I know?"

Skip continued to study the war map as General Hanalin glared at him. He stood straight up, looked at Carol, then at Hanalin. "There's a communications link in your wall."

General Hanalin shouted, "ENOUGH!"

Skip looked at him. "They should know; they've earned the right!"

Carol stared at Chin. Chin shrugged her shoulders. General Hanalin went to the right corner of the inside wall of the living room. He took out a folding knife, opened it, and cut away a section of wallpaper. He opened a metal door. Behind the door was a code-encrypted handset.

Carol almost dropped the tray. "*What the hell!*"

"Hell is right! You see, Carol," Skip said, "from 1955 through 2005, we've been secretly constructing defensive and offensive missile silos in strategic locations. We have nuclear missiles at Fort Devens, Massachusetts; Maquire Air Force Base, Fort Dix; New Jersey, and Air Combat Command; Langley AFB, Virginia."

Skip stopped to study the map as taskforce personnel began moving scale model ships around the Atlantic and Pacific Oceans, listening.

"We have ballistic and nuclear short and long range missile silos at Air Force Space Command, Peterson AFB, Colorado and Air Force Special Operations Command, Hurlburt Field, Florida."

Skip placed his index finger of his right hand on Germany. We have nuclear missiles at Ramstein AFB, and sixty field, mobile nuclear and ballistic batteries at Heidelberg and Fulda, Germany, which have already been deployed."

Skip looked to General Hanalin. "You want to finish?"

General Hanalin sucked down a gulp of air, exhaled, then continued. "We have long range ballistic and nuclear missile silos at Air Missile Special Operations, Caguas, Puerto Rico; Air North Special Operations, Fort Greely and Fort Wainwright, Alaska; and Air Pacific Special Operations at Upolu Point, Hawaii, Lipoa Point, Maui, Kaena Point the northwestern point from Pearl Harbor on Oahu, and Mana the west point of Kauai, Hawaiian Islands. This control panel is a fail-safe mechanism; if any launch cannot be carried out, I can do it from here."

Chin staggered to the table next to Skip, "Casualties?"

Skip could not look at her. She shook his left arm, "*Casualties?*" He closed his eyes. "A close guestimate is three hundred million; half the world's population."

Skip stopped to take in some air. "President Short has no idea why I had selected the six senators. Their predecessors were instrumental in assisting the military in creating the missile system we now have. These six senators had been handpicked to continue funding the mission."

Everyone in the room stood rock-still. Carol breathed out her statement, "Nuclear holocaust!"

Chin Lee and Skip's eyes locked on each other. "Now I understand," she said, "you hate war...WAR."

He nodded. "That's why I had fought the Cold War the way I did; trying to avert this catastrophe, but our enemies just won't leave us the fuck alone...so now, half the world is going to be wiped out...for what?"

Little Pentagon
Fort Ritchie, Maryland
Sunday, October 17
0515 hours

President Short, Vice President Aims, and military leaders who had been secretly moved to the Little Pentagon were in the war room viewing the movements as information was being fed into the fortification from signal sources. Junior officers and enlisted personnel were moving and removing ships and planes from a huge map on a table, which depicted the world. Toy vehicles and soldiers represented US, allied, and enemy units and their locations were being moved along the lines of battle.

Vital information had not been available regarding the bulk of the Soviet forces such as their locations; at least none that might have leaked out to the enemy, but all key elements of the allied forces had received encrypted transmissions from a source in space.

The Commander-In-Chief was not truly in charge of the operation, but was more of a bystander. The ones in charge were the officers in the field and at the key Command Centers. They were keeping the president informed of battle situations, as information became available. This is how communications would flow during the entire war.

European Space
Sunday, October 17
0530 hours EST
1730 hours European Time

Star Wars systems had accepted the code-specific operations

functions, which had been uploaded into its main frame circuits two days earlier. It had taken twenty-four hours for the satellite to acknowledge each code and sever its umbilical cord to the NSA control systems. Star Wars was in complete control of all of its functions by Sunday morning. It began transmitting images to the communications system at NSA; however, there was no response. In accordance to protocol, Star Wars rerouted the images and information to the control center at the Little Pentagon at Fort Ritchie, Maryland.

The satellite was passing over the European Continent at 0530 hours EST, 1730 hours European time; its jamming and surveillance devices were working overtime. The duty officer, Major Reighly had hurried from the war room to alert the president and Admiral Smith of new developments Star Wars was sending. He banged on the bedroom doors ordering all personnel to the war room immediately.

President Short studied the war map for several seconds as did Admiral Smith and his staff. The president looked up from the map, "What's happening, Bill?"

Admiral Smith and several naval strategists had been rounded up from the Naval Academy in Annapolis to take charge of naval operations at the Little Pentagon.

Ignoring the president, Admiral Bill Smith said to the duty officer, "Major Reighly, where are these images coming from?"

"Star Wars, sir."

"They're being interposed from Star Wars?"

"Yes sir!"

Admiral Smith looked down at the map. He looked at President Short who was standing on the admiral's right. *What could he say to the president? There wasn't a gentle or easy way to say it, but simply to give him the facts.* "We're in trouble, Mr. President. Russian military forces are massing along their border with Finland. Russian naval forces have deployed ground troops in Kaliningrad on the Polish border, and there are forces massing along the Latvia and Belarus borders." Admiral Smith pointed to those places on the map as he explained to President Short.

"What I fear, sir, is that if the Soviet Communist forces show any sign or indication that they are winning, or will win this war, then Russia will attack."

More images began to appear on the map showing Russian troop movement in Leningrad, Lovozero, and Kovdor.

Admiral Smith gave orders to Major Reighly. "Major, notify General Hanalin of these new developments, immediately."

"Yes sir."

Admiral Smith studied the map with grave speculation. "We will not have anything to stop the Russian navy if they gain the open sea."

As if the situation wasn't bad enough, Major Reighly returned to the war room with trepidation etched on his bulldog face. He collapsed into a chair near the table supporting the war map. He could not look upon the faces of the people in the room. He spoke to the floor. "General Hanalin said…" He had to pause so he could breathe. "He said that only one-third of our forces are in position. "'The good news,' he said, "'is that Skip had anticipated Russia's involvement. If they attack, they'll never know what had hit them.'"

Major Reighly looked up at his audience through sad eyes. "We're not ready, Mr. President. If the Soviets attack now…we're not ready."

First Lady Short had been standing in the doorway. She stepped into the room clearing her throat. "Ladies and gentlemen, here is fresh coffee." She placed the tray down on a small table left of the war map table. "So, it looks like we are behind the eight-ball again. That's good!"

Everyone in the room stared at her while she poured hot coffee into the twenty cups on the tray. She strong-armed the tray and began to move around the room as each person took his or her cup of coffee. "It seems to me that you have lost sight of who we are," she said with a smile on her face.

She smiled at her husband, and then turned to Admiral Smith. "I believe all of you have forgotten something; we Americans are a come from behind team." Her smile was contagious.

Carol's House
Harlan, Kentucky
Sunday, October 17
0600 hours

Skip read the messages from the Little Pentagon three times as he stood before the war map studying locations of forces.

"Here," General Hanalin said, "we just received this info from "Sky Eagle.""

He read the printout. He looked back at the map. "ONLY *HALF* OF OUR GROUND FORCES ARE IN POSITION!"

General Hanalin nodded.

Skip crumbled up the printout and threw it at General Hanalin. "I hope the enemy doesn't decide to attack today."

Skip went upstairs to be alone. He activated a code-specific number and waited sixty seconds. "Da?"

"Dad, it's Skip!"

"My boy, things do not look good."

"What's going on with your military?"

Heavy breathing came from Kristine's father. "Our senior generals think that we should be ready, either to assist the Soviets, or finish the war for them."

Skip took thirty seconds to process this information. "Dad, withdraw your forces. Remember 1974 and '86?"

Now it was his father-in-laws turn to hesitate. "Yes!"

"Withdraw your forces, Dad. Please!"

Both men waited, breathing into their respective cell phones. "Good bye, Dad." Skip closed his cell phone, and returned to the war room. General Hanalin went over to him. He asked in a low voice, "Will he remove his forces?"

Skip stared at him; then he smiled. "He's been warned."

Soviet Command Post
Tyson's Corner, VA
Sunday, October 17
0625 hours EST

General Igor Aloyoshenka, who had taken command since Bardolph and Deniska had been killed, stood in the war room of his bunker system studying his world map. He was a realist; he understood that his forces would now be hard-pressed to win, but victory was still on their side. He smiled. "Soon, it will be over. We will have achieved our goal."

His twenty-five officers and soldiers agreed, and laughed, slapping each other on their backs. "Yes, by Christmas," General Aloyoshenka said.

The Soviets' belief of a swift and decisive victory had been based on the element of surprise, disarming the Americans, decreasing US forces, and setting up a global attack. However, their deceased military leader, General Bardolph, had made a grave error in judgment—he had attacked the one person in the US arsenal who could undermine their goal of world domination.

The only thing that had gone right for the Soviets was Russia's attack and occupation of Georgia in 2008, allowing the Soviets to man its two ballistic missile bases and arm their 30 SS-20 ballistic missiles. These missiles were part of the SS series ballistic missiles which the Soviets had sworn had been dismantled and removed in accordance to Intermediate-Range Nuclear Forces Treaty of 1987 (INF).

The INF Treaty stipulated that the Soviet SS-4, SS-5, and SS-20 and the American Pershing II ballistic missiles and ground-launched cruise missiles deployed in parts of Western Europe, be dismantled and removed. The SS series missiles were intermediate-range land based ballistic missile systems deployed in western parts of the Soviet Union with independently targetable warheads.

The Soviets had lost access to their two missile sites when the Berlin Wall came crumbling down in 1989, and Georgia gained its independence. The Russians had sent a message to the Soviets in November 2008 when they had sent a naval contingent into the Gulf of Venezuela protesting US presence in the region.

Now, the Soviets were in control of the bases in Georgia, and the Russian military leaders had moved their forces without authorization from Moscow. They would sit back and wait to see how the war developed. Then they could urge Moscow to allow them to engage the Capitalists.

These maneuvers by the Russians were messages for the Soviets. The massing of their forces and by allowing the Soviets to take control of their missile sites in Georgia, a country north of Turkey, which the Russian military now controlled, were simple ploys to let the Soviets know that if the war was going well, then there would be additional forces available.

Monday, October 18
0300 hours

Elements of the US Naval Combat Power included its Aircraft Carriers, Carrier Air Wing, Guided Missile Cruisers, Guided Missile Destroyers, Guided Missile Frigates, Nuclear Attack Submarines, Fleet Ballistic Missile Subs, and the US Marines. While ships moved out to sea, the Marines would be deployed on the ground along the East and West Coasts and the Gulf of Mexico.

US Naval Strategy focused on a Blue Water Strategy designed to fight a set battle at sea and maintain a sea-line of communications. The Blue Water Strategy was used against the Japanese and during the Cold War against the Soviet Union. When the Berlin Wall crumbled and the Soviet Union dissolved, the US Navy redirected its power inland and focused on a strategy called "Forward from the Sea." However, like all US military powers, the navy had continued to train, employing both strategies. The navy will utilize these two strategies during the upcoming war.

US Air Force operations included deterring potential adversaries from engagement. If deterrence proves ineffective, then the air force will use all means to defeat the enemy. Therefore, the air force retains a significant amount of all US nuclear weaponry. Fighters use internal guns as well as Sidewinder air-to-air missiles and radar guided advanced Medium Range Air-to-Air Missiles. The combined task force of the US Air Force fighters and bomber and naval planes command the skies with an impressive fighting force of over twenty thousand screaming eagles. The air force also conducts intelligence gathering, which can be directed to field commanders in seconds.

The alert notification of an attack against North America was the responsibility of the joint command between Canada and the United States. The North American Air Defense Command (NORAD) was established May 12, 1958, during the Cold War threats. A series of radar detection lines were put into operation along the Alaskan frontier. These systems are assigned to the Cheyenne Mountain Operations Center in Colorado. In the 1980s the systems were upgraded to include the Canadian Air Operations Control Centres at Canadian Forces Base North Bay, Ontario, and in March 1981 the name was changed to North American Aerospace Defense Command. When the alert went out and authenticated, all NORAD planes, to include the Strategic Air Command forces went airborne carrying nuclear bombs and missiles.

At approximately 0300 hours eastern standard time the US 2nd Fleet weigh anchor steaming out of Norfolk, Virginia, for the Atlantic Ocean to marry up with the British Navy. One third of its complement branched off to link up with the US Coast Guard to defend the US Atlantic Coast.

At precisely the same moment, the 3rd Fleet steamed out of port at San Diego, California, heading out into the Pacific Ocean to marry up with elements of the 7th Fleet, which had left Yokosuka, Japan a day earlier. These fleets would attack the North Korean and Soviet fleets that will attack and land ground troops on the US Pacific Coast and Alaska. The 6th Fleet would be supported by elements of the British Navy in the Mediterranean Sea.

Yet, in the war rooms at Harlan, Kentucky, the Little Pentagon, and Cheyenne Mountain, Colorado, naval personnel began moving model ships around on the war maps. The problem with the ground forces still persisted; only one half of forces on the North American continent were in position, while the remainder of the US ground forces was still hundreds of miles from their assigned positions.

Monday, October 18
0445 hours EST

A combined force of seventy million Communists open fired on North America and Germany at Bremerhaven. The war, which all humanity had feared since the 1950s, had begun. The German navy had left port twenty minutes prior to the Soviet subs firing their missiles at the port of Bremerhaven. The Soviets had positioned six nuclear subs fifty miles northeast of Bremerhaven directly above the Netherlands in the North Sea.

One third of the British navy was steaming up the English Channel entering the North Sea past Great Yarmouth. Another one third of the British navy was taking up a defensive position in the Celtic Sea thirty miles south of Ireland and Great Britain. The remainder of the British navy was linking up with elements of the US Sixth and Seventh fleets heading to intercept the Soviet navy, which was now steaming south toward the North American and European continents from their berth in the Arctic Ocean sixty miles north of Greenland.

US nuclear subs had left Pearl Harbor two days earlier, and had moved, stealth-like, into position forty miles west of the Soviet subs off the coast of California. North Korean Forces had massed at the DMZ poised to crush the American forces and invade South Korea with the aid of five million Chinese forces. The North Korean missiles were aimed at targets in Alaska, Washington, and California. At precisely 0445 hours, the Soviet spies at the nuclear missile base at White Sands, New Mexico were killed. Air force personnel were repositioned, and the codes the spies had uploaded into the firing systems deleted. The proper firing sequence and coordinates for the offensive and defensive missiles were reprogrammed. The Fail-Save system was deactivated so the four senior air force leaders at the site could simultaneously insert and turn their keys in order to fire the missiles. The top-secret codes had been uploaded using the cryptic key-code books—all was ready. The four officers began to sweat while waiting for the order to activate the missiles. The order would come from the North Warning System (NWS) communications tracking station at Elmendorf Air Base, Alaska, which is part of the North American Aerospace Defense Command (N.O.R.A.D). Canadian East and West Sector Air Operations Control Centres located at Canadian Forces Base (CFB) also received authentication of attack.

At approximately 0457 hours the radar systems at White Sands detected incoming missiles as the order from Elmendorf was authenticated. At 0458 hours, 24.30 seconds the New Mexico desert erupted with earthquake force as the early morning sky was blasted into daylight from the white flames of the missiles, which would go down in history as the first shots of the war fired by the Americans. North Korean offensive in-coming missiles were systematically destroyed while the US offensive missiles were being launched against North Korea.

Wednesday, November 24
1900 hours

It had been a bloody struggle. Four days into the fray, Star Wars engaged its laser cannons against the Soviet ground forces deploying at Bremerhaven. Denmark, Norway, and Sweden had fallen.

By the end of the fifth day, Soviet ground forces aided by its air force were moving through the Netherlands, Germany, and Poland. Washington, D.C. had fallen; Baltimore, New Jersey, New York, Maine, and Massachusetts were under siege, as was the entire West Coast, including Alaska.

South America had fallen. Thousands of US, South American, and Mexican forces were fighting in the mountains around Mexico City.

While combined free world air forces and navies were destroying the Soviets air and sea power, the Americans were drawing the Communist forces into the Cascade Mountains, the Alaskan Tundra, southwest deserts, Rocky and Appalachian Mountains, and systematically putting the enemy to death.

On Thursday, November 18th, twenty million soldiers of the free fighting forces landed at Norway, Sweden, and the Netherlands driving the Communists into the sea.

All of the missiles had been deployed. Millions lay dead. Out of fifteen million Communists who had attacked South Korea, only twenty thousand limped back across the DMZ to a wasteland of destruction.

On the mountain peaks above Carol's house, Skip and Chin Lee and thirty thousand soldiers were engaged in the final battle of a seven-day struggle.

Harlan County, Kentucky
Thursday, November 25
1635 hours

Harlan lay in a hollow. During the coal mining wars of the 1940s, Harlan had become know as "Bloody Harlan." Now, it lay peaceful, under two feet of snow. During the past seven days its countryside had exploded into violence again as its residents and militia met the Communist opposition, and Kentucky erupted into a fight for survival. Now, all that could be heard was the sounds of wounded Americans who had taken part in the action. All of the enemy soldiers had been put to death according to Skip Daggard's plan of operation.

Skip Daggard and Chin Lee sat in the snow on a ridge overlooking the quaint town.

"Where did they all come from?"

"What do you mean?"

She turned her head to the right and stared at him. They were sitting close together so she leaned forward and kissed him. When she sat straight up again, she said, "All of these Americans!"

Skip chuckled. Then he went quiet and still as he stared out over the bloody landscape.

Generations of wars flashed through his mind. Battlefields of the American Revolution and the American Civil War: Lexington, Bunker Hill, Yorktown, Bull Run, Shilo, Gettysburg, and many more. The bombardment of Fort Sumter, the burning of Washington, Battle of the Bulge, Normandy, the Ashau Valley, Khesanh, Hue, Bataan, Pearl Harbor, Kuwait, Iraq, and a thousand other war-torn pieces of real estate across the world.

"Like I tried to tell you over a month ago, Chin, the Americans will not go quietly into that good night. Freedom is only a seven letter word, but it's the most powerful word in the American language."

Skip waved his right hand sweeping it from left to right with his palm up. "They came from small towns like this one; from villages, farms and hamlets. They came from cities, valleys and the plains. They came down from the mountains and ridges and up from the hollows. They stood their ground and died along the Appalachian, Rocky, and

Cascade Mountain ranges, and they met the enemy on the deserts of Arizona and New Mexico. Well…you get the picture."

Chin sat next to him. She could feel the heat from his body as she surveyed the carnage all around them, but it was the passion in his words which had made her look at the country and people before her. She realized that she was finally beginning to grasp the meaning of his words.

"They didn't come for themselves, Chin. They came to express their right to die, not live. They came to fight for the right to pass the baton of freedom on to the next generation of Americans, and that, Chin Lee, is what had been given to the colonists in 1783; a right of passage… freedom, the right to choose. And you…why did you defect…fight? Was it just for revenge? But during this past month you tasted it, touched, and inhaled it. You lived free to choose, and you chose to fight along side of us.

"Actually, your people did us a favor; one that we couldn't seem to manage on our own."

Chin looked at him quizzically. "I do not understand."

Skip exhaled a long, heavy, deep sigh. "We knew our country was in dire need of another revolution in order to restructure our government, get it back to the way it should be, back on track. We just weren't sure on how to go about it. With the aid of the Communist OPFOR (opposing forces), the US will be provided a tremendous opportunity."

She pulled back from him. "I see! So now you can rebuild your government."

"Exactly, but not rebuild it; just repair it."

They chased each other around in a circle throwing snowballs at one another. Then, without warning, Chin turned on him and tackled Skip. They rolled around for a few minutes laughing. She began to ask a question, but realized, from the vacancy in his eyes that he was gone.

He reached out for her after a few minutes had passed. "Do you know why we celebrate Thanksgiving?"

Chin looked at him puzzled to what had prompted such a question. "Yes, I do."

He smiled at her. "Bet ya' ten deep-throat kisses you don't."

She took up a sarcastic pose. "It is because of 1620 and the Pilgrims. So there, smart ass."

He jumped to his feet. He began to jump up and down for three triumphant minutes. "Ha! You owe me ten deep-throat kisses. It was President Lincoln who issued the proclamation in 1863. But," he conceded, "you were half right, therefore, you owe me five and I owe you five. We both win."

A light snow began to fall, and from valleys, hollows, and ridges around Harlan, and from all over the United States, Thanksgiving fires were being lit, and free Americans were sitting down to dinner.

Tomorrow...tomorrow the burial parties would go out from the northern tip of Maine on a U-shaped curve across the country to Seattle. But tonight in camps, cities, hollows, and mountaintops, and in small towns and villages, the citizen soldiers will laugh and cheer, smile and cry, and give thanks to each other and fallen friends and family members...and... to God.

As Chin Lee and Skip Daggard rose and began to brush the snow from their clothing, Chin wrapped her arms around him, gently placed her hands over his ears, and pulled his face to hers. After giving him his five rewards, she asked him as they began to walk down the hill hand in hand, "Who are you, Skip Daggard, and what in life had brought you to this place?"

He took a sideways glance at her as they continued to walk. "Well, Chin, that's a long story. If you have the time, I'll tell you all about it.

"I have the time," she said smiling back at him.

He smiled at her. She returned the warm affectionate glance. "I believe that you must give *me* my rewards first."

Skip took her in his arms and gave her five deep, passionate kisses.

They stood in the blowing snow. She was glaring at him, but he was looking off to the east. Without looking at her he said, "It all started when I turned down a free scholarship to become a soldier. The day I informed my mother, she threw such a shit-fit, so I didn't go into the military police, instead, I went into communications, and that's how I became an operative."

When he looked back at her, she could see sadness in his eyes. "I want to know all of it," she said above the wind.

Skip studied snowflakes as they fell. He looked at Chin. She could see by the distant stare in his eyes that he had gone somewhere. He was looking past her; his focus was on his past. His head moved in a slow lowering motion until he was staring at their feet. "I used to wear glasses." He raised his head until he was staring into Chin's brown eyes.

She wanted to pull away from him, strike out at him, "*What*," was all she could muster. Then, she witnessed the deep sadness in his blue eyes.

He stepped forward taking her in his arms placing his face on her shoulder—he cried. She held him tight as if trying to merge their bodies into one. He continued to download for thirty seconds as they held each other in the light falling snow.

"Kristine talked me into the laser operation back in 2007. Now, I don't even use glasses for reading."

Chin knew he was leading somewhere. She'd have to allow him to explain in his own way. She held him and listened.

"There is so much that I remember and that I will share with you, but the one that reeks of irony is the war the Soviets called in November 1974. Due to their moles in the 3rd Armored Division..." He lifted his head pushing her away with a gentle movement so he could look into her eyes.

"Their spies had been diligent in their work. They had uncovered NATO's best kept secret and moved to battle positions. Then those spies discovered the 3rd Armored Division's top-secret battle plan. We were going to nuke them. The Warsaw Pact Forces packed up and went home."

Skip smiled at her confused stare. He lifted her chin with his right hand with a gentle touch. "And that, darlin,' is another story which I will share with you."

Their feet made crunching sounds in the snow as they walked and slipped down the hill laughing. The wind died down and the snow settled into a gentle shower. Chin directed a hard, chastising stare at him. She shook her head in frustration.

Skip smiled at her. "Like I said, honey, if you've got the time, I have so much to tell you."

She tried to rush into his arms, but stumbled. Skip caught her. She smiling at him, "I have a lifetime," she declared.

Skip cringed at her words as he slipped his right arm around her shoulders. They continued to walk down the hill; their progress was slow in the knee-deep snow. Her question had evoked memories. No matter how hard he fought to repress certain events, trigger mechanisms managed to bring the past back to life.

"I've decided to go into the military," he said to Bryanna and her mother while driving out to Route 46 from Morristown as a steady snow fell, two weeks before Christmas 1966.

Bryanna turned her head as if the motion was labored. She glared at him through her sensual, brown, Italian eyes. Her pleading was plain to see.

On a warm day in May 1967 he told his mother, "I'm going into the Military Police in the army…"

It was her reaction and pleading which would affect the rest of his life.

Skip felt a gentle tug on his arm. He shook his head as snowflakes fell against his cold face.

"There's a lot to tell, Chin. Are you planning to stay?"

Chin wrapped her right arm around Skip's left arm. With eyes of love, she smiled at him. "I am staying, Skip Daggard.

He slipped his left-gloved hand into her mitten-covered right hand and smiled at her. "You *do* know that being married to me can be hazardous to your health?"

They both laughed and giggled like kids in puppy love. Chin chased Skip around in a circle, and then he chased her. They fell in the snow as he tackled her and he gave her five more passionate kisses.

Somewhere down below in the town a dinner bell was ringing. Skip held out his hand and helped Chin gain her feet. The cold air was shattered by the crisp report of a rifle shot as Skip pulled Chin to her feet. She slammed into his chest throwing her arms around him. He reached out to hold her as she began to slide down to the ground.

A soldier popped up from his hiding place under the snow and cut loose with a burst of five rounds, "Got him, Chief!" Skip wasn't listening. He was staring into the fading light in the brown eyes of Chin Lee. He cradled her in his arms as he let his knees fall to the snow-covered, frozen earth.

The sounds of footsteps crunching in the snow were barely audible to Skip's ears as General Hanalin, Carol, Tim, and several soldiers surrounded them.

Skip supported her back with his left thigh, her head cradled in his left arm. He began to feather her thick, raven hair with his fingers of his right hand, while looking into her eyes.

Chin looked long and deep into his eyes. "We did have a chance, did we not?" She witnessed the vacancy in his sky blue eyes. She coughed and spit up blood.

Skip wiped the red saliva from her lips with a gentle touch. "Yeah, I believe we could have made a go of it, Chin."

They smiled at each other as tears began to swell up at the corners of her eyes. "You promised to tell me about your life."

Skip smiled. "I will. I will come back here every spring when the grass is green and the flowers are in bloom. I will sit right here and tell you how I gave up everything for war, and of all my adventures, and how it all began when I was shipped out to Vietnam."

"Chin," General Hanalin said. "I want you to know that your friend, Wong, is safe."

Snowflakes turned to water beads on her face. She reached out to take General Hanalin's hand. "Thank you!"

General Hanalin leaned forward placing his right hand on Skip's left shoulder. "She's gone. She died free, Skip."

"Yeah, she did, didn't she?" With a light touch, Skip closed her dead eyes as his tears splashed on her face. "We'll bury her right here, Mac. We'll put her on ice until the spring, and then we'll bury her right here in the soil she fought for; right where she died."

General Hanalin and Tim helped Skip rise to his feet as he laid her gently onto the snow. Skip turned and stared at Hanalin. "She had learned what we had learned, didn't she, Mac? She had learned that freedom isn't free...that freedom comes with a price."

The snow fell creating ghostly shadows of the company of soldiers, with fixed bayonets, as they moved over the battlefield.

"And you can tell me as well, Skipper."

Skip spun around, "*Bryanna!*" He charged forward toward the woman who began to rush toward him. They embraced each other in a bear hug.

"You're a genuine bastard, Skip. You should have given me a chance."

"Bryanna! Oh Bryanna!" He held her tight.

With gentle hands on her shoulders, he pushed her away. "I did give you a chance, Bryanna. I gave you a chance at life."

He moved her at arms length studying her face as his tears dripped unchecked from his eyes. "It could have been you there," he told her pointing to Chin's form lying cold in the snow. "It could have been you!" He thought of Kristine. He sighed.

"I let you go, Bryanna so you could live, and you have. But, what are you doing here?"

She stepped forward hugging him. "Mike was killed in the battle for Morristown. As I held him in my arms near the Ford Mansion, you know, Washington's Headquarters, he said, 'Go to him, Bryanna. Go to Skip! He's in Harlan, Kentucky.' Then he died."

They squeezed each other as a gentle snow of small flakes was falling all around them. Bryanna pressed her right cheek against his. She softly whispered in his right ear, "Do you remember the last movie we saw before you left for Vietnam forty-two years ago?"

Skip could see them walking down the aisle to their seats in the third row from the back of the theater. "He whispered to her, "I remember, *Dr. Zhivago*."

Bryanna began to cry. Between her sobs she began to sing in his right ear, "Somewhere, my love, there will be songs to sing, although the snow covers the hope of spring."

Skip broke out in a torrent of tears, and he answered in song, "Someday we'll meet again, my love. I will come to you, and you will come to me, out of the long ago."

They sang and cried and squeezed each other not wanting to let go.

She faced him. "Are you finished with it, now?"

He smiled as they wiped away each other's frozen tears. He nodded, then said, "Can...can I come home?"

She began to cry again as she caressed his face. "You *are* home, Skipper...you're home!"

They walked down the hill arm-in-arm as the snow crunched beneath their feet.

T.S. Pessini

**Please read on to experience a sampling of
NOVEMBER SPIES
by T. S. Pessini**

**Frankfurt, Germany
I.G. Farben Building
Captain Hanalin's Office
Friday, January 10, 1975
2400 hours**

"Do you see that little girl walking up the street, pushing the baby carriage?"

"Jesus, man, how long you been in the bush?"

"Shut up you idiot! Look at her face. See her step? That girl's on a mission. SH—it! Lock and load and shoot the bit..."

BOOM!

My eyelids flashed open. I sat frozen with my head resting on the desk listening to the noises of my room. It took thirty seconds for realization to set in. "Another damn nightmare. Will they ever end?" I lifted my head, wiping sweat from my forehead.

I stared at the top-secret documents for a few minutes then closed the file. "What the *hell* am I doing here? I'm a spy killer, not a damn analyst." The need for mobility caused me to stand. While stretching and twisting my torso, I inhaled a faint aroma of Captain Black. "Old Mac is still smoking his pipe."

The army issued, white-faced, brown-rimmed wall clock struck midnight. "Damn, it's twenty-four hundred hours on a Friday night in Frankfurt, Germany. I should be on the strip partying instead of searching through documents hunting for a security breach and possible spy activity.

Glancing around the captain's office, I began to wonder about its lack of furnishings. A cherry wood coat rack with brass hooks was strategically located just inside the door, standing like a lone sentinel, near the left corner. One large oak desk sat in the middle of the room facing the door. A maroon Captain's chair rested behind the desk for Captain Hanalin's use and a wooden chair had been placed three feet in front of the desk so an occupant would be facing the desk. A desktop calendar and a black cup containing three yellow pencils and two black army-issue ballpoint pens were strategically located on the desk. One large window in the east wall provided sunlight and a view to the rear area of the I.G. Farben building, while one large window in the west wall looked out on the massive parking lot, allowing sunlight to filter into the room from that angle. Hanalin's office appeared to be a twenty by twenty-foot square.

The desk, which was provided for my use, was a gray colored metal desk with two drawers on the right side, and a center drawer. My chair was metal, painted gray, and covered with a gray leather cushion and backrest.

Standing between my desk and chair with my right arm across my chest and my left elbow resting on the back of my right hand, I massaged my chin with the fingers of my left hand worrying over the question, "What am I doing here?"

I haven't uncovered any significant information in the documents, which I've reviewed, nor has Captain Hanalin provided me with any plausible explanations.

I moved away from my desk and began to stretch twisting my torso left and right several times while mentally analyzing the documents. Nothing jumped off of the pages providing me with a hint of mischief; however, I had only managed to browse through messages from January 1970 thru January 1971. The info was just routine bullshit. Even the top-secret files were normal procedures and operations.

Some messages covered field exercises, dealt with after-action reports, and addressed problems and needs within organizations. There wasn't any indication how Moscow acquired NATO and the 3rd Armored Division's (AD) best kept top-secrets dealing with unit strengths and battlefield positions and defense responsibilities and nuclear use probability.

The 3rd AD and its sister Panzer division were assigned to defend the Fulda Gap: the major invasion route into Western Europe. The Romans and Alexander the Great, to name a couple, had plunged through the Gab during their conquests. When NATO and the Warsaw Pact forces had rushed to their battle positions in November, the American and German units realized that the Soviet 8th Guard had increased its military power threefold.

The bottom line was frightening. The Warsaw forces had restructured their units so that they out-gunned and out-manned the NATO forces. The final analysis: NATO forces would have been annihilated within forty-eight hours if war had begun. It would have taken seventy-two hours for reinforcements to reach the battlefields…too late.

As I paced, I began a systematic, mental analytic review of the last one hundred pages of classified documents marked ASA TOP-SECRET. These documents had come from an Army Security Agency (ASA) field unit—SSG Ackerman's. Something was prodding my brain with nagging sensations trying to pull information from my subconscious. Perhaps I was too tired for my brain to comprehend any significance, yet my intuition would not allow the nagging, pulsating sensations to rest. Something, there was something but what? I couldn't grasp anything tangible or concrete, yet there was something.

I paced back and forth in front of my desk. "What was it that Captain Hanalin had said? Oh yeah, "I believe we have had a breach in communications security (COMSEC) measures."

There was nothing in these documents to indicate such a breach. Yet, something kept pulling at me. "Oh hell," I said throwing up my arms in frustration, and turned toward the front window.

I approached the room's eye using slow, steady steps. Once I reached the left side of the window, I pressed my left shoulder against the cool, white wall. Extending my fingers, I slid my right hand between the infantry blue curtain and the windowpane. It took me thirty seconds to move the curtain enough so I could peer out at the parking lot below. Snow was floating down from the blackish sky like small pieces of cotton balls. Four Military Police officers in Battle Dress Uniforms (BDU) were patrolling the parking lot. Two were afoot; two in a jeep, which was camouflaged in a real tree pattern. The driver kept his vehicle ten feet behind the foot patrol while the other rider manned an M-60 machinegun. His index finger was in position close to the trigger. The butt plate was drawn snug against his right shoulder. As I studied their patrol techniques for a few minutes, memories flooded forth from my subconscious.

"Shit! I'm forty-five minutes late for duty. That's piss-poor behavior, Skip Daggard," I admonished myself.

It was one of those humid, bug-infested nights. I had to squint, clamp my mouth shut, and use a hand as a windshield wiper in order to fend off the assault of millions of clicking, chirping, wing-flapping flying insects. Our compound floodlights were on, but gave off a small amount of brightness because of the denseness of the bugs. I finally made it through the massive wall of insects to the double-steel doors of our communications center.

I shook my head thinking that that was an old road not worth traveling again. I resumed my surveillance of the MP's on patrol. However, I couldn't push the memory back into the recesses of my subconscious mind. Beads of sweat seeped out from the pores on my forehead. My breathing became labored as my body began to tremble.

I pushed open the right door of the double steel doors and slid inside. When I closed the door and turned toward the center of the room, Mark, the on-duty MP was standing behind the MP desk glaring at me.

"Damn, Daggar, what the hell are you doin' here?"

I removed my hand from the curtain with a slow, undetectable withdrawal. As beads of perspiration formed rivulets across my forehead, I fell against the wall for support.

Mark pointed his Colt .45 at my head.

"What the fuck, over, you gone crazy, Mark?"

"Skip, go inside and I'll call you when you can come out for your badge."

That was against procedure. No one could go through the interior double steel doors without a badge. I took another step forward, and that's when I noticed the three huge shadow boxes sitting on the left corner of the countertop.

"When will the horrors leave me alone? When will that damn war end?" I squeezed my eyes shut while clenching my fists trying to suppress the onslaught of the memory. Gasping for breath, I lost the struggle.

"I'm warning you, Skip—go inside."

"What the hell is going on, Mark; what's in those boxes?"

Tears began to form at the corners of Mark's eyes. A sensation of fear and dread shook my body. My brain shouted, "Right, face...do as Mark has ordered."

I couldn't. I had to know what was in those boxes.

My desk lamp was like a lighthouse on a sea of darkness warning me of dangerous waters; warning me, but the disaster had already occurred. If I had only known, I would never have pushed Mark. I had learned a horrible secret in Bang Pla, Thailand, on a bug-infested January night 1969, about "special orders" to protect the code...top-secret orders ordering Americans to kill Americans.

Those shadow boxes contained five hundred rounds of .45 cartridges; the number of officers and enlisted soldiers at our site. Each cartridge had a name on it. I had walked in on Mark while he was lining up cartridges in accordance to the six names on the evening "special orders."

I stood in front of the MP horseshoe desk as Mark began to push cartridges into the black, metal clip of his weapon. He had loaded a brass cartridge with his name on it first—it would be the last bullet fired. Next, came the one for the Duty Officer, then the one for the Duty Warrant Officer. Mine was the fifth round loaded.

As I sat at my desk gripping documents, trying to steady my trembling hands, Mark's voice came as a whisper in the night across six years of nightmarish dreams.

"You once asked me why we MPs never socialize with you MI types. This is why, Skip." He said as tears made water tracks down his cheeks splashing on the countertop. "We hadn't been assigned to this AO to protect you guys. Our mission is to insure that none of you are taken as POWs."

I can still see him standing behind the counter in his green jungle fatigues, loading cartridges into the worn, scratched, black paint-chipped clip crying. Damn, we were both crying as he said, "you have to promise me, Skip, promise me you will never tell anyone."

Ever so softly, I answered his whisper with my own into the darkness of Captain Hanalin's office. "I have kept my promise, Mark. But during the past six years, I too have had to protect the code."

I wiped tears from my face and picked up a folder stamped TOP-SECRET in red. The dates were written in black ink on the right tab—Feb 1, 1971-July 31, 1972. Two locations had been written across the top of the manila folder: ASA, FRG (Federal Republic of Germany), mobile units ECHO-BRAVO; and Field Station Augsburg, FRG, section BRAVO-NINER. As I began to study documents from these two units, I realized that linguists of two US intelligence agencies had been zeroed in on the same grid coordinates, which happened to be the Soviet Embassy in Bonn, Germany.

There were two things I had learned from the Army Security Agency (ASA) mobile units' documents. First, the unit had been setup and operating from a location one hundred miles east of Bonn; and two, the documents clearly indicated that parties within the 3rd AD intelligence framework had been transmitting cryptic information to the embassy on a weekly basis.

What I picked out of the encrypted information from the cryptographers in Augsburg grabbed my attention. The army linguists were intercepting the same cryptic info as ASA. However, the air force linguists in TANGO-ROMEO section at the field station had catalogued telephone transmissions, in English, at another set of grid coordinates on a quarterly basis but on alternate days. These transmissions were in code, spoken over a dedicated LIMA, LIMA (land line) to NATO HQ in Brussels, Belgium. The transmissions had also been intercepted by the Soviet Embassy in Bonn.

My question came forth on a slow stream of profanity. "How the fuck did anyone in the Soviet Embassy know where the land line was located, and how the HELL did they tap into the dedicated circuit?

I sat at my desk in the dim light feeling my rage erupt as I shouted out, "What the fuck, over! Don't these people communicate with each other?"

Leaning back in my chair, I clasped my hands together, resting them on my head and stretched out my legs, contemplating these startling facts. Giving up my contemplation, I sat up leaning to my right. I opened the top, right drawer of my desk and retrieved a topographical map of Germany. I unfolded the map spreading it out over my desktop.

Using the grid coordinates on the army topographical map, I was able to pinpoint the location of the LIMA line transmissions. It was a small village occupying a mountain peak on Friedberg Hill. Its elevation is about 1,200 meters. The only US military installation in the area is located twenty miles southeast of the base of the hill in the town of Friedberg. It's the post where Elvis Presley served during his two years tour in the late 1950s.

By themselves, these incidents didn't seem to mean much. Put them together and their meaning is significant: The Soviets had been receiving valuable information about US and NATO operations from someone at the 3rd AD Headquarters in Frankfurt and Friedberg Hill for about three years, and perhaps are still receiving pertinent info.

I jumped to my feet, sending my chair rolling across the floor. *"S-h-it!"* I spit out the world. I couldn't believe it. The evidence was here in plain sight and analysts had missed it. I began rifling through boxes searching for files marked TOP-SECRET until I found all the files dated April 1973 thru November 1974. I laid the files out on the floor highlighting pertinent lines indicating the coded communications between the 3rd AD and the Soviet Embassy.

Kneeling with my palms on the floor, I stared at the proof Captain Hanalin was looking for, a breach. The evidence left no question… no doubt—spies were at work in the security section (G-2) of the 3rd Armored Division and had been since 1971. I leaned back on my heels staring at the highlighted information. A slight creak caused me to raise my head. I drew my .45 from my shoulder holster resting my left hand on my desk, placing the butt of the handle in my left palm for support as the door to the office began to open slowly…I cocked the hammer of my weapon.